In the hallway, a sound chilled her...
...a sound of slow-moving footsteps.

She told herself it was only her imagination working overtime in the spooky atmosphere of the old building. But her intuition was keenly tuned, too. She felt she was no longer alone.

With trepidation, Terry began to move toward the stairway. Wanting out, wishing she didn't have the dark basement between her and the outside, she made her way down to the second floor.

Turning at the landing, scanning the deepening shadows, Terry's heart began to pound wildly. One of the shadows had moved. Someone *was* here, watching her.

''Who's there?'' she called, shining her light into the shadows.

The figure of a man emerged abruptly. The beam of her flashlight caught a pair of dark eyes, the meanest eyes she had ever seen. Baring his teeth in a snarl, the man began to move toward her.

S0-AGF-696

ABOUT THE AUTHOR

Regan Forest lives in the desert near Tucson
but has also spent many years overseas. She is
very adept at creating stories that combine
romance and suspense. Her fascination with
ghost towns led Regan to visit Jerome,
Arizona, and resulted in her decision to use it
as a setting for her third exciting novel for
Intrigue, *A Walking Shadow*.

Books by Regan Forest

HARLEQUIN INTRIGUE
24–ONE STEP AHEAD
48–HEART OF THE WOLF

HARLEQUIN TEMPTATION
80–THE ANSWERING TIDE
95–STAR-CROSSED
123–DESERT RAIN
152–WHEREVER LOVE LEADS
176–A WANTED MAN

Don't miss any of our special offers. Write to us at the
following address for information on our newest releases.

Harlequin Reader Service
901 Fuhrmann Blvd., P.O. Box 1397, Buffalo, NY 14240
Canadian address: P.O. Box 603,
Fort Erie, Ont. L2A 5X3

A Walking Shadow
Shadow

Regan Forest

Harlequin Books

TORONTO • NEW YORK • LONDON
AMSTERDAM • PARIS • SYDNEY • HAMBURG
STOCKHOLM • ATHENS • TOKYO • MILAN

With gratitude for his help and suggestions,
this book is dedicated to Chief of Police Jim Allen,
a real-life hero who lives in Jerome's deserted,
"haunted" hospital with a dog,
a black cat and a gun.

Special thanks to Patrolman Skip Straus.

Harlequin Intrigue edition published February 1988

ISBN 0-373-22084-7

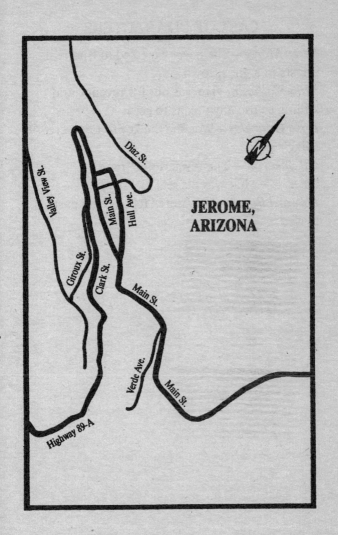

JEROME,
ARIZONA

Diaz St.

Valley View St.

Giroux St.

Main St.

Clark St.

Hull Ave.

Main St.

Verde Ave.

Main St.

Highway 89-A

CAST OF CHARACTERS

Terry Morse—She never expected to find real ghosts in a ghost town

Mike Calhoun—He was out for revenge and willing to use any means to get it

Rosa Gonzales—Was she the key to the secret of Mike's past?

Gil Spearow—The mysterious "man in black"— what was his real identity?

Howard Boyce—He wanted to keep the past buried

AUTHOR'S NOTE

Jerome, Arizona, is a registered National Historic Landmark. It began as a mining community in 1876 and reached a population of around fifteen thousand in the 1920s. Mining operations were closed in 1953, and by 1955 the population of the town had dropped to under a hundred. It had become a ghost town.

At present, restoration is in progress. The location of the town, with its breathtaking view of the Valley of the Verde River, and its pleasant climate, make it desirable to artists and retirees. Legends of ghosts abound, but it is no longer possible for the public to explore abandoned buildings at will. Those not under reconstruction are carefully protected.

While the setting is authentic, liberties have been taken for the sake of the story. The Beyer House, while typical of the houses in Jerome, does not actually exist, nor does the hotel managed by Rosa Gonzales. The United Verde Hospital, still owned by the Phelps Dodge Mining Corporation, is one of the outstanding landmarks of Jerome. Closed in 1951, it remains abandoned and incredibly well preserved.

There is no similarity between characters in this book and any actual persons, living or dead.

Chapter One

A street lamp burned through the billowing darkness. In its white, eerie light, shadows of tree branches spread like giant spiderwebs across the walls of deserted buildings, and trembling silhouetted leaves swayed and danced in the wind.

Terry Morse rubbed her arms and shivered. "Ghosts," she whispered into the cold, dark cracks of night. "The ghosts are everywhere."

The structure before her had once been a grand apartment building. Now its broken window panes and falling plaster echoed sighs of inhabitants long gone. From a garden grown high with weeds came the faint, dusty scent of lilacs.

This place was so incongruous, Terry thought. Ghost towns weren't supposed to have street lamps lit on spring evenings, or music playing in the saloon down on the street below, or inhabitants living in the husks of crumbling buildings, but this one did. She thrilled to the ghoulish dance of the leaf shadows on the wall. The ghosts surrounded her; this town called Jerome was everything she'd hoped, except for one unwelcome surprise: it was virtually hanging—and hanging precariously—on the side of a mountain.

Mingus Mountain was so steep that the streets of the old mining town, winding up, one above the other, resembled terraced rows. Near the main business center, stairways allowed pedestrians faster access to the streets above and below. Most of the houses were built with entrances to the first floor on one street and doorways to the second story on the street above.

The town had died. Jerome, Arizona, once a thriving mining community, located between Sedona and Prescott, had died some thirty years ago, yet a heartbeat remained, and Terry could feel it. Fascinated, she walked the curving length of a deserted upper street, looking at the lights in the Verde Valley far below.

There were no other lamps on this upper street—only the one lighting the stairs, and it was far behind her now. Shining her flashlight into the shadows between the dark houses, she was walking into clots of darkness so dense that she miscalculated the bend of the street and the sudden drop of the curb. A sharp jab of pain caused her to lose her balance and the flashlight fell from her hand as her knee twisted.

Terry swore out loud to the whispers of wind. How could she have been so stupid—shining her flashlight everywhere but in front of her, when she knew she should be careful about her knee? Her fascination with the ghost-inhabited shadows had caused her temporarily to forget.

Her flashlight had gone out when it hit the pavement with a crack. Fumbling around, she found it, but it was useless to try to get it to work now. The bulb must have broken. She looked back in the direction she had come. The lighted stairway was far behind her, two unlit, uphill blocks away, at least. Ahead there was only darkness.

Wincing with pain, she clutched the railing lining the sidewalk and looked down onto the street below. The roof of her hotel was about at eye level, but a good two blocks away. Small white lights from its entrance on Main Street were visible. But Main Street was straight down and there were only a few lights down there. Her problem was getting to a stairway.

A streetlight shone faintly from this south end of the lower street, and in its pasty light Terry made out the shadowy outline of steps. If she kept going, guided by the rail, she could reach that dark stairway more easily than she could get back to the lighted one. A glance behind her was all that she needed to convince her that the lighted stairs she had climbed up here were too far back to attempt without a flashlight and with her knee hurting like this. She'd have to use the darkened stairs. If she took them slowly enough, she could feel her way down. Toward the bottom, where the lower street lamp shone, there was some light. If she could just make it that far.

Don't panic, she told herself. *You can get down.*

The saloon music had faded into the night. Water trickling through a pipe on the hillside and the barking of a dog in the distance were the only sounds in the darkness except for the rustle of wind in high branches. Carefully Terry descended the steep stone stairway, clutching the handrail tightly, giving her weight to her left leg. The light from the old street lamp provided some help. It gleamed softly on the metal railing and on the water trickling down rocks on the other side of the rail. But the steps were wrapped in shadow; it was impossible to tell how steep they were or whether or not they were broken.

For all her caution, when Terry was three-quarters of the way down the stairs, the injured knee buckled and she lost her balance. Her grip on the railing wasn't strong enough to prevent a fall, and in those split seconds she thought of nothing but the hard, pebbly concrete at the bottom of the stairs. Her brain exploded in panic; her eyes closed, but she didn't scream.

The concrete was soft! Dazedly, she realized this wasn't possible. Something had broken her fall. A soft material brushed her face as she turned her head. Someone had caught her.

A tangle of sensations held her mind suspended in confusion while her body was suspended in the grip of something she hadn't heard or seen. Scent of a freshly laundered shirt. Awareness of breathing that was not her own. Awareness of incredible strength, not her own. Terry's eyelids blinked open. A tremor of fright shivered over her like a cold breeze. She was staring into the face of a ghost!

Silver eyes. Silver hair, blown by wind. In the eerie white light of the street lamp, a scar came visible as he turned his head—a jagged scar shaped like a seven. Fine straight features, incredibly handsome features. For several seconds Terry couldn't feel the warmth of a human body touching her or the strength of human arms cradling her as if she were weightless. She saw only the ghost that appeared out of the darkness and saved her from a dreadful fall.

Slowly logic prevailed. Ghosts didn't have warmth. There was warmth in the arms that held her, but none in the shine of silver eyes. Too stunned to utter a sound, Terry only stared into the strange, pale eyes.

A velvet-deep, masculine voice broke through the silence. She could feel the voice rise in the man's broad chest as he held her.

"Are you all right?"

"Yes." Her answer was a weak whisper.

He lowered her gently and released her to the night's chill.

Trying to keep her balance on shaking legs, Terry stared. "Where did you come from? I didn't see anyone down here."

The man looked at her the way one looks at an exasperating child. "Why the devil would you try to come down these steps in the dark?"

His voice was as cold as his eyes. He may as well have been the ghost she first imagined, Terry decided, for the way he affected her. The scar on his temple appeared sinister, but, she realized before she recoiled from him, a man can't help a scar. As he stood looking down at her five-four height from his six feet or more, he blinked the veil of hardness from his eyes, and the cold, hard eyes began to soften.

She pulled her bulky sweatshirt down over her hips and sucked in her breath. "Thank you for catching me. I might have broken my neck if you hadn't."

"I'm sure you would have."

Terry was aware that she was staring; she couldn't stop herself.

He gazed at her quizzically. "Is something wrong?"

"You just...startled me. In the sudden light I thought you were a ghost."

This admission brought a smile of genuine amusement. It was a sincere smile, not a mean one.

"This street corner may well be haunted," he said. "But not by me." He stood a moment longer in silence before he turned and started up the stairway with no further hesitation, as surefooted in the darkness as a night-prowling cat.

Hugging the mountainside, Main Street sloped gradually toward the tiny business section. Terry started walking toward the sparse, dim lights of town, gritting her teeth at the pain in her knee. The pressure of her weight hurt her badly. Those two blocks may as well have been two miles. She'd taken only a few painful steps when the voice boomed out of the darkness behind her.

From the stairway he called back, "I thought you said you were all right."

Turning, she could see nothing but shadows on the stairs. "I am all right. Really."

"Hell, you can barely walk!"

"I'll make it. I'm just...slow."

She could feel more than see him move back down the stairs. He crossed under the pale light again, approaching her. A strange discomfort formed in Terry's solar plexus. Behind the warmth of his amused smile something about this man belonged to the darkness, to the shadows; Terry felt it. She wanted him to remain part of the night shadows, like a bad dream should remain part of the night. It wasn't that he was sinister, but he was mysterious, like the night.

His shadow moved over her, dwarfing her. "You did hurt yourself in that fall."

"No. No, I recently injured my knee in a car accident. It isn't completely healed yet, and I turned it up there." She made a gesture to the street directly above. "I didn't think I could walk all the way back to the lighted stairs. That's why I was trying to get down here."

It was impossible to see his face clearly as he had his back to the light.

He began gruffly, "You should never have..." Then he stopped.

Terry started walking slowly, uncomfortable under the scrutiny of his eyes.

"You shouldn't try to walk on that leg," he said.

She knew he was right. Walking on her leg after such a painful twist was the worst thing she could do. But there wasn't much choice. Sighing resignation, she looked up the crooked block to the lights of the saloon, and thought about the steep stairway in the small hotel.

"Is it swelling?"

"I..." she touched the knee. "I think so."

He moved around in front of her. "I've had paramedic training. Mind if I check it?"

Without waiting for permission, he knelt in front of her and touched the knee gently through her jeans. "There is some swelling. Walking will make it worse. I'd better give you a lift back to the hotel."

"How did you know I was going to the hotel?"

"There's no place else you could be going, except to the saloon, and you don't look like the type for that. Unless your car is parked in town and you're driving back down the mountain tonight."

"No. I'm . . . going to the hotel."

"My Jeep is just around the corner." He helped her to the curb, where there was a low stone wall to sit on. "Wait right here. Don't move."

She had had no chance to respond to his command before he had disappeared into the shadows of trees where the street curved into darkness. His manner was gruff yet gentle at the same time, his eyes so strange.

Right now a ride uphill to the hotel would be a godsend. Walking all that way would be torturous. Terry hated nothing more than feeling like an invalid, and during the past three months since the accident she'd felt that way all too many times. Like it or not she needed the help of this stranger; he knew it too.

She heard an engine start, and in moments he was pulling up to the curb in a blue Jeep that had chipped paint and no glass in the side windows. The earlier harshness in his voice had given way to genuine concern when he jumped out and offered assistance.

His arm around her shoulders felt almost hot. So did his chest as she leaned into the softness of his dark shirt. He felt big and solid.

She stammered, "This is very nice of you."

He shrugged as if he didn't know how to answer, if indeed an answer was called for, and she thought, *If I were a stray dog with a hurt leg he'd do the same for me. He doesn't consider it a favor or even a duty; he just does it because he happens to be here and I happen to be in trouble. He is like the wind, touching me as he goes by.*

They rode in silence past unpainted two-story frame houses, some empty, some in stages of restoration. The wind had died down and the breeze carried scents of spring, lilacs and orange blossoms. The lights of a town called Cottonwood sparkled down in the valley. This ghost town sat so high up on the mountain that it presented an eagle's eye view of the vast river valley and beyond.

She asked, "What makes you so sure I'm a tourist?"

"What else could you be?"

"I'm not exactly a tourist. I plan to stay for several weeks, maybe months."

This seemed to surprise him. "Stay where? The hotel?"

"Yes. It's absolutely charming. I love it. You must live here. How long have you lived in Jerome?"

"Years."

"How many years?"

"About eight."

"Really? Why would...do you like living in a ghost town?"

"If I didn't, I wouldn't."

Obviously he wasn't a man who thrived on conversation, although he looked over at her and smiled and it was a nice smile with far more warmth than pity.

The street was deserted. She looked out at the darkwindowed buildings. "It's hard to believe that fifteen thousand people lived in this town once. How many are there now?"

"About four hundred. There were fewer than that when I came."

"I was told the population got down to fifty people in the fifties, after the mine closed. Is that true?"

"Yes."

He pulled up directly in front of the hotel, which had no pretentious entry, only a door beside a curio shop and a small sign in the shop's window. In seconds he was out of the driver's seat and offering her his strength for help in walking.

Leaning on him, Terry limped into the quaint, freshly painted lobby. The hotel manager, Rosa Gonzales, rose in surprise. Terry saw her look at the man with alarm, yet it was to Terry the old woman spoke.

"Is something the matter, Miss Morse?"

"I hurt my knee and was lucky enough to find a ride," Terry answered. She tried to keep her voice light, but she felt near tears from frustration, for now ahead of her were the stairs of the hotel. All these damn stairs!

The man, too, was looking at the narrow, carpeted staircase that led from the street level to the hotel rooms above the curio shop. He led Terry to the landing and before she realized what was happening, he was lifting her, almost effortlessly, into his arms.

"Which room, Rosa?" he asked.

The elderly woman blinked and hurriedly picked up a key from the desk. "Room two." She rushed to get ahead of him. Layers of petticoats rustled under her long blue skirt as she led the way.

Carried in strong arms up the steep flight, Terry momentarily closed her eyes. An image of Scarlett O'Hara being hustled up to her bedroom by Rhett Butler presented itself in living color to her mind's eye. *Lord, I'm dreaming this. In real life I couldn't find myself carried to my room by a stranger who only minutes ago I thought was a ghost.*

Amazingly, he wasn't even puffing at the top of the stairs as he followed Rosa Gonzales into the room and lowered his burden onto the bed.

Rosa switched on a lamp. The man turned around to face Terry. In the soft amber light of the antique lamp, he appeared far less ghost than human. His eyes were more blue than silver. His thick hair was streaked with as much black as gray. The scar on his temple was somehow less pronounced. And he was younger than she'd realized, easily only in his thirties. But the human was scarcely less frightening here in this safe yellow light than the ghost had been in the windy shadows. And Terry wasn't sure why. He was a little too good-looking, a little too perfectly built—with broad shoulders and husky thighs in tight jeans—to be quite real. He looked at her then, and now, through pale, mysterious eyes that seemed friendly enough, yet still disturbed her.

A man like this wouldn't live in a ghost town without some reason, Terry thought. The place was so dead, so isolated. What could his reason be?

The blue eyes squinted as he looked down at her in the strain of silence. She met his gaze. "I wish I knew how to thank you."

"No thanks required."

"You were very kind to help me." Terry pulled her right leg up onto the bed and proceeded to rub the throbbing knee over the thick denim of her jeans. She noticed his eyes shift from her face to her leg. So intense was his gaze that for a moment she thought he would bend over to touch her injured knee again.

But he kept distant, with his body and his voice. "Do you need anything?"

A fleeting moment caught unexpected softness in his voice, unanticipated empathy with another human being, something calm and real, the same something she had seen in his smile under the street lamp. Then, as now, the softness was fleeting. He seemed so guarded.

"Thanks for your concern," she answered. "But I don't need anything more. I appreciate the lift."

She observed a quick exchange of glances between the man and the old woman. What passed between them in the glance was impossible to translate, except that there was some meaning there, something private between two people who knew each other better than they would have her believe.

"Look after her, Rosa," he said, and left the room so abruptly that his exit was awkward.

If Rosa Gonzales knew what had prompted the rushed exit, she showed no signs of being bothered by it. Smiling, she crossed the room to close the drapes. Her dress, narrow in the bodice with an ankle-length skirt and ruffled sleeves, would have been in fashion at the turn of the century. When Terry first saw the hotel manager earlier that afternoon, she'd assumed the dress was a costume worn for the benefit of tourists. It might be. Yet the simple gingham gown suited the trim, white-haired woman so perfectly Terry now wondered if she ever wore anything more modern. Perhaps she never had.

"Mrs. Gonzales..."

"Call me Rosa, please. Everyone does." Her Spanish accent was so slight Terry noticed it now for the first time.

"Rosa, who is he?"

"His name is Mike Calhoun. He lives in Jerome, down on the far south end of Main Street." Rosa sat down on the edge of the bed. "How did you hurt your knee?"

"In an automobile accident several weeks ago. Tonight I turned it because I wasn't careful enough about keeping my flashlight beamed on the street and I stepped off a curb, up there—on the high street. Tell me about him."

"About Mike? I know very little about him."

"Does he have a family?"

"No, he lives alone in a building that is still partly in ruin." Rosa smiled. "I thought he might offer to have a look at your knee, since he's a trained paramedic and there's no doctor in town. If you need a doctor—"

"No, I don't." Terry looked away, then back at the old woman. "Does he work as a paramedic?"

"I believe so, from time to time, in the valley, if one is needed. Why don't you get comfortable, Miss Morse?"

"Terry."

"Terry. There's a chill in the room. Why not get ready for bed, dear, and crawl in under the warm quilt, and I'll bring you some tea."

"Tea sounds wonderful!"

Rosa's full skirt brushed the frame of the doorway. Alone, Terry looked around a room decorated over half a century ago with furniture which had become a valuable collection of antiques. It was a step back in time—stepping from her sports car into the mystical world of the past that was Jerome, Arizona.

She undressed and put on silk pyjamas and examined her tender, swollen knee with mounting frustration. The knee shouldn't have weight on it for several days, and just how could she accomplish that?

It wasn't going to work, she decided. All these cursed stairs. Damn, how could she have made such a mistake?

Rosa returned with a tea tray and proceeded to pour. "Either you are in pain, dear, or you're very upset about something." She set a china cup on the bed table.

"Both. But mostly I'm upset, Rosa. I had my plans all made to stay in Jerome. To work here. Now I don't see how I can stay."

The older woman poured a cup of tea for herself, which she carried on its saucer to a rocking chair across the room. "You mean because of your injury?"

"Yes. My knee will never get well if I have to climb stairs all the time."

"You want to work here?"

"I'm a cartoonist. I want to draw a real ghost town in my syndicated comic strip, and Jerome is perfect, better than anything I ever dreamed I could find. Only I didn't do my homework well enough. I didn't realize this town is perched on the side of a mountain the way it is, with the streets on top of each other."

Rosa said, rocking, "It has been called the home of the nineteenth century cliff-dwellers. You've probably chosen the most vertical town in the United States."

Terry sighed, brushing back pale blond hair from her shoulder. "It's going to be impossible. I'm so disappointed I could cry. I've never seen a place so intriguing, so full of ghosts. The empty buildings, the echoes, the incredible view of the valley. I just love it! And here I am stuck in this room with steep stairs between me and the world. Is there any other place in town to stay, any level place? I'm okay if I can walk on level ground."

"There is another small hotel, but like this one, it's over a shop, and the stairs are just as high." Rosa gazed into her teacup. "I wish I could help you."

"Damn," Terry swore softly. "Already I've nearly killed myself here. I tripped on the stairs between Main Street and the one above. Mike Calhoun happened to be walking at the bottom and he caught me when I fell. How, I don't know. I didn't even see him until I hit him." She gazed at the kind, dark eyes. Rosa had been so friendly from the first moment Terry had walked into her hotel this afternoon. She assumed it was merely small-town hospitality, but now it seemed more. Rosa seemed genuinely interested in her.

"When I first saw him I thought for a second he was a ghost," Terry said with a grin. "But he's much too strong to be a ghost. I never saw a man so strong. He carried me up these stairs without even breathing hard."

The old woman laughed. "Well, my dear, you're not very big. You must weigh barely a hundred pounds."

"I weigh a hundred and fifteen, which isn't that small for someone who's five feet four. People always think I'm smaller than I am—and more fragile. Do I look fragile to you?"

"I think delicate is a better word. Yes, you look rather delicate, in a feminine way."

"Oh lord, I hope you don't mean *dainty*! When I was a kid, whenever I got my knees dirty, my mother always told me a girl should be dainty and oh how I hated that word. I'm not delicate. It's the light hair, maybe, damn wispy hair, or my small frame, but I'm not delicate."

"Your features are." Rosa looked at her in an almost mocking way as if Terry's protests were groundless. Rosa's voice was musing and kind. Her smile came with ease. "I've heard Mike Calhoun called many things, but never a ghost."

"What is he usually called?"

Rosa shrugged. "I've heard him called a loner."

"Loner? Or lonely?"

The woman's eyes darkened. "I don't know."

"Yet he's a paramedic."

"A volunteer—when he's needed. Otherwise he prefers to keep to himself."

"He's young, Rosa. Surely he has a girlfriend."

"Yes, I suppose so. He spends time in the valley. I've seen him walking with a young woman now and again. I don't ask about his personal life. Here in Jerome people come for reasons of their own. We don't ask where they come from or why they come unless, like you, they volunteer the information. That's just how it is here. I've known Mike for eight years and I don't even know where he lived before he came. I don't know why he came. I've never asked and he's never said."

Terry studied with artist's eyes the face of the woman in the rocker across the room. Her white hair was drawn back in a neat bun, her face quite free of wrinkles except around the eyes and throat. The eyes of the artist saw a woman who had been unusually beautiful in her younger days. Rosa was beautiful still. There was a serenity about her.

"What about you, Rosa? How long have you lived on this mountain?"

"All my life. I was born in a shack on Cleopatra Hill, above town, where there used to be hundreds of miners' shacks, though you can't see any trace of them now. My father worked in the copper mine. When I was seventeen I went to work as a maid for the wealthy family of a banker. And when everybody left, I stayed. I've worked in this hotel off and on since 1956."

"You never married?"

Her brow creased, then smoothed again. "No, I never married."

Terry thought, *She was in love once, though.* Rosa Gonzales had known tragedy; her dark eyes couldn't have said so more clearly. But Terry wouldn't ask.

Rosa sought to change the subject. "Tell me about your comic strip."

"It's called *Morse Codes*, and it's been syndicated for four months. It's more of an adventure series than anything else. I like to do mysteries and such. That's why Jerome is such a great setting. I plan to call it by its real name and draw real places here." She sat back. "I can see satire, too. For instance, I'm told the residents want to restore this town. And if they do, it will still be old-fashioned and nice but it won't be wonderful and ghosty then. It won't be spooky like it is, and walking the deserted streets in the dead of night won't be a great adventure anymore."

Rosa blinked. "You're going to say all that in your comics?"

"Among other things. Mainly, I'm going to create some local intrigue. Danger."

"There's nothing dangerous here. All we really have left is the tourism. Small shops. A handful of people have come to retire or to paint. Jerome will never be the exciting town it was when the mine was here."

"You have no idea why Mike Calhoun came? Does he have a business or anything?"

Rosa rose from the chair, holding her teacup with one hand and smoothing her skirt with the other. "I know little about him," she said gently. Pouring more tea into Terry's cup, she added, "But when I see him again, I must tell him you mistook him for a ghost. This will amuse him, I think."

"I did tell him, and you're right, it made him smile. His hair was so silver under the street lamp—that was what I saw first. He's much too young to have gray hair. How old is he?"

"Only thirty, I think. His hair was much darker when I first met him. I must go, Terry, and let you rest. I'll look in on you in the morning."

"It's not fair for you to be running up and down these stairs waiting on me. I can't have that."

"These steps are nothing for me; I'm up and down them all day, doing up the rooms, repairing small things. Don't be in too great a hurry to leave Mingus Mountain, my dear. You haven't been here long enough yet to really see it."

"I guess I'm not going anywhere until I can walk. You're awfully kind, Rosa. Thank you."

Leaving the fresh, hot cup of tea, the old woman took up the tray. "If you need anything, my room is just at the end of the hall. I'm here all the time. Sleep well."

Settling back into the pillows, Terry thought, *Eight years in a town this size, and Rosa doesn't know any more about the guy than that? Could Rosa be telling the truth? Why did she try to change the subject so fast every time a question about Mike came up?* Thinking back on their conversation, Terry realized she wasn't imagining it; Rosa did subtly change the subject, every time. Rosa didn't feel comfortable talking about Mike Calhoun. Yet she seemed to like him. There was *something* between them to initiate the exchange of private glances that Terry had witnessed when they thought she wouldn't notice.

She was a professional at studying the changes and expressions of the human face; it was a requirement of her job. Lying in the dark, listening to the creeks and groans of the old building, Terry replayed the scene in her head. There was no question about it—Rosa was hiding something she knew about Mike Calhoun.

Chapter Two

From the front porch of the half-empty building where he lived, Mike Calhoun could smell the morning fragrance of lilacs. Hyacinths blooming along the crumbling stone wall had been planted decades ago and came back each spring with the lilacs to remind him that another winter was gone. Season after season life passes, he thought. Delicate as the flowers were, they refused to die, refused to give up. They waited through each long winter to feel again the warmth of sunshine in the spring.

He too had waited. The bitterness never passed. Shadows of the horrors of his past never lightened. Yet mornings gradually dawned brighter, through the years. Slowly he had come to see sunrises and sunsets for the beauty of each one. Slowly he had learned to live each day for itself, realizing that each day had music that belonged only to itself and paths forming out of itself. The paths seemed to lead nowhere, except toward his prime life's purpose: revenge.

This morning's sunrise held the image of a woman's face. Ash-blond hair that looked almost white in the street lamp light. Eyes as blue as a summer sky, frightened eyes. What was she frightened of, he wondered. Of him? She had clung to him tightly when he had carried her up the stairs, her arm around his shoulders.

He didn't know her name. It didn't matter. She was part of a world he didn't live in anymore. Part of what he couldn't have. She was real and her life was real and no doubt her dreams were real. While his dreams had been stripped from him eight years ago when his two closest friends had betrayed him, turned on him, condemned him to a life of exile.

Revenge made a powerful purpose for a man's life, he thought, seething in hot coals of bitterness. His survival depended on it, his victory would be chartered by it. Victory—retaliation—it was all the same. Mike was sick to death of looking over his shoulder whenever shadows moved behind him. One way or another, he intended to finish off his enemies before they found—and finished—him.

The view of the Verde Valley from his front porch was magnificent, but Mike thought less about the sunlit view this morning than of Howard Boyce. It was getting close to the time to make a move against Howard. *Soon,* he thought. *Soon.*

He leaned back against the step, hands behind his head, his lips set tight. *Howard, you're as good as dead. You should have thought twice about making yourself an enemy of a convicted murderer, old buddy. Because murderers sometimes escape.*

An ache down inside reminded him that escape was not the same as freedom. Not the same at all. Eight years was a hell of a long time.

With a heavy sigh, Mike shielded his eyes to the sun's glare as the slim figure of a woman in a long skirt came into view. She waved to him from the street. Rosa? Rosa never came here to see him; she was terrified of this house. Odd she'd be here now, so early in the morning.

She ascended the three small steps to the wooden porch and sat down on a chair. He got up from the step carrying an empty coffee mug.

She asked, "Do you have any more coffee?"

"Sure. Let me get it for you, since I doubt you're willing to venture inside."

"You're wrong today, Mike. I want to see what you've done to the inside—the renovations."

"You actually want—"

"Yes, yes," she interrupted with nervous impatience. "Oh, mind you, it's not something I'm looking forward to, having to go inside this...this place. But you've made me curious."

He offered his arm, gallantly, protectively. She grasped it tightly.

"Don't worry, I'll be right beside you. I promise there's nothing to be afraid of."

The woman hesitated.

He said, "Something's going on. You wouldn't have all this sudden curiosity without a reason," and then gently, "You're trembling, Rosa. I've told you a thousand times there's nothing in this house that can hurt you."

"Oh, yes, I know. You insist it's all superstition. But people say they've heard frightening noises from this house as recently as last week. That isn't superstition."

Mike's arm encircled the old woman's small shoulders. "It's a fine old house. You'll like what I've done to the inside of it."

Allowing him to lead her from the front porch through double entry doors, she answered, "I notice you aren't denying the noises."

He only smiled, as if no comment were called for.

The house sat close to the street, on the far southern end of Main Street. Like all the others, it faced east to the valley. The two-story white wood structure was in need of paint again, but in comparison to many of the old buildings nearby, it looked solid, even painted. A balcony stretched across the upper story at the front and side. And at the back, the upstairs level opened onto the upper street, so that the entrances to the two upstairs apartments were actually on a different street from the two apartments below.

They stood in a narrow front hallway, which was lighted by a high window over the door, and a second high window at the top of the stairway. Before them the steep stairs led up, but the stairway was blocked at the bottom by a barricade of boards that stretched from one side of the hallway to the other and that were nailed in place. To their right was the open door to one downstairs apartment, and to their left, the closed door of the other.

"Why have you blocked off the stairs?"

"It isn't safe to go up there," he lied. "The floor isn't solid. Somebody could fall through and get killed."

"I assume that's why the doors and windows upstairs are all kept shut."

"Sure. I can't have people wandering through here until the building is safe." He guided her toward the open door. "As I've told you, I've just finished renovating the downstairs. This is my apartment."

Once they were inside the apartment door, he could see Rosa breathe easier. Her shoulders relaxed. She pulled away from him and walked through the living room in fascinated delight, looking at the paintings on the walls, the comfortable overstuffed furniture mixed with a few handpicked antiques, and all accented by colors of blue and white and mint green.

"It's quite lovely, Mike."

"I thought you'd like it, if I ever got you in here."

"I'm surprised a man has such imagination and good taste."

"Thanks, I think."

Some papers were strewn out on the dining table in the L of the living room. Rosa wandered through the small kitchen, which had been freshly painted and accented in blue, and into the one large bedroom that held only a double bed, a single dresser and a love seat. A huge oil painting of an old-fashioned picnic scene, with its restful hues of yellows and blues and lavenders, dominated the room. For a few moments Rosa stood in silence before the painting.

Mike spoke finally. "You have a funny look on your face. Do you like it?"

"Yes. What surprises me is that you like it, too." She turned to face him. "There is a great deal I don't know about you, my dear. A very great deal, isn't there?"

He evaded the question, as he always did. "There's an awful lot I don't know about you, too. Things from your past you won't talk about."

"It sounds as though you wonder."

"Sure I wonder. I know something pretty terrible happened while you were working in the Rayburn house. I've seen how you gaze at that house sometimes. I wouldn't ask, though."

"Nor would I. What a pair of misfits we are."

"It's a good alliance, Rosa. I've always thought so."

"Yes. Good for us both. I would like to see the other apartment."

As they walked across the hallway to the other door, he reached in his pocket for the key.

"There still might be a slight smell of paint, since it's been closed up." Mike proceeded to the window and opened the wooden shutters. The room flooded with light.

"Oh, my! It's even nicer than yours."

"I learned from doing mine, and had more time to plan what I wanted to do in here."

It was the same plan, in reverse, with the same kind of look, a blend of antiques and country charm. On the walls hung paintings of the Verde Valley, obviously paintings he'd purchased from local artists. The dominating color in this apartment again was blue. But here it was accented in tans and browns and white. Rosa muttered praise as she walked through.

"And now that it's finished, who is going to live here?" she asked.

"Nobody. At least not for a while."

"Why not?"

"Because I'm still working in the building."

"Why would that matter? You're working upstairs now, aren't you?"

Mike scratched his head. "Yeah. But it's noisy work, dust and all . . ."

"Suppose there was someone who didn't mind all that? Would you rent this place temporarily?"

"Nah. Not now. Eventually, maybe. But not now."

"I know someone who needs it very badly."

He looked at her puzzled. "Who?"

"Terry Morse. The young lady you carried upstairs last night. She wants to stay in Jerome for a while, but her injured knee makes it impossible for her to negotiate the hotel stairs. And I have the feeling this girl wouldn't mind the fact that she's staying in a haunted house."

"Forget it. I don't want anybody in here."

"You're a hermit. That's what your problem is. Why fix this apartment up and leave it empty?"

"I told you, I'm working on—"

"Oh, I know what you told me. But Terry wouldn't bother you."

"No. Definitely no."

"Why not?"

His face darkened with discomfort. "Because she might go upstairs."

"*What?* Who could possibly get up there? You've got it so barricaded a lumberjack couldn't get up there. Are you trying to keep people from going up or the ghosts from coming down?"

"Ghosts go where they want."

Rosa studied him. "Michael, I've worked for you loyally for eight years, running that hotel of yours so not a soul in this town suspects you own it. I've covered for you more than once when you wanted to keep curiosity seekers out of this house. And I've never asked a favor of you that amounted to more than a ride down the mountain. Now I'm asking something. I like that girl. And she has an important job she wants to do here—drawing pictures of Jerome for her comic strip. It's not going to kill you to let her use this apartment for a few weeks. Good heavens, she's not going to bother you."

He scowled. "A few weeks? You're sure that's all it is?"

"You're the landlord. If it doesn't work out, just tell her. But it will. She's very nice."

"She'd be...alone here while I'm gone."

"Can something hurt her here?"

"No, not if she doesn't... No, nothing can hurt her. But I just don't like it, Rosa."

"You're afraid of a girl. I'm ashamed of you."

He finally smiled, a forced smile. "You're making me sound like a monster."

"You are a monster if you don't do this for her. This lovely place sitting completely empty."

"Maybe she's afraid of ghosts."

"Are there ghosts here? Are you admitting it?"

He hesitated. "Yes," he answered honestly. "There are. And they might frighten her."

"They don't frighten you."

"I'm used to it."

"You said nothing could hurt her!"

"I didn't say nothing would scare her."

Now Rosa seemed uncertain. "Then the ghosts are still here! The ones we knew about when we were children, the awful stories. The ghosts *are* still here!"

"Rosa—"

"Aren't they?"

He walked to the window and looked out onto the street below and wouldn't answer.

She came up behind him. "Paul Germaine said he talked to you a few days ago, he and Jim Smith, and you admitted to them that the house is haunted."

"What could I say, Rosa? People keep... keep hearing things. They talk."

"They've always talked about this house."

He nodded. "Terry Morse wouldn't like it here. I promise you she wouldn't."

"Perhaps not. But shouldn't she have the say about it? If you never plan to open up this house to anyone, why are you renovating it at all?"

He couldn't reveal to her the answer, so he stood mute, looking at the sun reflecting from broken window panes of deserted houses across the street until he felt her touch on his shoulder.

"I'm going to tell her about this apartment anyhow, Mike. At least give her the chance to use it if she wants. I wouldn't stay here myself for a million dollars, but I'm old. I've grown up fearing this house. She is young, and she came here in search of ghosts, and somehow I don't think she'd be any more afraid than you are. When you say nothing can hurt her, that's what I believe; I know you. I know nothing about you, but I know you." She patted his shoulder as if the decision were made. It *was* made. "We can furnish bedding and towels and dishes for her from the hotel, with no bother to us at all. You know, dear, if we aren't here on this earth to help people, what are we here for?"

FROM THE WINDOW of her hotel room Terry could look out onto the Main Street of Jerome. During the day tourists came and parked their cars and strolled the streets, browsing in the small shops. It wasn't like nighttime when everything closed up in a cocoon of silence save for strums of guitars and activity around the saloon.

Hobbling around the room, not wanting to put pressure on her right leg, she set up her drawing equipment on an antique walnut table in front of the window and went to work. Closing her eyes, Terry let the images come, but of all the faces she'd seen in this town, one dominated every thought—the face that had appeared so mysteriously out of last night's darkness.

While she sketched, the face came clearer and clearer—eyes so pale they were white on paper, hair streaked black with white, and the wicked scar on his left temple. Terry held the series of drawings out before her and studied them. No character could be better for her story. He was handsome and mysterious. A man who was part of a ghost town, who looked like he might prefer the darkness to the light. Yet there was something else, too—a sparkle in his eyes—friendly concern for her, friendship—she was sure it was friendship—with the elderly woman who managed the hotel. Rosa liked him. She wouldn't talk much about him, but she liked him. Terry felt Rosa was a woman who chose her friends carefully. That mysterious darkness about the man didn't seem to bother Rosa.

It excited Terry. He would be her model—his handsome face, his silver hair, his light eyes that reflected friendship one moment and secrets the next. Sketching a likeness of Mike Calhoun, Terry named her comic strip character Rod Lightning, a movie star with a sordid past who hid from prying reporters and curious fans by taking up residence in the isolated ghost town of Jerome. He was going to get into trouble here, and he was going to meet the adventurous amateur sleuth, Clover Mae, who would no doubt be saving Rod from sinister villains before long.

She drew Rosa as a young woman, a miner's daughter in Jerome. Her name became Louisa and her beauty was envied by every female in the valley. Terry had the freedom of mixing the present with the past and playing with the values changing from one decade to another.

Gazing out of her window, the artist captured on paper the likeness of a man on a bench playing his guitar with a dog sleeping at his feet. She sketched a boy gliding down the slope of Main Street on a skateboard.

Spreading out her drawings confirmed what she had sensed from the moment she drove up Mingus Mountain— there was a wealth of material here. It was her habit to copy likenesses of living faces in her cartoons, and the faces of Jerome were diverse, fascinating. Even if she could stay only a few days, they'd serve to provide a story for a month or so. Her editor, Thomas Hingle, loved the Arizona ghost town setting and was waiting impatiently for her to express mail the first of her roughs.

Perhaps, she thought, she could stay in Cottonwood or even in Sedona, the resort town on the other side of the valley, and drive regularly to Jerome. It wouldn't be half as good as being here for every sunset or the full moon, but it would be better than having to return to Los Angeles. In this vast Arizona valley she could recuperate from the accident, breathe fresh air into her lungs, and enjoy the silence and the peace, and produce a hell of a good story for her editor.

There was a tapping at her door, and Rosa opened it, carrying a tray. "I knocked softly this morning," she said, "and got no response, so I knew you wished to sleep late. I've brought you something to eat. How do you feel?"

Terry quickly shuffled the papers into her working folder to make room for the tray on the table. She wasn't ready for anyone to see any sketches yet—particularly someone who might recognize people she knew. It was too soon for the people of Jerome to know that caricatures of their faces would become familiar to millions of households all over America.

"I'm better, thanks, Rosa. The knee always responds well to rest. This is awfully nice of you. Are you going to join me?"

"Yes, for coffee. I want to talk to you." She uncovered Terry's breakfast of omelet, toast, orange juice, and grapes, and poured coffee into two cups.

"This looks so good! And smells wonderful. How do you have time to do all this for me with a hotel to run single-handedly?"

Rosa smiled and pulled up a chair. "I have a total of four rooms and at the moment yours is the only one that is occupied. Did you not wonder how an old woman could run a hotel alone? There is little to do. Any large chores I delegate to the owner, or to Juan, my nephew who is not really my nephew; I only call him that." Rosa spread a worn carefully pressed linen napkin across Terry's lap. "It must have been a serious automobile accident you were in."

"Umm," Terry nodded, taking a sip of orange juice. "I was rear-ended by a truck at an intersection. It bent the frame and totaled my car. The seat lunged forward and slammed my knee against the dash. While I was in the hospital I learned my comic strip was going to be syndicated. I couldn't even jump up and down; all I could do was scream, which isn't a popular thing to do in a hospital." Terry smiled as she buttered her toast.

"The ghost town material you want to do—was it planned before you were hurt?"

"No. I was going to go on a raft trip down the Colorado River. When I couldn't do that, I started looking for an unusual setting where I could spend a few months working and recuperating. An excuse to get out of the city."

"You'd like to stay several weeks?"

"I'd love to, Rosa, but I can't with this damn knee."

She nodded. "There is one place available that doesn't have stairs—"

"There *is*?" Terry set down her cup, spilling the contents onto the saucer.

Rosa's hand went up. "There's a problem about it though, Terry."

"It's expensive."

"No. I believe the cost would be exactly what you'd be paying if you stayed here at the hotel, and it might be far more comfortable, depending..."

The woman seemed genuinely distressed at whatever she had to say. "Depending on what, Rosa? What?"

"Depending on how you feel about the ghosts. It's a lovely, newly decorated apartment, but it happens to be in the Beyer House, the most haunted house in all of Jerome."

"Oh!" Terry burst into relieved laughter. "Is *that* all? But that's wonderful! What could be more exciting?"

"You must understand fully before you make a decision about it, dear. It truly is haunted. I've heard stories about this house since I was a young girl. This morning was the first time I've ever had the courage to set foot inside."

"Why did you go inside? Oh, for me? To see it? Did you really?"

"Yes. And I will admit the apartment is charming."

Terry was becoming too excited to eat. "Do you *really* believe in ghosts?"

"Certainly I do. But I realize young people often are drawn to the challenge of trying to disprove what people for centuries have known—that the dead still walk among us. I believe you'd be safe in the house; the owner assures me there is no actual danger from the ghosts. But he did warn that you might become frightened of them."

"The owner? Does he live there? Does anyone live there?"

"Yes, the owner lives in the apartment just across the hall. The two upstairs apartments are boarded shut, still in a state of ruin."

"Does he have a family there? The owner?"

Rosa smiled. "You know the owner, dear. It's Mike's house. He's been renovating it himself, and it's half-finished. But I must warn you that he isn't always there. He travels some. You would be alone in the building sometimes. That's the part of this that I don't like. You would sometimes be alone in that building."

"Mike Calhoun lives in the most haunted house in all of Jerome?" Terry tilted back her chair and raised her arms in a gesture of delight. What she had to hide from Rosa was the fact that the mention of ghosts didn't have the same impact on her as the mention of Mike Calhoun's name. It sent a little shiver of excitement through her, just the sound of his name. She wasn't sure why.

"I take it he isn't bothered by ghosts himself, then. Did *he* say I'd be scared of them?"

"Yes, he did."

"He did, did he? He's just daring me to do it. That's it, isn't it?"

"I don't think so. I think he meant it."

Terry couldn't help but notice the genuine concern in the old woman's eyes. Either she was absolutely serious about all these warnings or else something else was bothering Rosa. Or both.

"I'm not afraid of ghosts."

"I didn't think you would be."

"When can I move in? Can we go there now?"

"If you think you're able to manage."

"I can get down the hotel stairs on my rear end with one leg in the air if I have to. I guess I'll have to, but the sooner the better. This is so great, Rosa! I'll have a wealth of material for my story. Thank you so much."

Sighing, Rosa got up from her chair. "I'm not sure you should thank me. Local legend says two people were murdered in the Beyer House."

"I love this. I really love this. And I love taking Mike's dare."

"It wasn't a dare."

"He may not have thought so, but it was. He seems nice. You like him, don't you?"

"Yes, I do. What little I know of him. And I trust him if he says the ghosts won't hurt you. He ought to know. He's been there nearly eight years now, with them. And he seems none the worse for it. Except..." Rosa's voice faltered, and she would not continue.

Terry prodded, "Except what? What did you start to say? Come on, Rosa, tell me."

The old woman turned toward her with an unreadable expression on her face. "Except," she finally continued with strained reluctance, "that in those eight years his hair has turned gray."

Chapter Three

An hour later Rosa helped her to her car while Juan, the teenager Rosa called her nephew, followed with Terry's luggage. He got behind the wheel to chauffeur her the short distance to the Beyer House.

It stood apart from the other houses, separated by a vacant space where the adjacent building had crumbled and was gone. Only a distance of a few feet and three steps separated the narrow front porch from the street. And the vacant apartment was on the ground floor. Seeing the house, Terry's immediate thought was of her good luck in acquiring a place to stay at street level, but that was before the spell of the house came down over her.

It was hard to identify the feeling that gripped her when Juan pulled to a stop at the front. She opened the car door and sat looking up at the looming house—great white walls before her. Paint was badly chipped on the railings of the upper balcony, which shadowed the front porch. Branches of a tall cottonwood overhung that high railing, pushing at the walls and the tightly boarded windows above. A disturbing, unnatural silence seemed to prevail over the entire building and the garden surrounding it.

Terry realized that the boy, Juan, was staring up at the house too. He had come around to assist her, and had stopped, following Terry's eyes in their first daylight glimpse of Jerome's most haunted house.

Her young escort took her arm as she limped toward the double doors of the building's entrance. There he hesitated.

"What's the matter, Juan?"

"This house. Many people have heard weird sounds coming from here at night."

"You're not afraid to go inside, are you?"

He was afraid, she could see, but his manly pride wouldn't allow him to admit it. With jaw set tight, the boy opened the doors for her.

They stood in a narrow entry hall. Before them was what would have been a stairs landing, had it not been partitioned off by boards that ran from one side of the hall to the other, completely blocking access to the upper story.

She looked about in the light of the open doorway and produced a key from her purse. "Rosa said it's the door on the left."

She half expected the door to squeak. It didn't. Instead it led her into a pleasant room with freshly plastered and painted walls and beautiful antique furniture. Through open slats at the window, sunlight streamed in, flooding everything with a soft yellow glow.

Juan's hands felt tense on her arm as he impatiently helped her to the sofa. As soon as she was seated there, he backed toward the front door.

"I'll get the suitcases now."

He took the bags into the bedroom, constantly glancing about as though he expected something to grab him. "Do you need anything more?"

She wanted to say, *This is a lovely house, Juan. See, there's nothing awful or ugly.* But she didn't say it because he was bouncing on one foot, then another, wanting out, and she knew her evaluation would convince him of nothing. "No, thank you, Juan. I'll be just fine. I appreciate your help."

Accepting a bill from her with a forced smile, he looked around once more, quickly, before he turned and almost ran from the room.

Alone then, Terry limped to the window to open the shades. In the L of the living room was a dining table, a perfect place to work in excellent light. Exploring, she found the kitchen tiny and quaint with its newly varnished hardwood floor, white walls and blue and white checked curtains. The window of the kitchen looked out on a side garden where grass had been planted and was kept neatly mowed. It was a hundred times better than the hotel room where she'd thought she'd have to stay, and it certainly wasn't the sort of place that ghosts would be attracted to. It was all so silly—the superstition about ghosts. But it was fun. And it was going to make a great adventure for Rod Lightning to flash his handsome self into.

Rosa had promised to send sheets and towels and a few dishes from the hotel, which meant poor Juan was going to have to come back. It seemed bizarre for anyone to be frightened of this pleasant place. Of course, maybe all the house wasn't this nice. Much of it was obviously still in ruin.

While she stood at the living room window gazing out at the valley, she felt a presence behind her and turned swiftly. Her breath caught in her throat at the sight of the large form that filled the open doorway. Juan had left so fast, he hadn't even closed the door. "Oh, you startled me."

Her landlord was leaning on the framework of the door. "Will it do?"

"Yes, it's lovely. It was good of you to agree to rent it to me."

"I don't think I actually did agree. Rosa sometimes bullies me."

She laughed. "I can't quite see you being bullied by a tiny little old woman."

"Nevertheless, that's how this happened. I hadn't planned to have anyone here until the building is restored."

"Why not?"

"Because of noise and dust from my working."

Her eyes narrowed in a direct gaze as she took a step nearer. "Why do I get the feeling that isn't the whole reason?"

He met the challenge of her gaze. "No, it isn't. The house is dangerous on the second floor. The...floor is bad and the wiring is strung around. I don't want anybody to go up there for any reason. A person could get hurt."

"How could anybody *get* up there? You've got it completely blocked."

"Yes."

"How do you even get up there to work?"

A flash of anger crossed his eyes. "That doesn't need to concern you, does it?"

"No, it's your house."

His shoulders relaxed slightly. "Rosa told me your name."

"Oh, I'm terribly sorry! I didn't get a chance last night to introduce myself and—"

He interrupted, without smiling. "Have you been warned that this building is haunted?"

"Rosa believes it is, and Juan couldn't wait to get out of here. I was told ... Rosa told me you said I'd get frightened if I stayed here. Did you really say that?"

"Yeah."

She grinned, hands on hips. "The ghosts, I suppose."

"I suppose."

"I thought it was a dare."

"No. The opposite. I was trying to talk you out of coming." He plunged his hands into the tight pockets of his jeans; only his fingers would fit in. "Terry, I promise there's nothing in this house that can hurt you. If there was, I wouldn't have you here, however bullied I was into agreeing. In this apartment there is no danger whatever. Please remember that, if you should get scared. I mean, if you should hear or see anything strange."

She expected a laugh or at the least a smile with this last remark. None came. Sobered over his less-than-welcoming behavior, she looked away, at a painting of red sandstone cliffs that hung on the far wall, then back at him. "And *will* I hear or see anything strange in this house?"

"Possibly."

"What things?"

"Noises, maybe. Cats get up on the balcony sometimes, and bats get in through some of the attic windows. And the...uh...ghosts might get started with their...uh...their carrying on. But look, I'm right across the hall if you need me, so there's nothing to be worried about."

Pushing away from the wall, he stepped toward the door. "Sorry, there's no phone here. I've no need for a phone. Rosa said she'd see that you have what you need."

Terry stared. He was telling her—perfectly seriously—that ghosts lived here! What *wasn't* he telling her? There was something; she could feel it. "Wait."

He turned. "Yeah?"

"Rosa told me you often leave town."

"Rather often, yeah. She was supposed to make that clear, so you'd know there isn't always somebody here. But you don't have to be worried. Jerome is the safest town I've ever lived in. There's nothing but good people here."

"The living ones, I assume you mean."

This made him smile. "The ghosts are okay, too, Terry. They say there aren't bad spirits on this mountain. Anyone will tell you that."

He left quickly, as if he wanted to give her no chance to question him further. Through the open doorway, Terry watched him cross the narrow hall and enter his own apartment.

Strange sounds? Juan had mentioned that people heard sounds. How noisy could cats and bats be?

There was something about the way Mike Calhoun talked about the house that made her nervous. He had admitted he didn't want to rent the apartment to her. Yet he had completely furnished it *before* he finished the upstairs. That didn't make a great deal of sense, somehow. To furnish an apartment he didn't want anyone to rent. And she hadn't liked the tone of his voice when he was so explicit about not wanting anybody upstairs. No, he sure as hell didn't. Why would he need such an impenetrable barrier to the upstairs of his own house?

Well, Terry scolded herself as she unpacked her suitcases in the bedroom, she had no right to complain if she met odd people in this town. What could she expect, coming to a place like this, a town barely alive? Mike Calhoun had no visible means of support, yet he owned this building and was renovating it. She had written a check for the apartment rent, not to him, but to Rosa and it was Rosa who wrote the receipt. There must be more connection than mere friendship between the two of them, just as she'd guessed last night when they exchanged quick glances in the hotel room. Why else would he let Rosa bully him? Yet Rosa insisted she knew almost nothing about him.

Juan came with sheets and towels and a few dishes later in the day. She heard a car drive up, but when she walked out onto the front porch, it was Mike, not Juan, who stood there holding the large box.

She asked him, "Wouldn't Juan come in?"

"He preferred not to. So I thought I ought to help him out."

He followed Terry into the house and set the box on the dining room table.

"Juan is really frightened of this place," she said. "I could see his face turn a shade paler when he came in."

He tried to shrug it off. "You know kids. I hope this will be everything you need."

"It was kind of Rosa to send it over. And kind of you to save Juan from having to come in."

While Terry looked up at his pale eyes, she began to ask herself what it was about those eyes that seemed to look right through her. What was it about his smile that made her feel she had walked right into summer? Yet seasons could change very quickly in his smile; it could become winter very fast.

He was saying, "I was going to stop in a minute anyway to tell you I'm going to be out of town tonight, and possibly tomorrow night."

She felt a small wave of fear, one she never would have expected. She'd believed at least she wouldn't be alone here the very first night. Why would he go away so soon when he'd promised he'd be there if she wanted him?

Trying to keep her voice casual, she asked, "Is this something you just decided?"

"I didn't decide it. I've been called out of town. An emergency."

"I thought you said there's no phone here."

"I get my calls at the hotel. Juan or somebody else runs over to tell me. He told me just now, so I'm gonna have to hurry. You'll be okay, Terry."

"Sure. Of course I will." Intellectually she was sure of it. But all this talk of ghosts could set any disbeliever just a little on edge.

He could sense her apprehension and she knew it.

"There's nothing to worry about," he said, unbuttoning his shirt.

She turned with a smile. "Hey, do I look like somebody who would worry over a few old ghosts?"

He was still unbuttoning his shirt, getting ready to change clothes, when he paused just long enough to turn back from the doorway. "Take care of the knee."

"Oh. The knee will be fine with a little more rest." *Where are you going?* she had wanted to ask, but she hadn't had the chance. She wondered who had called him away at a moment's notice. A girl? Anything was possible with him; there was no point in guessing.

THE APRIL NIGHT WIND billowed down across the mountain and through the high windows of the Beyer House, rattling the broken panes in the attic windows and moaning through the hollow rooms above her. Floorboards creaked. An owl screeched in tree branches above the garden. The eerie atmosphere wrapped itself around Terry and she welcomed the stimulus of its melodrama while working late at night with her sketches spread out on the dining room table.

Her character, Rod Lightning, was a close likeness of Mike Calhoun, no question of that, but he lacked that mysterious quality of Mike's, the something in his eyes that seemed to absorb moonlight better than sunlight. Perhaps, Terry thought, studying her sketches, she ought to put more emphasis on the scar.

For two days and two nights she neither saw nor heard any sign of Mike. Nor did she hear anything unusual from the empty caverns of the building. By day the old house was wonderfully silent and her apartment was sunny; she had never had an environment more conducive to creative work, and the sketches were going very well.

But at night while she listened to the wind in the high eaves and the mournful wail of an owl, Terry thought irrational and disturbing thoughts about the man whose house she was living in. Was he more phantom than man? His voice, so raspy deep it sent its vibrations surging through her bloodstream, seemed to ride more smoothly on darkness than on light. Like a secret. He carried with him the weight of a heavy secret; she could feel it.

By the third day of minimal activity, her knee was sufficiently rested that it was no longer hurting. This meant she could drive down the mountain to the town of Cottonwood to express mail the first of the comic strip panels to her editor. She shopped for groceries before she headed back to Jerome, and it was odd how heading back up Mingus Mountain already felt a little like coming home.

Was Mike down in the valley, she wondered. With a woman? Rosa had hinted he might have a girlfriend in the valley.

That afternoon, wearing jeans and an oversize pink shirt, she sat on little bleachers of the park on Jerome's main street and sketched more impressions of the town and its faces and its old buildings.

When she returned to the Beyer House, Mike was home, in the garden on his hands and knees, planting something.

From the porch step she called to him, "It's a warm afternoon, Mike. Do you want to share some lemonade with me?"

When he looked up, wiping perspiration from his forehead, his hand left a dirty smudge. "Sure."

"I'll just be a few minutes."

In the kitchen, she set the container of frozen lemonade she'd bought this morning in a bowl of hot water to thaw. Then, because she felt dusty, Terry ducked under the shower before she changed into a yellow summer skirt and white cotton blouse trimmed in lace.

Within twelve minutes she was standing on the porch with a tray of lemonade and cookies and thinking, *This is so quaint. My first experience with quaintness.* But somehow it fit. The whole world around her, this funny little town that had once been a big town, was quaint. Trying to brush the dust off the old porch table with her hand wasn't effective, so she spread paper napkins under the dishes.

"I'll be right there," Mike called, patting down the soil. He poured water over his newly planted seeds and picked up the empty bucket.

Diligently, he wiped his hands on the seat of his jeans and then on his gray T-shirt before he sat down across from her. The smudge of dirt on his forehead was still there. An image of him as a little boy playing in dirt flashed into her mind. He *had* been a child once, with the mischief and the dreams of all little boys.

"Hey," he grinned. "This is damn nice of you."

"I'm glad you're back."

"You weren't scared in the house alone, were you?"

"Of course not. But this building certainly does creak, doesn't it?"

"It's been in the process of dying for a long time."

"I'm glad you're not going to let it die. It really is quite beautiful."

"Once it was."

She handed him a small glass of lemonade. "You travel a lot, do you?"

"No." He tasted, licked his lips, and gave a nod of approval. "I get called away once in a while."

"Oh."

Neither his voice nor his manner invited questions. Every time she asked something, she half expected her question to be ignored. Terry remembered what Rosa had said about people not asking questions in this town.

Mike offered, after an awkward silence, "I work with a volunteer search-and-rescue team. Any emergency in the valley, I'm often summoned, especially for searches because I know the area pretty well."

"And because you're a paramedic."

"Yeah. Well, I work as a volunteer with an ambulance crew in Cottonwood."

"That's where you've been now?" The question was out before she realized she was being inquisitive again.

He nodded. "A little kid wandered away from a camping area in Oak Creek Canyon."

"Did you find him?"

"Yeah. Finally. He's okay, just exhausted." Mike reached for a cookie and sat back chewing. "Rosa tells me you draw a syndicated comic strip."

"I have a little character, a self-proclaimed sleuth named Clover Mae Sibley who travels around the country in her motor home seeking men and adventures, which are the same thing. She gets involved in other people's lives and scandals and finds mysteries to solve."

"And Clover Mae Sibley is presently in Jerome."

"Yes. She's getting involved with a decadent, devious movie star named Rod Lightning."

"Good God."

"You might get a kick out of Rod," she grinned, refilling the glass he'd emptied already. "Rod is . . . interesting. Incredibly handsome."

"I'll look forward to meeting them both." Mike wiped his lips with the back of his hand. "Did you make this lemonade?"

"I thawed it. Does that count?"

"Sure. I don't think I've had lemonade since I was a kid. It tastes like a summer afternoon."

"Today feels like a summer afternoon."

"Umm hmm, it's warm for April."

Terry noticed him looking at her as he had the first time he saw her in the light of the street lamp when he was literally holding her in his arms. He seemed to be seeing her for the first time, once again.

She asked softly, "Why are you looking at me that way?"

"What way?"

"The way you are."

He cleared his throat. "I was thinking how long it's been since I've done anything like sit across from a lady on an April afternoon drinking lemonade and eating chocolate chip cookies."

"You look pretty content sitting here."

"It makes me feel . . . alive."

This remark jolted her, because it came as sadness glazed his eyes. *Secrets are in his eyes.* She could sense secrets more strongly this moment, here on the sunny porch, than at any time yet. *Eight years,* Terry thought. Rosa said he was only thirty; that meant he'd lived on this isolated, half-alive mountainside most of his adult life. Why? Why would a young man come here? Why did he stay?

"Mike," she said carefully. "What ever brought you to this town?"

He cocked his head sideways and sighed as he folded and unfolded the paper napkin in a way that made her realize this was not a welcome question. But it was too direct a question for him to ignore. She waited.

"I was traveling," he answered. "I stopped at a little bar in New Mexico, somewhere in the middle of nowhere that had a fantastic view of the distant mesas. There was a guy there, another traveler, who told me he knew of a place even more isolated than the place where we were sitting. A real ghost town, he said. He described Jerome, Arizona, and I wanted to see it, so I came. And I decided I wanted to stay."

She eyed him warily. "It was the isolation that appealed to you?"

"And the atmosphere. This mountain. I like this mountain."

"Eight years is a long time."

Mike didn't answer, but at her remark his jaw muscles tightened. Watching him with scrutiny, Terry saw a shadow enter his eyes. Dark, frightening. His fists clenched and unclenched and he shifted in his chair.

For some reason, he did not like being reminded about how long he had lived here. It seemed to make him angry. Yet he'd stayed by choice, *hadn't he?* Terry tried, with little success, to contain her mounting curiosity about this man. He talked as though his life had begun eight years ago in a bar in the vast, dry deserts of New Mexico. She wanted to ask what had happened before eight years ago—before that isolated, roadside bar—but she couldn't. Every instinct was telling her it would do no good to ask. Rosa didn't know. No one knew. And no one ever would. The certainty with which this intuition came over her frightened her. Whatever had happened to him must have been very bad. It had driven him to a mountain full of ghosts.

She said, watching his clenched fist gradually relax while he leaned back in the chair, "You consider this valley home now, don't you? You've explored it enough to be considered an expert on the terrain."

"I spend a lot of time outdoors. The weather here is good all year and I enjoy hiking."

The anger that had gripped him, if it was anger, moments ago, had subsided. Once more, his eyes had changed like the seasons. He'd been reminded of something he didn't like, but now it was gone. He was back with her again, and his voice was easy, friendly.

Because his negative reaction to her probing had been so fleeting, Terry decided to risk one more question, just one more. She asked, "Where are you from originally? Why were you traveling?"

He hesitated, then shrugged, not looking at her. "Why does anybody travel? I wanted to see America."

What were you running from? she wanted to ask, but she couldn't. He hadn't answered her question; somehow she hadn't expected him to. Yet he'd tried to be nice about it. There was a certain sincerity in his smile that warmed her—a gentle something in his smile and sometimes in his eyes. That gentle something came now as he looked at her and moved closer to her to better see the view of the changing colors of the late afternoon sky.

"There's something about this town," she mused, "that's utterly fascinating."

"I agree."

In the long silence that ensued, she felt his thigh brush her leg. It seemed deliberate. He moved his hand over hers and gazed on the landscape out beyond the street below. Every house was built with a porch or balcony that overlooked the vast Verde Valley. Beyond, down the slope of the mountainside, was a view of the old high school, which seemed to rest on a ledge at the edge of the town, the first large building a traveler passed on reaching the city limits.

Far to their left, resting in a hillside cradle just below the town, was the enormous, sprawling shell of the Little Daisy Hotel. From this distance, it didn't look like a shell, but a living building. It's proximity to the old mine site, just above it, was testimony to the function this big hotel had once. It was the mine that drew people to Jerome in its prosperous years, and the hotel must have been a hub of activity then.

"Incredible view, isn't it?" he asked in the husky voice that stirred her every time she heard it. "The sun looks different on the distant cliffs every hour of the day and every season of the year."

Terry had marveled at that view a hundred times, but not now. Her attention focused on the warmth of his hand over hers and the warmth of his thigh against hers. She was keenly aware of the rise and fall of his chest under his tight T-shirt as he breathed. The rhythm of his breathing broke with the heave of an enormous sigh. She began to liken a closeness to this man to walking a live volcanic crater—a sleeping crater, outwardly benign, but under the surface, alive, rumbling with discontent. Threatening. Dangerous.

A shivery thrill coursed through her, not unnoticed. Mike's silver-blue eyes turned from the valley to gaze at her, silently questioning the reason for the shiver. The pressure of his hand increased on hers. His breathing changed still again. Self-consciously, she lowered her eyes, looked at their hands—his hand square and masculine, streaked with red-gray dirt from the garden, covering hers.

"Forgive me if I stare at you sometimes, Terry. Your beauty sort of astounds me."

"I'm not beautiful."

He sighed deep in his throat. "Through my eyes..." His voice melted into a whisper so soft she couldn't hear how he finished the sentence.

"Through your eyes," she murmured, feeling strangely dizzy, "through your eyes, everything must look silver."

This made him smile. "Sunlight in your hair looks silver." Touching her ash-blond hair with his fingertips, he gazed at her for a long time in silence, which didn't seem like silence to either of them.

It was he who forced his gaze away. He lifted her hand and kissed it softly. His voice trembled slightly when he said, "Thank you for the lemonade," and rose, brushing his hair from his eyes.

"The pleasure was mine."

Terry watched him for a few minutes from the porch as he worked a posthole digger in the garden. He hadn't said what he was doing it for, either planting a tree or building a fence, but it was hard work in the dry soil. His T-shirt darkened with perspiration and his muscles strained. Once or twice he glanced back up at her.

The vertigo left by his nearness remained, making her think her knees wouldn't hold her when she got up and tried to walk. For a moment she'd been sure he was going to kiss her. There, in the white lazy moments of the spring afternoon, he'd wanted to kiss her and she knew it. He'd wanted to and forced himself not to. And he had left her with the strangest feeling that the day—and the whole world with it—was incomplete.

JUST BEFORE MIDNIGHT Terry was awakened by a noise so hideous she sat straight up in bed with her heart pounding. A hyenalike howl drifted down on the night air from some distant part of the upstairs. She shivered. Whatever that howling was, it certainly wasn't a cat. And it wasn't human.

Chapter Four

Echoes billowed through the dark hallway like gusts of wind. Inhuman moans snarled out from the vacuous corners of the building. Trembling in her bed, Terry knew, suddenly and horribly, why she had been warned—by Rosa and by Juan and by Mike—about the sounds in this house.

The night was cold. She slipped into her robe and switched on all the lights as she made her way through the bedroom and into the living room, to the front door.

Opening the door with caution, Terry heard the ghostly echoes in the hallway getting louder. The moans were coming from upstairs. Something hideous was up there!

Although the hour was late, there was a light under the door of Mike's apartment. Terry glanced at the shadowy hall staircase and jumped back, her hand in front of her, as a dash of silver-white light appeared on the ceiling over the boarded entrance to the steps. The light began to wriggle and take on the shape of a human figure—definitely a male figure. It hovered, floating in front of the high window over the upper landing for a few seconds before it slowly disappeared.

Terry recoiled, less in fear than in disbelief. She couldn't trust what her own eyes had just seen. *My God,* she thought, *this house really is haunted!* And Mike knew she'd find out that it was. No wonder he didn't want her to come. Yet...it couldn't be! There were no such things as ghosts. Yet she had seen one! There had to be some logical explanation for this. There had to be, and there couldn't be. All the denial she could conjure up couldn't cancel what she had heard and what she had seen. Fleeting as that white figure was, she had clearly seen it!

For a few moments, it was hard for her to think. Was her secretive landlord upstairs? The stairway was completely blocked, so he couldn't have gone up that way. Yet he'd told her he often worked up there, renovating the upper story; he must get into the upstairs rooms from the street above, somehow. And he must be up there now, because surely he wasn't just sitting behind the closed door of his apartment pretending there wasn't something grim and diabolical happening this minute in this house!

The hallway seemed as cold as ice. Terry knocked on Mike's door, waited nearly half a minute, then banged on the door with her fist. Gazing up at the ceiling, wondering if the ghost was going to reappear, she was unsure whether or not she wanted it to. The hall ceiling was dark now, so dark that it would be easy to tell herself she had only imagined the white figure floating there.

In response to the banging, Mike opened his door finally and stood barefoot, wearing blue jeans and a white T-shirt, his body filling the entire doorway.

Surprise mixed with relief flooded her. "Mike! You're here!"

"Yeah. Where else would I be at this time of night?"

His deliberate nonchalance angered her. What kind of stupid game was he trying to play? "I thought maybe you were up..." She glanced at the black stairway again. "What's that hideous noise up there?"

His eyes moved involuntarily to the stairs and he scratched his head as if he didn't know how to answer.

"Noise?"

She stared at him. "Don't tell me you didn't hear anything!"

"My stereo was on."

"I didn't hear any stereo."

"I wouldn't blast it in the middle of the night. I use earphones."

She swallowed. "Don't do this to me! You're the one who said there were strange sounds in this house."

"Yeah," he conceded. "And I told you not to worry about it if you heard any."

She could sense his discomfort; he wasn't that good at hiding it.

"It's more than just sounds. Just now I . . . I saw something on the stairs."

"Saw what?"

"I think you know what. You must know! A strange light. It looked . . . like a ghost."

He glanced at her and then away, and had nothing to say in response.

This bothered her greatly. "What the hell did I see?"

"Probably a ghost." His eyes slowly began to soften. The noise had stopped and the house had fallen into deathlike silence.

"Have you . . . have you seen it?"

"The figure above the stairs? Yeah."

"Well, what *is* it? It can't really be . . ." she stammered, then finished decidedly, "It can't!"

"You're shivering, Terry. Why not come inside? I'll make you a cup of coffee."

Before she had a chance to answer, a clanking noise like a rattling of chains came from the top of the house, followed by a hollow thud. Horror-struck, Terry slid quickly past him and into the safety of his apartment. He closed the door after her, showing no visible reaction to the ghoulish sounds.

She turned to face him. "You can't say you didn't hear *that*."

"Sure I did. I'm not deaf."

His stereo wasn't on, she noted, although he may have shut it off during the half minute it took him to get to the door. Or maybe he was getting dressed in that time. He sure was doing *something*. Unless it was true about the earphones and he simply didn't hear her knock until she started pounding.

She glanced about an apartment furnished much like her own, the same floor plan in reverse, done in similar, but more muted colors. His dining table, like hers, was strewn with papers and books, and she found herself wondering what sort of books they might be. Books always told a lot about a person. What other clues could she possibly find about a man who ignored the sounds of wild and wailing ghosts in the attic of his house and casually admitted he had actually seen a ghost? He acted as if all this were a common occurrence. Perhaps it was, in this house.

Between the living and dining areas a grillwork of black wrought iron bars formed a room divider. There was no such divider in her apartment, but here it matched the light fixture over the table and formed a design in shadows against the wall.

To Terry's astonishment, Mike approached her without hesitation and encircled her in his arms protectively, as he might have done if she were a child.

"Terry, I told you nothing could hurt you here. Those noises...they're nothing."

"And that...thing I saw?"

"It was nothing. Just light and shadow."

"You said it was a ghost. I wish you'd make up your mind."

The warmth of his body flowed into hers; chill of the midnight left. She remembered his warmth from the night he had carried her and from this afternoon when he had touched her. When he touched her now, she lost the feel of the floor under her feet, as if something lifted her, rendered her weightless. A tingling sensation began in her stomach and rose to her throat. She felt helpless, no longer in control of the moment or of the night.

He smiled, hugging her. "I'm trying not to scare you. You said you don't believe in ghosts so I'm trying to make you feel better."

"Are you telling me this house really is haunted?"

"You saw it, didn't you?"

"Yes, but . . ."

"But you don't want to believe it."

"Of course not! Well—" she shrugged "—maybe everybody sort of *wants* to believe in ghosts. It's sort of . . . fun, you know."

He smiled softly. "I know. So why fight it? You're staying in a haunted house, and I'm guaranteeing that the ghosts are perfectly harmless, so why not just enjoy it." His voice was so deep and soothing, almost mesmerizing.

But it wasn't quite enough. She protested, "But, Mike . . . what's up there?"

"Noises. People have heard noises in this house for over fifty years. I've only been here for eight, so what do I know about it? There are noises, that's all."

"And that doesn't bother you?"

"They've never hurt me any." He walked away from her and into his kitchen, from where he called, as if nothing had happened, "Is instant coffee okay?"

"Whatever you have."

"I'll just put on some water to heat, then."

When he came back, the softness was in his eyes again. Terry could tell he was frustrated, whether he tried to hide it or not. He didn't like the fact that she had seen the ghost, she thought. He didn't like having to try to explain what he apparently couldn't explain, except that the house he lived in was haunted and had been for a great many years.

"Mike, If you want to know what I think, I think there must be something alive upstairs."

"There's nothing alive up there, unless it's a squirrel or a cat or a bat."

"Well, it can't be *dead*! Whatever is causing those sounds can't be dead!"

He entered the living room again, his laughter more nervous than amused. "Hey, kid, you chose to live in a haunted house in a ghost town and you don't look like you're enjoying it. Stop trying to explain everything and don't be so skeptical. If the ghost decided to let you see him, then what the hell? He just did, that's all."

Flinching, she raised her hands in frustration. So he wanted to make light of it, did he? She could play, too. "Oh, I get it! You're keeping an insane relative locked in an upstairs chamber and you're trying to cover up the truth. Right?"

"The wife, yes. I read the same book."

"He should have told her. He was wrong not to tell her."

"What?"

"Mr. Rochester should have told Jane Eyre about the mad woman upstairs."

"Wouldn't she have lost respect for him and left?"

"I don't think so, not if he'd been honest from the start. Because she..." The words halted by themselves and fell away into the room's sudden silence.

Mike finished the sentence for her. "Because she was in love with him."

"Yes."

Those words, sighed from his lips, greatly unnerved her, for he spoke with his gaze riveted on her eyes. Terry stared back. "He should have trusted her."

There was a long, disturbing pause.

Then his eyes glazed once again and the glaze put distance between them, as he meant it to. "Letting you move in here was a mistake. Rosa is so damned persuasive, but I knew better."

"Why? Because I ask questions?"

"I don't blame you for asking, considering what you saw." His eyes raised toward the ceiling as if he were waiting for something more, but it had been very silent up there ever since Terry had come into his apartment.

Through the open window came the plaintive chirps of a cricket. Moonlight shadowed the wall with blowing leafy branches and reflected the lacy shadows of the branches in a wall mirror. Frustration clouded Mike's pale eyes.

Terry said, "I'm sorry if you regret having me here, but it's done and I am here."

"I don't regret having you here the way you mean."

"But you have secrets . . . like Mr. Rochester?"

"Forget Mr. Rochester. He was a fool."

Sensing how deeply bothered he was by this conversation, Terry moved closer, angry with him one moment for his secretive attitude, wanting the warmth of him near her the next. "Something's going on in this house. What could be so secret you can't tell me?"

"Damn it, I have told you. You just don't want to accept it."

"You're saying this house is haunted; that's your explanation for everything?"

"Yes. You saw it for yourself, yet you keep asking me to explain what I can't explain. I don't know what you want from me." He rubbed his chin and would not look at her. "There are ghosts here and I . . . and that's all I can say. You were warned about it before you came. If it bothers you that much, then the best thing is for you to leave."

"Leave?"

"You shouldn't be here at all."

Terry was stunned. "I should leave because the house is haunted?"

"If you can't accept that, yes. I don't want to be hounded about it."

She drew back, blinking. "Pardon me for having the curiosity of a normal human being!"

Mike ground his teeth, scolding himself bitterly for allowing Rosa to talk him into this. He turned to look at the woman who stood in the soft lamplight wearing a white cotton robe, barefoot, her shoulder-length blond hair brushed back carelessly. And he knew why he'd given in to the moment of weakness. No woman had ever affected him quite the way this woman did. Something in her smile, her laughter, the way her voice tended to drop into a whisper at the end of her sentences, something about her—everything about her—left him vulnerable and unable to think rationally. She took his learned and practiced caution from him as the sun lifted moisture from dew-drenched leaves, so softly, so gently.

"Terry, please understand. I don't want you to leave. I just think it's better."

"Because your house is haunted," she said sourly. "Harmless but haunted."

"Yes."

Her voice softened to a whisper. "I don't want to leave."

"Then don't. But if you stay, you'll have to accept and ignore the ghosts and stop asking a lot of questions I can't answer."

It was a great deal to ask and he knew it, and she knew he knew. But he was giving her an ultimatum. No, actually, he was giving in, with a condition. Ridiculous as it sounded, this was his condition for letting her stay: no more questions about ghosts. If he knew anything about them, if he had seen more than she had seen, he wasn't going to share it or talk about it. If there were legends, stories, she wouldn't get any of them from the man who owned the house. And there was some reason for his silence. Something guarded.

Mike's odd attitude, more than the ghost she thought she'd seen, made Terry uneasy. Yet she had to stay; there was no place else to go. And she was far less afraid than angry and far less angry than intrigued. "All right, Mr. Rochester. I won't ask about your ghosts."

He winced. "I'll get the coffee."

Moments later he returned from the kitchen with two steaming mugs. "You're not limping anymore, are you?"

"My knee feels pretty good. I've been very careful not to overdo."

"That's good." He set the mugs down. "Look, I'm... uh...glad you're staying. You bring a certain warmth to an old house that hasn't known any warmth for decades. The coffee's black. Do you want some milk or sugar?"

"I do like a little sugar, but I don't want to be a bother." She picked up one of the mugs. "I'll get it myself; I'm sure I can find it."

"There's a sugar bowl on the counter," he said, settling himself on the sofa.

His kitchen was neat, for a man's kitchen. There was no clutter except for a few dishes stacked in the sink. She set down the mug and opened a drawer to find a spoon while she looked at the Indian baskets decorating the walls. The kitchen was almost identical to hers, the oak cabinets, counters of white and blue tiles, fresh curtains over the window and the glass in the back door that led out to the narrow side gardens. There were a few plants in his kitchen, and an extra door, a louvered door she hadn't noticed at first—a pantry door, perhaps. He hadn't bothered to build a pantry in her apartment. Curious, Terry stared at the narrow pantry door.

He called, "Did you find the sugar?"

"Yes." She turned back and joined him in the living room and sat beside him on the couch, leaning forward, warming her hands with the coffee mug, her hair falling over her face.

Mike gazed at her. She seemed so small, and her features were delicate; her hair and her eyes were pale, yet there was a sparkle to her, an aliveness that generated from her. Enthusiasm for life, for her job, for challenges. Her mouth was small, her eyes large and wide apart, her skin flawless. How easily he could picture her in lace. Misty lace, like her blue eyes. Yes, he thought, she would be beautiful in lace. Here was softness: her hair, her skin. He wanted to touch her. This moment he almost ached to touch her.

His hand moved to her shoulder, a gesture of comfort, as if to reassure her everything was all right. He could feel her tense at his touch, but not from fear. It was her awareness of him as a man that had caused her to tense. Mike had seen how her eyes sometimes fixed on him. The attraction was mutual; it was impossible for either of them not to sense that. And impossible to ignore it.

Terry trembled at Mike's touch. It was very slight, but he didn't miss it, and he felt his power over her. That power brought forth sensations from days long past—sensations he associated with the strength and needs of manhood.

There had been women in these eight years—women who never really knew him. Women who might have loved him, had he allowed it. Women he could not love, even if he'd tried. Temporary affairs. He was allowed nothing more than temporary affairs by the rules he lived by, for in a sense he remained a prisoner, not free to love or be loved, not even free to feel.

Until now, when the sensations were stronger than he'd ever felt them, ever, even in the faraway days of his youth. This woman stirred him harder, deeper, than his pent-up body aches could cope with. She made him remember what it was to be alive. To hope and plan and think of new days and Christmases and the innocent, smiling faces of children. To think the thoughts of men not chained to shadows. To think the thoughts of men not condemned to life in prison.

Now, suddenly he was aware of a woman's softness. He set his coffee mug on the table. His hand moved over the smooth skin of her arm as he shifted nearer to her, and his lips almost brushed her temple. Almost. With force, he stopped himself.

She moved slightly, unconsciously, toward him, touching her arm to his. And the warmth of that subtle touch surged through him like a rush of hot blood.

Mike fought back the urge to kiss her. He had no right to kiss her. He felt her body so near his own, and the fight became a raging inner battle. The room seemed to go dark and light and dark again. He was aware of the scent of her perfume. Aware of her breathing—slow, deep breaths. Aware of her heart beating so near his own. Aware of his own body, tortured. And of her body, trembling.

She wanted his nearness, he knew; she even wanted his kiss. But he couldn't. It was too unfair. He gazed down into blue eyes and touched her cheek carefully with his fingertips—a touch that spoke his feelings.

He whispered, "Don't be afraid, Terry."

"Of you?"

"I meant of the house. You're not afraid of me, are you?"

"Maybe a little. Because I don't know who you really are. Sometimes I get the feeling you're someone...else."

Mike caught a glimpse of the shadow of the wrought iron room divider against the wall. With the light behind it, the divider formed a pattern of shadowed bars like the bars of a prison cell. He tensed, jolted into reality by a grim trick of light playing on shadow. Suddenly the wisps of Terry's hair burned his cheek like prickles of fire and he had to draw away. She turned her head in inquisitive response to his sudden change, but he couldn't look at her. It hurt to look at her. All he could see now were the shadows—the bars—somber reminders that he was imprisoned by a past he couldn't let go of.

Of course she didn't know him! She didn't even know his name. Sometimes for days on end now, after eight years, he didn't think about his real name. But he never forgot for more than an hour the faces of the two men who had forced him to discard his christened name and live in exile. Gil Spearow, who himself had disappeared, and Howard Boyce, the flashy young state legislator destined to keep winning elections. So the world thought. The world didn't know about Boyce's real connection with a convicted murderer named Calhoun, but it would. And Boyce's world would rock. Crumble. It was for this Mike lived. And for this, the macabre secrets that placed a barrier between him and the woman who sat so close to him tonight. The shadows of the bars on the wall had reminded him of what he dared not allow himself to forget.

"What is it, Mike?" Terry was asking. "What's the matter?"

"You're right when you say you don't really know me. You know nothing about me."

"You know nothing about me, either. That is, except that I came from Los Angeles with a sore knee and I draw little pictures for a living."

"You're right. That's not much."

"Ask me anything. I'm twenty-eight. I've been engaged twice, never married. I studied art at UCLA and free-lanced my cartoons, and did a strip in a few small papers until I came up with Clover Mae Sibley and got a terrific agent and then my big break, just this year. I grew up in a small town in California and I've never adjusted to the noise and congestion of a city and never will. Oh, and I like history. I want to learn everything about the history of Mingus Mountain.''

"That's it? Your life story?"

"Yes." She squinted at him. "You don't want to talk about yourself, though, do you?"

"There's nothing of interest to tell."

"Oh really, Mr. Rochester." She sighed in near defeat. "Why did you come to Jerome?"

"I told you. It seemed like a good idea at the time."

"Did you come to escape your past?"

He nodded, while a tightness grabbed his chest. It was dangerous to get close to anybody; he knew that. And he'd better keep remembering it. Tonight, sitting so close on the sofa smelling the perfume on her skin, he was too close.

"I won't pry, Mike. Rosa told me she's known you for years and knows nothing about you, so who am I to pry, having known you for only a few days?"

He was silent.

She pulled her robe tighter around her, showing discomfort at his subtle, but definite withdrawal. There was a certain fascination in mysterious men—the kind of fascination she was trying to create in her character Rod Lightning—but Mike was too mysterious even for Rod. Mike was literally a walking shadow. Terry wondered how he would react when he realized she had drawn him, scar and all, mysteries and all. And now there were ghosts to draw. She only hoped he had the sense of humor other people had about her caricatures. Surely he would. Comics were all in fun.

She said, "It's terribly late. I'd better go back to bed."

"I won't be around for a few days, Terry. If you need anything, just ask Rosa. There shouldn't be any ghosts disturbing your sleep while I'm gone. This—" He forced a smile. "This zombie jamboree tonight ought to placate the ghosts for a while so they'll be quiet."

She swallowed. *What did Mike really believe about that thing on the stairs? About those screams?* She'd agreed to his stupid rule: she wasn't allowed to ask. Or to yell at him for making remarks like the one about the zombie jamboree. "Are you leaving on another search-and-rescue?"

"No. I'm going fishing."

"Fishing? When did you decide this?"

"What do you mean?"

"Nothing." *What good is it to ask?* she thought. He was leaving to get away from her, wasn't he? There was tension between them that he didn't want to have to deal with. She could feel it, and she was certain he knew she could feel it.

He did. Mike had decided to go fishing moments ago, after experiencing emotions that had sent his needs soaring and his senses pleading and his heart wondering. He had decided it because he had wanted so desperately to kiss her, and he had to get away from her to cool down. He knew the woman beside him could come close to reading his thoughts, but he didn't try to justify his sudden decision to leave town or explain it in any way.

Terry rose, picking up the two mugs from the coffee table, neither even half-finished.

"It's okay, leave them," he said.

"I'll take them into the kitchen for you."

In the kitchen, she set the mugs in the sink and rinsed them. But she wasn't looking at the dishes; she was looking once more at the narrow louvered door on the inside wall. Now she realized what it was that bothered her; the door had a lock on it. People didn't lock pantry doors.

Mike had gotten up off the couch and was closing the window. Swiftly, to satisfy her mounting curiosity, Terry moved in front of the pantry door and tried the handle. It wasn't locked.

Feeling a little guilty, glancing behind her to make sure he wasn't looking, she opened the door just far enough for a peek inside.

What she saw made her draw back in alarm.

Chapter Five

The door opened to a stairway. It was narrow and steep, and too dark for her to see very far up, but it could lead only to the apartment above Mike's. So this was how he got upstairs. There was one puzzle solved.

Why am I starting to shake? Terry wondered, as a weakness crept from her knees upward. *It's only a stairway.* She quickly shut the door for fear he might catch her snooping, but the weakness lingered.

Why should a stairway upset her? Because it led up *there*—to where the ghosts were moaning. Was it possible Mike had even been up there tonight, instead of listening to his stereo as he claimed? The noises had stopped when she came in. But they hadn't stopped when she was talking to him in the hallway, and Mike had looked up and winced when that rattling sound came from the high rafters. So *he* couldn't have been responsible for the noise; it was some-one—or some*thing* else.

From the window, he turned around as she returned from the kitchen and crossed the living room to the front door. "It's getting pretty chilly outside, Terry. Is your apartment warm enough? If you need heat—"

"No, it's fine. Really. I can't sleep in a room that's very warm." She tried to keep her voice casual and not let him know that she didn't want him to leave on his damned fishing trip. She didn't believe in ghosts, but tonight she had seen one. The "jamboree," as Mike chose to call it, was real enough to make staying alone in this house different than it was before. Terry wasn't really frightened because there was nothing to indicate any danger. Actually, she was excited about the mystery of what she'd seen and heard; this house presented elements of high adventure. But part of the adventure was not knowing what to expect next, and when Mike was right here, so calm and reassuring, the possibility of seeing the ghost again was welcome—just to prove to herself she'd really seen it. Being alone in the house would make her more apprehensive; that was a little too spooky. She was irritated with him for leaving, but she couldn't say so, because if Mike had had his way tonight, she wouldn't be renting the apartment anymore at all.

Well, one good thing about his going away—she might have a chance to do some snooping around. She didn't see how, with all the barricades he'd put up. Certainly Mike was satisfied that neither she, nor anyone else, could get up to the second story. But he didn't know how resourceful she could be, or that she had happened onto one of his secrets—the narrow door in his kitchen.

"Well, enjoy yourself," he said. "If you like trout, maybe I'll cook you some in a few days."

It was unnerving the way he could change so fast from one mood to another. The only explanation she could come up with was that he was a very good actor; good at concealing his thoughts, his true feelings.

There had been truth in his embrace tonight. Warmth in his arms. But something had held him back and not allowed him to get any closer. Only his arms, and his hands—not his lips—had touched her. What had pulled him back? Something remembered?

Her apartment seemed unusually quiet when she was once again lying in her bed thinking of the sounds of a house that everybody said was haunted, and thinking of the man across the hall. As the midnight hours became the hours of pre-dawn, was he asleep over there? Or was something pressing on his mind to keep him lying awake the way she was?

WHEN TERRY WOKE at eight o'clock silence still prevailed over the house. She listened carefully for any sounds coming from Mike's apartment, but she could hear nothing. When she opened the shutters she saw that his Jeep was gone. Of course it would be. Getting up early was one of the main requirements in the game of fishing. Something fishermen always had to do. She supposed it had something to do with the habits of fish.

Yawning, Terry went into her kitchen to make coffee. She stretched. It was a great day for working—quiet, sunny, with a freshness in the morning air. How hard it was to think now of what had gone on last night, those awful noises. Now it was like a dream—not just the noises, but all of it. Mike's closeness. And the wild, stormy, scary, beautiful sensations his touch had brought—these, too, were almost like a dream against the cold light of morning. But unlike a dream, the memory wasn't going to fade. Not in a day or a year or ever. One never forgot the embrace of a man like him; one couldn't.

It was hard for her to work that morning, hard to concentrate. Her mind was on the promise she had made not to ask questions. Why was Mike so afraid of questions? He insisted that the house was haunted, but he didn't want to talk about it, and this was odd. Most people loved to talk about ghosts and speculate who the ghosts were and how they died and why the spirits stayed around; it was all part of believing in the spirit world. Maybe he didn't want curiosity seekers in his house, bothering him, but that wouldn't explain his refusal to discuss it with *her*, or his suggestion that she leave.

He just expected her to accept what she'd seen and drop it, but that was simply asking too much. Who could possibly drop it?

Why had Mike gone to such trouble to barricade the stairs so heavily, assuring himself that no one could get upstairs? For safety, he'd said. Unsafe floors. But might another reason be that there was something up there he didn't want anyone to know about? Something to do with last night's noises? If that was true, whatever he was hiding in the attics of the house was hideous—so hideous that even a few innocent questions had prompted him to suggest she move out.

Curiosity stung and nagged her, and the more she thought about it, the more curious she became. There had to be a way to get upstairs. But there wasn't any way—except through Mike's kitchen. Even if she broke into his apartment, the stairs door might be locked. It was no use. He'd gone to great lengths to make this place snoop proof.

Still, he didn't know she had discovered the stairs. That was the one thing he hadn't anticipated.

Terry thought about it all morning until she couldn't stand it anymore. There was a heavily guarded secret upstairs; there must be. And it might have something to do with the fact that Mike refused to talk about the ghosts. Why did that story about the madwoman in the tower keep popping into her head? Did the groans belong to the fleeting ghost figure she had seen on the stairs? How could they?

Daylight offered safety and courage. And defiance. At least she could *try* to learn something. Feeling like a burglar, Terry crept out into the hall and tried Mike's door. It was locked. Of course it would be if he was going out of town for several days. She walked around the outside of the house, checking the windows. His bathroom window was halfway open. It was large enough for her to crawl into but too high to reach without a ladder, and even if she were to find a ladder, people might see her crawling into Mike's side of the house. The living room window, too, was open, although he had closed the inside shutters. Maybe those shutters weren't locked.

On the front porch, Terry looked around to see if any people were in sight, and satisfied they were not, she reached through Mike's window and pushed at the wooden shutters. They gave. This was incredible luck. Entering through this window would be a cinch.

She slid through the window into his living room and closed the shutters behind her. Silence came down through the shadows.

In the kitchen, where sunlight shone softly through the blue chintz curtains, Terry discovered with a start that the stairs door was no longer visible. Mike had completely concealed it by pushing a tall cabinet in front of it. This confirmed her suspicions that he *was* hiding something upstairs; he was so determined that no one find a way up there. So she *had* caught him off guard the other night. Maybe he had been using the door and hadn't had time to hide it.

Propping her back against the side of the cabinet, Terry braced her feet and pushed backward with all her strength. It gave more easily than she expected because the floor was slick and smooth.

She stared at the exposed door, pausing with her hand on the handle. Now, if only...

Luck was with her; it wasn't locked. On examination, it appeared that the lock had not been properly fitted yet; it was only half-installed, so he couldn't lock the door even if he wanted to. Maybe that was the reason for concealing the door behind the hutch.

The stairway was steep and narrow and dark. Frantically searching the kitchen for a flashlight, Terry turned up a drawer full of them, tested for a bright one, and then, with her heart beating wildly, paused with deepening fear at the bottom step. *Calm down, kid!* she demanded of herself. *Just remember the knee, and take it slow and easy. And don't panic.*

The wooden staircase moaned under her weight. Shining the light in front of her, she saw that the lumber was not old. Mike must have built these stairs himself; they weren't part of the original house. Slowly she ascended, favoring her knee even though it was not hurting, and shining the light in circles at her feet and up the dark passage. It was so deathly quiet in the narrow passage that she could hear her own breathing. Except for the creaks on the stairs, it was like a vacuum of soundless, dark space, and the walk up seemed to take forever.

She emerged into the kitchen of the apartment above. At least she assumed it was the kitchen, because it was the same shape as the room below, with the same wide, low window facing the garden, but there the similarity stopped, for the room was in ruin. The window was boarded from outside, but enough rays of sunlight shone in through the cracks to produce an eerie light, enough light to see by. Bits of yellow and red wallpaper clung to the walls. The flooring was torn away where heavy appliances had once sat, and under the boards was thick, raw lumber.

Carefully, she made her way through the kitchen and into the living room. Here, too, were signs of decay and ruin. Mike had been truthful when he said he was doing some work up here, because there were new, wood-framed windows stacked against an inner wall and there were small piles of fresh lumber, some tiles and some plumbing pipes.

Nothing unusual—certainly nothing that could cause last night's awful noises—was here. A large broken mirror leaned precariously on one wall, and piled on the floor was some electrical equipment, which she couldn't identify a use for—some wires and switches. Certainly no evidence of ghosts, only of a man doing renovations on an old building. He would have had to hook up lights in order to work, she reasoned, because the boarded windows let in so little sun. Evidence that he had been doing just that was everywhere; electrical wiring was strung all over.

Terry could feel a small tingling in her knee, and wondered whether it was the result of the climb—of strain on that knee, or whether it was apprehension, even dread of the truth. There must be something up here that Mike was guarding so fiercely. What was it, though? *Where* was it?

Remembering what he'd said about the floor being dangerous, Terry walked carefully, making certain with every step that there was something solid beneath her feet. There were some badly damaged boards in places, but they felt perfectly solid.

The front door of this north apartment hung loosely on one hinge. She ducked through it and stood in the upper hallway, between the two apartments. Now a flashlight was no longer necessary, for the high window at the top of the stairs let in the sun. That high window had not been boarded shut, because it was too narrow for any human to crawl through. A cat or a squirrel could get in. But neither of those could howl and rattle chains and cause a ghostly figure of a man to appear near the ceiling.

The door of the south apartment—the one directly over hers—had fallen or been removed and was propped against the wall. Plaster from the ceiling was everywhere, leaving a white-gray dust that rose in tiny billows if she didn't pick up her feet. If the downstairs rooms had been in this same state of disrepair, it had taken a tremendous amount of work to renovate them. Eight years worth of work, evidently.

Pushing into this apartment, Terry shone her light in, and drew a breath of surprise. In the center was a table with a dustcover and a chair next to it. On the opposite side of the room, in the L, was a second table, also with a sheet covering it.

An odd feeling came over her. These things didn't fit. Terry carefully lifted one of the sheets. The flashlight beamed on a collection of electronic and stereo equipment, all kinds of contraptions. This paraphernalia could have nothing to do with renovating the building—it had some other use.

There were tapes, and there were wires leading around. And small speakers, several of them. In one corner was a machine that resembled a projector.

Terry felt her body go cold. The sounds she heard must have been on tape! Could that ghost have been on *film*? It must have been. Damn him! Mike had rigged this building to make it appear haunted.

But *why*? Why on earth would he do that? Was he eccentric? Or crazy? Or *what*?

She fought down the burning urge to force him into a confrontation. If she did that, he'd kick her out of the apartment, and she needed to stay long enough to get the Jerome material she wanted.

There were a couple of other things to consider, too. If she didn't confront him, she'd have more chance of learning what this was about. Rumors had abounded concerning this house for fifty years; that part was true. Hauntings evidently had been reported here long before Mike had ever come. If she was to admit trespassing in his apartment, and up here, he'd be so angry, he would make her leave, and then she'd never know what all this was really about. Maybe he was just plain crazy! But at least she'd know. And now she wouldn't be afraid, either. He'd told the truth when he said the noise couldn't hurt her. It was all a stupid trick.

And yet nothing added up. If Mike was up here last night, he'd done some fast moving to get back down while she was waiting at his door. He *could* have, but it wouldn't have been easy. Or there may have been someone else up here, working these machines. These machines didn't look as though they'd been used in a while; dust was thick on the covers. The tapes were scattered around carelessly. When Terry tried to turn on the projector, it didn't work. This bothered her, and she fumbled with it for a while, changing plugs on the several electrical extensions Mike had run up from downstairs. Finally, she realized the machine didn't even have a bulb. It hadn't been used; it was broken.

Worse than the discovery of this equipment was the growing certainty that it couldn't have been used last night. So what the hell was going on? Feeling a little shaky, Terry replaced the dustcovers carefully and proceeded through the other rooms. She found mirrors, some sheets of cardboard and sheets of tin—an odd combination of things that could all add up to the conclusion that Mike was indeed *haunting* this building himself. But what reason would he have and why wouldn't he tell her? Why make such a big secret of it? Why build a secret stairway?

Another thought screeched through her brain, one she didn't want to deal with. Yet, unwelcome as it was, the thought had come. Could Mike be trying to exorcise ghosts out of this house? Good heavens, Terry thought, I'm losing my mind. I could end up as crazy as he is if I let this stuff get to me. The evidence was here that the noises were on tape and the ghost on film. It was here, and it wasn't! What she had seen last night couldn't have been produced by that dusty, broken machine, and a search through all the rooms of both apartments produced no other.

It was eerie. And strangely frightening. Lingering up here was starting to feel like wading through a pool of madness.

It was not easy to make herself move slowly out of the darkened rooms and down the narrow stairs, but her safety depended on keeping her head and moving with caution every step of the way. If she were to fall now, it could mean getting badly hurt.

Extra care was needed, too, to be certain everything in his kitchen was exactly as she had found it—the hutch in front of the door, the flashlight put away. On impulse, Terry did a quick search through his closets and under his bed, looking for more electrical equipment, especially a movie projector. There was nothing. His two closets were half-empty; she was surprised at how few worldly possessions he owned.

It was not easy trying to close the shutters from outside after she had crawled back out onto the front porch. She had to do it with a piece of wire, hooking it on the bottom and pulling.

In her apartment again, Terry paced, making calculations and decisions. She was consumed with guilt for having invaded Mike's privacy; never in her life had she ever done anything like that. Curiosity about ghosts was a strong motivator, but it didn't excuse what she had done—not even if she was being deliberately tricked, which must be the case. Yet she couldn't be sure. *She just couldn't be sure.* That ghost on the stairs . . . if Mike had made it appear, *how* had he done it?

It would be unwise to mention anything she'd found to Rosa. A curious relationship existed between Rosa and Mike, although Terry couldn't begin to define what it was. Surely Rosa couldn't know if Mike was faking the haunting of his house. No, Rosa honestly believed it was haunted and so did Juan. And apparently everybody else around here. It was bizarre that Mike would pull something like this. He seemed so intelligent and stable.

But secretive, so damned secretive. *Am I afraid of him?* she asked herself. Does it bother me that he has a master key and that he could get into my apartment whenever he wants? *Does it?* The question was impossible to answer because when she was near him, Mike was not frightening. His eyes sparkled with genuine concern for her welfare, and his smile was sincere. That other side, though, that dark side, was also real. What more proof of this than the grim secret she'd just discovered upstairs?

Sleep didn't come easily that night. Scenes from the movie *Psycho* kept flashing in her head. The creaks of the house, so familiar now, didn't seem quite the same as before. She found herself listening for sounds of Mike moving around, but he was gone. There were only darkness and silence. How could he have been so sure it would be silent when he was gone? The idea returned that maybe the ghosts were real and he was trying to somehow drive them out, but that idea came from confusion and fatigue and desperation. And the fact that the machines she saw hadn't been used last night.

"Damn!" she swore aloud. Terry reflected on her flight into the unknown. What she'd discovered here was far worse than anything she could have anticipated. Even Mr. Rochester wasn't as sinister as this! Mr. Rochester's secret wasn't the condition of his own sanity!

MIKE WAS AWAY for a week. During that week there were, of course, no reappearances of the resident "ghosts." Terry phoned her editor from Rosa's hotel to learn that the first of her Jerome panels had been published on schedule, two days after she mailed them from Cottonwood, and the material was enthusiastically received. Her knee had sufficiently improved so she could walk into town.

It was a gradual uphill slope along Main Street from the Beyer House, which sat at the very end where the mountain curved, to the hotel in the center of town. Above were other houses on the upper street, and above that street, still another street. And still higher up the mountain loomed the great hulk of a building that had been a hospital, with its high balconies all looking out to the valley beyond. Terry always looked up at that building with longing, waiting for her leg to be well enough to make those steep climbs and get up there to explore. She had already driven as far up as she could by car. She'd reached the entrance, but there was a steep stairway to the doors at the top, which appeared to be boarded shut. By now the layout of the town was familiar to her. Driving the narrow old streets was all the touring she could do; climbing around in the old buildings was going to have to wait until she was better.

There was no need to drive the three or four blocks along Main Street between the Beyer House and the hotel because the uphill slope was smooth, a pleasant walk. That much exercise was needed. She took up the habit of eating lunch at a small cafe in town, and sometimes Rosa would join her. Terry almost dreaded Mike's return, for, suspecting what had caused the hideous growls and shrieks in the night, she didn't like the idea of having to hear them again. After he came back, she probably would. Over and over she puzzled, why would he do it? *Why?* And then, the question always rushed in: *did* he do it—or didn't he? Was she going to have to look at him and study his light eyes and think unwelcome thoughts of madness?

On the sixth day when she walked home from town a feeling of unease came over Terry—a sense that she was not alone on the quiet street. Turning, she noticed a man half a block behind her, strolling as slowly as she. The man hesitated when she turned, which made her wonder if he was watching her.

Or following her. *Don't be silly,* she scolded herself. The atmosphere of the ghost town was playing on her runaway imagination. The man was only walking there on the street, as tourists often did. Yet when she turned a second time, the man came to a startled halt. He *was* watching her!

In tight black pants and a leather jacket, he formed a dark silhouette against the sun. He wasn't dressed like a tourist, nor like one of the penniless drifters who frequently came through town.

Trying to talk herself out of the obvious conclusion that he was following her, Terry thought about turning back to town rather than returning alone to the big, empty apartment house.

It was a gut feeling, instinct. Suppose the man wanted something from her? What he could want, Terry couldn't imagine, but she had learned to go with gut feelings like these warnings that the man back there was someone to avoid.

Turning back meant having to pass him on the street. It shouldn't bother her to do that, on this fine, bright spring morning. Yet she hesitated. And once again lectured herself that she was being paranoid over nothing.

She quickened her pace, wanting to get home as quickly as possible, frustrated to discover that as she walked faster, so did he. The distance between them shortened. Her heart was beating faster by the time she reached the Beyer House, yet rationality prevailed, keeping her on the safe side of panic. There was no reason anyone should follow her. If he was, there was a simple explanation for it. No one in this town knew her; certainly no one had any reason to harm her.

Unless, of course, they believed she was associated with Mike Calhoun in some way. Unless, of course, the secrets in Mike's eyes had to do with...strange men in black leather who followed his tenants around.

No wonder I make my living creating wild adventure stories, Terry told herself as she approached the quiet old building she temporarily called home. *I've sure got the imagination for it!*

Terry's quick glance back from the door confirmed that the man was still there, and coming closer. In the drafty hall, she fumbled in her handbag for her key while the echo of a man's heavy boots sounded just inside the building's entrance. A black shadow darkened the doorway, cutting out the glare of the sun. Terry's palms began to sweat. The damn key was so hard to turn in the old lock.

For some moments the man in black didn't move. He simply looked at her from behind dark glasses.

Struggling with the key, she faced him, wishing his eyes were visible. "What do you want?"

Still the man stared as he stood spread-legged on the porch just outside the double doors, in the shadow of a large elm whose branches overhung the entrance. It startled her when he took a step forward and pulled a crumpled, folded newspaper from his jacket pocket.

"I'm looking—" the stranger finally answered "—for the person who draws a cartoon in this paper. Name of Terry Morse. I was expecting it to be a man, but in town somebody pointed you out and said you are Terry Morse. Is that right?"

Terry didn't like him. Not his black clothes, nor his manner, nor his voice, nor the feeling of evil eyes on her, although she couldn't see the eyes behind the dark glasses. She sensed danger. If she was to open the door, might he push her inside and pull her into the apartment? It would be smarter, she decided, to stay in the hall. "Why do you want to know?" she asked, trying to steady her voice.

The man's answer sounded almost like a threat. "Are you Terry Morse or aren't you?"

"Now look!" Terry protested, backing up a step as he inched nearer. "I don't like the way you...the way you're..."

She could see his jaw tightening in anger. And for the first time the feeling overpowered her that he meant harm to her. She couldn't fathom why, but the man was dangerous. And he was getting closer to her by the second. There was no way to get away from him because he stood between her and the entrance to the building.

"Are you her?" the gruff voice muttered in so frightening a way that Terry, becoming desperate, bolted, and tried to run past him, knowing it was risky, but preferring action to the awful feeling of being cornered in the hall.

At that moment the door to Mike's apartment swung open.

"Terry, what—?" He ambled out into the corridor like a grizzly bear. At the sight of him, the man in leather coiled back like a serpent and slid out of the doorway.

Mike charged forward in pursuit, but the stranger disappeared on the side of the hill where there were a dozen old buildings to hide in. It was useless to try to find him.

Mike turned back to see Terry standing on the porch looking stunned and confused. "Who the hell was that?" he asked.

"I have no idea. He followed me from town. Said he was looking for me, for the person who draws my comic strip. But I can't imagine why...." Mike's broad shoulder seemed to her to form a wall of protection as he approached. Terry trembled. "You don't know how glad I am that you were home."

He scowled. "You've never seen that guy before?"

"No. He looks like a member of a motorcycle gang or something. I was getting a little scared."

Gently, he touched her shoulder. "Are you okay?"

"Yes, just a bit shaky. I wonder why he ran from you. Why would he run like that, Mike, unless he was up to no good?"

"He wouldn't. Something is damned strange here."

With shaking hands, she gave him her key so he could unlock her door, then followed him into her living room.

She slid onto the couch. "That man acted so weird! He followed me all the way from town, then he stood in the doorway staring—like he was trying to figure out what to do."

"Did he say anything?"

"He asked if I was Terry Morse. He thought it...I...was a man. He took out a newspaper."

Mike frowned and rubbed his chin. "You mean a paper with your comic strip?"

Terry sighed jerkily as she leaned back on the sofa. "Yes. But what on earth would he want?"

He sat down on the arm of the sofa. "How did he act?"

"Angry. He acted angry. And sort of mean."

Mike watched her in silence. "You're shaking. Why don't I get you a drink. Do you have something?"

"I have some sherry in the kitchen. And that doesn't sound like a bad idea, even though it's still morning. Will you join me?"

"Not quite this early, but I'll be happy to get it for you. Sit still."

"Thanks. First cupboard on your right."

Passing the table strewn with her work sketches, Mike paused abruptly and picked up a panel of drawings. "What the hell is this?"

The hard scrape of his voice startled her. "It's my comic strip."

"Is this supposed to be a joke?"

She rose from the couch. "I assume you mean Rod Lightning. Do you see a certain resemblance?"

"Resemblance? This is a drawing of me!"

"Well, I'll admit I was influenced. I always base my characters on the real-life people around me."

His eyes were wide and staring. She wondered why this would rattle him so; most people got a kick out of seeing their likenesses depicted in her cartoons.

"Why?" His voice cracked.

"Why not? Real life is the model for all artists."

While he looked back at the drawings, his hand went automatically to his left temple. "You drew my scar."

Frowning, sensing something terribly wrong, she assured him, "You were a physical model, Mike. So were a lot of other people in Jerome. Rosa too. But the character is nothing like you."

He muttered an oath that caused her to flinch. "Why the devil did you draw the scar?"

"Are you sensitive about it? You shouldn't be. It's really—"

"Damn it, Terry!" Angrily, he crumpled the page of sketches in his hand and tossed it to the floor.

When she tried to touch his arm, he drew away.

"I had no idea it would upset you so much."

He turned angry eyes on her. "These damn drawings have been published?"

"Yes. They've been out nearly a week."

"All over the country?"

"Yes."

He swore an oath so powerful that Terry physically drew back. Something terrible must have happened.

"And . . ." His jaw was tight as he spoke. "And Jerome . . . did you identify the locale? Did you actually name Jerome?"

"Yes, of course. I told you I was—"

Veins were standing out in his neck. She had never seen anybody more furious. "You're going to stop these drawings that look like me, and you're going to stop them now! You had no right to do this."

She stepped still farther back from him. "You're not only eccentric, you're also paranoid!"

"Call me whatever names you want, just keep my face out of your stupid comic strip."

"I can't take Rod out! My story line is already established."

"I'm not asking, Terry, I'm telling you. I want him out!"

Desperately, she grabbed his arm. There had to be some way to reach him, some way to reason with him. He was frightening her, making her wonder still again if he was crazy, but he was also angering her. "Mike, you don't know what you're asking me to do. You don't know how important this is. Surely it can't make that much difference if a silly little comic strip character bears a resemblance to you. So what if a few people in Jerome know it's you? They think it's fun. Mike if you'd only—"

"No, lady," he answered with eyes as cold as ice. "You're the one who doesn't understand. It may be your idiotic comic strip, but it's my face, and I won't stand for it."

"I don't believe this!"

"Believe this, Terry. If you don't listen to me and do as I tell you, you could get yourself killed."

"*What?* Mike, what are you saying? Are you threatening to kill me?"

His eyes were squinted, mean. This was a side to him she had never seen and never wanted to see again.

"I didn't say that. I said you could get killed. What you've probably done—with your stupid little pictures—is get *me* killed!"

He turned quickly and left the room, slamming the door so hard behind him that the whole building seemed to shake.

Terry stood staring after him, numb, terrified. His words were echoing in her brain like a reverberating drum. *What you've probably done with your stupid little pictures is get me killed.*

Chapter Six

Mike shouldered shut his apartment door, and slammed his weight against it. Involuntarily, his hands went to his head where sharp pains had begun stabbing at him the second he saw those damned drawings. His prominent scar was so blatant in the drawings! A groan of frustration rose in his throat and caused him to choke.

Coughing, he made his way to the kitchen, poured a glass of water from the tap with shaking hands and tried to drink it down. The choking only worsened, and he grabbed the edge of the counter, head down, until the spasm stopped, then forced himself to finish the water to soothe the catch in his throat.

Damn her! Mike slammed the glass to the floor in a fit of fury. He picked up a glass bowl from the counter and smashed it, too, to the floor, and it shattered in a spray of glass bits that crunched under his foot when he moved.

Eight years of hiding and now this had happened. Swearing, he slammed about the living room until his throbbing head compelled him to slump onto the couch. He had to think—try to think. There was no question Terry Morse had put him in danger of discovery. Those cartoons appeared in newspapers all over the United States. And she had identified the name of the town where he lived.

He could leave, just get the hell out of here. But if he did, then these eight years were for nothing. All the planning—his scheme to get revenge and his freedom at the same time—was for nothing. If he missed this chance, he'd never have another. If he left now, he might live longer, but what good was living like this forever? Without his belief that the hiding would someday be over, what good was life?

Sitting alone, head in his hands, Mike began to get a tighter grasp of the real horror of what these pictures had done. Howard Boyce and Gil Spearow, one or both, may have already seen them. By drawing him, Terry had connected herself publicly to a wanted man. And Mike at this point was unsure how many people wanted him. He knew of two men who wanted him dead. There were others who wanted him brought back to spend the rest of his life in prison. But it was the men who wanted him dead that were a danger to Terry. They'd have to eliminate anyone who even knew him.

A man had been following her this afternoon, carrying a newspaper, asking for her by name. Mike pulled at his hair in aggravation, trying to get a better picture of the man in his mind. The guy had run off before he got a real look at him, but Mike was pretty sure he'd never seen him. Still, he was following the person who drew the cartoons. *Why?*

Terry was in the middle of something terrible, and he didn't know how to get her out. What could he do, tell her he was a convicted murderer? That ought to get her trust. It might even get him turned in. His tantrum just now hadn't helped. In fact, he'd been so angry, he'd said far more than he'd intended. What the hell *had* he said? That she could get killed? Damn, why had he said that? For those few moments shock had blocked his reason.

He'd been insane, completely insane, he realized now, to let her move in here. It was too late to get her out; his enemies already knew where she was. They must know. Who else would seek her out and follow her home? And because of her, they knew where he was! It might be too late to save her. It might be too late to save himself.

IT HAD TAKEN TERRY a full minute, after Mike's stormy exit, to move. Then, zombielike, she had walked back to the table and stared at her pictures in the bright slants of sun that shone in through the window slats. The handsome face, the almost white eyes and gray hair. The scar. It was true anyone could recognize Mike Calhoun in these drawings. And that angered him, infuriated him. He didn't want to be recognized—by anyone, anywhere!

Why? she asked herself, setting down the paper and staring out at the branches of an elm tree moving in the wind under an almost cloudless sky. Was he a criminal or something? What did he mean her drawings could get him killed? Get *them* killed? He wasn't making sense!

But a powerful guilt was imprinting itself on every question, every thought. Whatever was wrong—whoever he was—the bare truth was that she had seriously invaded a man's privacy. The fact that she had never intended it didn't excuse her. She had been wrong.

Turning around, she stared at the closed door. With eyes sparkling contempt, Mike had slammed shut everything that had happened between them. But obviously a door slam wasn't going to end what she had started by creating Rod Lightning. It wasn't going to end his fury.

The door to his apartment was unlocked. She let herself in without knocking, and stood in silence staring at the man who sat slumped over, head buried in his hands, concentrating so hard on his agonized private thoughts that he hadn't heard her enter.

Near tears, she approached him and touched his shoulder. He jerked in alarm.

"Mike..." she whispered in a tear-filled voice. "Mike, what have I done?"

He barely moved. She knelt beside his chair, hand on his knee, and repeated, "What have I done?"

Finally he made himself look at her, and when he did, the anger began to ebb, for the sight of her face caused something to soften in him. She was frightened. And hurt. And defenseless.

And she was the only person he'd cared about, except for Rosa Gonzales, in the last eight years of his life. The only woman he'd allowed himself to think about and to want to dream about at night. The only one. Maybe, he thought while he looked at her tear-rimmed eyes, his caring had cost him everything, but he couldn't sit still and see her destroyed along with him. Just because of her association with him.

"Mike...?"

He straightened. "You had no way of knowing."

"I still have no way of knowing, unless you tell me."

"You have to stop the pictures."

She remained on her knees, looking up at him. "Are you a fugitive from the law?"

He stared at her.

"Why else would you be so devastated at the possibility of being recognized?"

He swallowed. There was no choice now but to tell her the truth—or part of it, at least. Nothing else could convince her of the seriousness of the situation and of the danger she was in. And anyway, she suspected. Lying wouldn't serve much purpose at this stage of the disaster.

"You're right," he said, half-choking, trying to get out what he had kept locked inside for so long. "I am a fugitive. I escaped from prison eight years ago, the same day I was convicted of first-degree murder."

Terry felt a chill move through her, from the top of her head all the way to her knees. "Murder?"

"I'm not a murderer," he said, brushing back his hair from his eyes. "I was framed. Oh, I know you're thinking I'd have to say that. You're thinking all criminals say that. I couldn't blame you for not believing it, but all the same, it's true. Two men lied to get me convicted. And it's those same two men who will come after me now. They want me dead. And I want them . . . alive."

"You think they'll find you because of the comic strip?"

"I think, Terry, that they already have."

She rose and began to pace. "The man who followed me? You think he has something to do with it?"

"Why else would anybody follow you?"

"What could they want me for?"

"To lead them to me, of course. You got yourself into something pretty bad, Terry. One of these men is a ruthless killer, and he'd kill anybody to get to me."

She turned. "Why? You have to tell me, Mike. Now that I'm . . . in it, as you say. You have to tell me."

He sat in silence for so long she thought he wasn't going to talk to her about it anymore.

She said, finally, "If they followed me, and already know where you are . . ."

"It's more complicated than that," he said. "I'm not sure these two men are still in contact with each other. In fact, I think one is trying to kill the other. I've tried to find one of them, find out where he is, and I can't, so I think he's been in hiding, too. But I'm not sure. I can't be sure."

"I don't know what you're talking about! Who's in hiding? One of the men who is after you is in hiding?"

"Yeah."

"And you've tried to find him? I thought he was trying to find *you*. Why—?"

"Because," he interrupted, "he's the only person on earth besides the real killer who knows I'm innocent." He sighed. "Sit down, Terry. I'll try to explain."

She waited while he stalled. Finally he began. "I grew up with these guys. We were kids together, and we went to college together. One of them, Howard Boyce, had a cousin who lived with him and the four of us were pals. One day over Thanksgiving vacation from college, the four of us were hunting. Howard murdered his cousin David. Cold, deliberate, premeditated murder, because David stood to inherit part of Howard's father's millions.

"Howard was always insanely jealous of his cousin. When the police saw through his story that the death was a hunting accident, Howard bribed Gil, the other guy, into framing me, saying I was the one who shot David. We'd traded guns; Howard had known enough to do that; he had let me use his new one. And because I'd had a couple of run-ins with David myself over a girl we both liked, the stories of the two so-called witnesses stuck. I was tried and convicted of first-degree murder. It was their word against mine. Howard's father was the richest and most powerful man in the county, an attorney. That didn't help."

Terry's face had paled. She was weak and shaking. "What was your sentence, Mike?"

"I was never sentenced. I escaped first. After I was found guilty, I pretended to faint and was taken to the infirmary. It was a wild try and even I couldn't believe it had worked. I was able to jump and grab the guard's gun and get away. I met Gil in the hallway. Stood facing him with the gun in my hand right after he'd lied his head off on the witness stand and I never wanted to kill a man so badly in my life. He knew it too. He threw his car keys to me so I could get away."

"Gil—the man who framed you—helped you get away?"

"Yeah. I never knew whether he helped me out of guilt or whether he did it to save his neck because he knew I could shoot him right on the spot. I told him if I ever saw him again I'd kill him, and at the time I meant it. And he knew I meant it."

She was wringing her hands nervously, disbelieving that what she was hearing could actually have happened. "And you actually...you got away and they never were able to find you?"

"Obviously not. I ditched the car after a couple of blocks and caught a bus to the roughest part of the city. Pawned my expensive suit for enough money for old clothes and a hat to cover my scar the best I could, and a little cash, and got a ride out of town with a truck driver. I knew the odds of getting away when I tried it. But it worked. I found this obscure, isolated mountain and tried to make a life here. Such as it is."

"Till I ruined everything."

"Yeah."

Tears rolled down her cheeks. Silent tears. She could say nothing. Mike's voice was forcibly controlled, although from time to time while he was talking, his voice broke. The story, she reasoned, was so rusted from having been concealed so long, unrevealed for so long, that it literally cracked when he had had to tell it. Still, his voice was controlled, while his eyes were not. His eyes frightened her. The anger was not gone—anger at her for what she'd done to him.

The glaze in his light eyes was more than anger, but Terry couldn't read what else was there. Could lies be there as well? It was hard to look at his eyes, and her gaze shifted about the room and then behind him to the arched doorway that led to his kitchen. The cabinet that hid the doorway to the stairs was in place just as she had left it when she sneaked in here and discovered the tapes and projector upstairs.

Seeing that hutch in the kitchen jolted her back into another reality—the reality of his madness. What else could it be but madness for a man to haunt his own house? And now the same man was admitting he was a convicted murderer and that there were men who wanted to kill him. Now that same man was telling her he was innocent of murder, that he had been framed. What was she supposed to believe?

What she could believe was his anger. And the intensity of his frustration. These were all too real. And all too frightening. What she could believe was that by drawing a caricature of Mike Calhoun, she had gotten him—and herself—in the worst kind of trouble.

She wiped awkwardly at the tears that stained her cheeks. "Your name isn't Mike Calhoun, is it?"

"No."

"What is it?"

"I can't tell you that."

"What . . . what's going . . . to happen?"

"You're going to stop the comic strip. And you're going to get out of this town as fast as you can."

She stared at him through her tears, and her chest ached. Her *heart* ached and she didn't know why. Fear? Guilt? *What if he was telling her the truth and he really was innocent?* She ached to confront him with what she had learned about the ghosts of the Beyer House, ached to know how he would react. And the ache inside her was becoming almost unbearable. She fought to control her mounting emotions, such conflicting emotions. Giving up the comic strip premise just at its onset could seriously jeopardize, maybe even kill, her young career. Leaving Jerome now carrying the weight of guilt over what she'd done to Mike was almost unthinkable. Not knowing was the worst of fates. Yet he seemed to think he wasn't giving her a choice.

"If they already know," she said in a thin, weak voice, "then what good is it to stop the story?"

"We can't be sure whether they know or not."

"But Mike..."

"You have to stop it, Terry. Today. I don't care what excuse you give your publisher. I want you to get over to the hotel and phone whoever it is that has the authority to stop it."

He rose. He had never looked so large to her; he seemed to tower over her as he looked down, the anger still burning his eyes. She had no choice but to get up too.

"All right," she agreed reluctantly.

He watched in silence as she wiped at her eyes again and turned toward the door.

Then she turned back again. "What are you going to do?"

"I don't know," he said. The harshness had left his voice. In its place was genuine uncertainty.

"Will you leave Jerome?"

"No."

Cold fear came over her. She blinked and stared at him wanting to scream, *Why not? Why not keep running, hiding, why stop now?* She wanted to ask, *What if they kill you?* But she couldn't. She could only stare back at him and wonder what he wasn't telling her.

Defeated, Terry left him, without closing the door behind her. She went back to her apartment to get her handbag. On the table was a folder with the latest finished panels. She gazed at them for a few moments, thinking that she hadn't yet made up her mind how Rod Lightning received that scar on his face. That damned scar. She had wondered if she'd ever get up courage enough to ask Mike how he got it. Now she'd never know anything—not even whether he was telling her the truth. And she'd never know why—or even if—he rigged the house with electronic scare tactics. She'd just have to drop everything and leave.

It was a lot to ask of her—just to leave. Why was she so afraid to confront him with what she'd found here?

This question was easy to answer. She had stepped way over the line of trust by sneaking into his apartment and up those stairs; he would be furious. Hell, she thought, he was already furious. He couldn't get much more angry with her than he already was. And she couldn't just leave without knowing. She couldn't. Especially in the light of what she had just learned about this man, she *had* to know.

He was in his kitchen opening a beer. Because his front door was still open, she let herself in again, and came up behind him again, unexpectedly.

"Mike..."

He didn't turn around. "I thought you were on your way to the phone."

"I am. But I want you to realize how hard this is for me. Unless I can figure out a way of dropping my character with no warning whatever, my strip will be in serious trouble."

"I can't help that," he said coldly.

She conceded with a nod. "I know. But since I'm going to do this and then leave this town forever, I want to...to tell you something first. You'll be furious, but I'm going to tell you anyway. I want a couple of answers from you."

He turned with a look of icy mistrust because he didn't like the threat of her tone. It didn't deter her; she'd already gone this far.

She braced herself. "I know what's upstairs."

He didn't seem to comprehend. He frowned and waited without moving a muscle.

"I'm sure you're deliberately haunting this house with electronic equipment. But why would you do something like that?"

The look on his face was one of disbelief. "What makes you think so?"

"I was upstairs and—"

"How the hell did you get up there?"

"Does it matter?"

"You'd better tell me."

"I discovered your—" she gestured toward the far wall of the kitchen "—your back stairs."

To her surprise there was no ensuing tantrum. Maybe he'd already had all he could stand for one day.

He fell into an awful silence, and since he was not looking at her now, she couldn't read the expression on his face.

Finally he asked, "What did you find up there?"

She let out a heavy breath. "You act like you don't know!"

"I don't. If I did, I wouldn't ask."

"I found stereo speakers, some tapes, and a movie projector."

Rubbing his chin thoughtfully, he asked, "Did you tell anybody about it?"

"No, not a soul. I thought it was something only an extremely eccentric man would do. I thought . . ."

"Thought I was crazy?"

"Are you?"

"Maybe."

She waited for him to continue. When he didn't, she took a step closer. "Mike, I know I shouldn't have snooped. It was a lousy thing to do. But if you'd been in my place, wouldn't you have been as curious as I? You must be awfully mad at me, and I can't blame you. It's just—"

"It may not make any difference now," he answered, and there was little anger in his voice, only defeat.

"I'm confused. I found that equipment, but it didn't look as if it had been used. The projector is broken. Yet the night before was the night I saw the ghost. What is that ghost—really? What are you doing with that stuff upstairs?''

"Nothing that would be of interest to you.''

"Then why are you guarding it so closely? Why the boards everywhere and why hide the stairs? And why did you try to talk me into leaving after I'd seen and heard the ghost? That stuff up there is very important to you. Why?''

"That's my business. You had no right to break into my apartment.''

"I know that! I also know you weren't sure of what I found up there, so that must mean I might have missed something. Mike, everybody says this house is haunted and—''

He interrupted, "I'm relieved you didn't tell anybody and I'd appreciate it if you wouldn't.''

"Why?''

"It would be too hard to explain.''

"Try me.''

"You're on your way to phone your paper, remember?''

"Another half hour isn't going to make any difference. Tomorrow's page is already in print. Mike, please. I hate to think the things I've been thinking.''

"Damn,'' he said in resignation, running his fingers through his hair. "Haven't I told you enough about me to hold you for one day?'' He paused, evading her questioning eyes. "Oh, what the hell. You already probably think I'm a murderer. I suppose now you think I'm a lunatic as well. I'm not crazy. That equipment up there—it's part of a plan of mine.''

He sighed and walked to the dining table and sat down. She followed him and sat across from him, staring at his hands on the table.

"When Howard Boyce and I were kids we used to take shortcuts to school through a graveyard. One winter evening it was almost dark when we walked home because we'd been kept after school for gluing the teacher's wastebaskets to the floor. Howard was afraid to walk through the graveyard, but it was a shortcut and I insisted. We started talking—or I did—about the ghosts that were reputed to live in the cemetery and Howard got so scared he wet his pants and began to run, insisting he'd seen a ghost and that it was after him.

"I didn't seen any ghost, but I was ornery enough to pretend I did, and I elaborated on it afterward to get a rise out of the other kids. Howard wouldn't even talk about it and he never would go near that graveyard again."

Watching Mike now, with the soft light from the window highlighting the scar on his temple, Terry observed the tension in the muscles of his forehead. The mere mention of Howard Boyce's name caused him to tense like this.

"Through the years," he continued, "other things came up to prove how terrified Howard is of the supernatural. It was an obsession with him. Once when we were in college some friends arranged a séance and invited him. Howard wouldn't even be in the same building. He confessed to me once that he knew the dead came back as ghosts and that he had seen them and the ones he always saw were evil and they were out to get him. He lived in terror of the living dead, even when he was a senior in college, and I know he still does."

"I see. . . ." Terry whispered.

"Yeah, you probably do."

She leaned forward, resisting the urge to touch his hand. "You want to set Howard up. But how on earth did you plan to get him to Jerome, to this house?"

"By convincing him that I'm dead. That my ghost is haunting this place and accusing him of the murder of his cousin. By the ghost insisting there is proof of Boyce's guilt. Howard, the up-and-coming state legislator, has a very ambitious political career planned for himself and everybody knows it. He used to say he was going to be President someday; that's how ambitious he is. This kind of publicity would get the imagination of a lot of investigative reporters, and it could ruin him. He'd have to try to stop that ghost's 'proof' from ever getting out.''

She stared. "Wait, wait, back up a little! How are you going to fake your own death?''

"I've been giving it a lot of thought, but so far no scheme is workable. I'm not sure. But in any case, the stories would be leaked to newspapers of a ghost here accusing a prominent state legislator of murder and conspiracy. Not naming him, but leaving Boyce no doubt as to who it is.''

"You think he'd come here?''

"He'd have to.''

"And then what?''

"Then I'd set up a séance, with witnesses, that would scare Boyce into confessing.''

She blinked. "I . . . I can't believe what I'm hearing.''

"I know it's a wild plan, but it's the only one I've come up with. I'll never get my freedom unless Howard confesses to the murder. And just how the hell would that ever happen unless he's scared into it? No matter how desperately and chancy this scheme is, at least it's something— some slim chance.''

"Could it still work?''

"No. Not if he knows I'm alive.''

She closed her eyes. "I'm so sorry.''

"There's nothing that can be done about it now. Except for you to protect yourself. Howard might suspect I've talked to you about the murder. I know what he's capable of when he's threatened and I don't want you having anything to do with me.''

She felt the ache again, stronger than before. "How can you be thinking about me at a time like this? After what I've done, how I've spoiled everything.''

"It's already done; nothing can change that now. What you can do for me are just those two things I asked before. Stop the pictures and then leave."

She nodded and rose slowly. "All right. But I still don't understand about that ghost."

"You didn't find everything. If you had, you'd understand easily."

"I looked."

He shrugged as if nothing could matter now, as if it were too late for everything. "Most of the equipment that's in use is concealed behind false walls. There's a projector in the ceiling of the stairway and speakers you didn't see." He closed his eyes. "The scheme is crazy; I'm not denying that. It was one hell of a long shot to start with."

"It might have worked."

"It might have. There was a chance."

He pushed his chair away from the table. "I have to talk to Rosa, so I'll walk to the hotel with you."

"Does Rosa know your past?"

"Does she know I'm a convicted murderer? No. I think she suspects I'm hiding from the law, but I've never told her so." He brushed back his hair as he followed her to the door.

They walked down the steps and onto the narrow sidewalk. The day was sunny and birds were singing and flowers were blooming in the old gardens on the hillside, but Terry felt none of the lightness of sun or spring. The day seemed as black as her spirits. She knew she'd not forget the pain of these moments for as long as she lived. And with horror one dark question stabbed her and wouldn't let her go: *how long does Mike have to live?*

She said, "You and Rosa are close friends."

"She's a special lady."

"Why does she collect the rent on the apartment for you and sign the receipts?"

"We're just running the House as part of the hotel."

"What do you have to do with the hotel?"

"I own it."

Her eyebrows raised.

He explained, "I had a source of money, from my family. I bought the hotel when I came here, along with the House, and then I cut all ties with my family so they could never be harassed about my whereabouts. They don't know where I live and I've not heard anything about them in all this time."

"What an awful way to live!"

"Yeah, but it sure beats prison."

As they neared the start of the business section of town, both, at once, spotted movement at the side of one of the deserted buildings. From the shadows a man was watching them. Icy fear overtook Terry as she felt Mike's body stiffen. She grabbed spontaneously for his arm, but Mike was no longer there.

Chapter Seven

With reflexes like lightning, Mike had bolted forward and now, already at a dead run, he was giving chase. It was him—the man in leather who had been following Terry. Now he had been following them both! And Mike didn't want him to get away this time.

Their mysterious stalker had a good head start. To make matters worse, a car screeched past, barely missing Mike as he lunged across the street, so that he had to pull back and wait while the driver shouted obscenities. This delay put Mike at a severe disadvantage.

There was no place to go but up. Terry could only watch helplessly from the sidewalk as the man in black scurried up the staircase of an old building, came out on an upper porch, and ran around to the side, which put him on the street above. Mike was the more agile of the two; he was able to close the distance between them a little, but not enough.

She couldn't see either of them then. But moments later, she caught sight of Mike emerging onto the higher street. There were too many old buildings up there for a man to hide in. Mike had lost the man in leather for the second time.

He stood at the railing looking down at her. Both hands raised in the air to give her the message that he had failed in the pursuit, and this was followed by a second gesture motioning her on in the direction of the hotel. She waited for him to get his breath and start down to join her again, but he didn't. Instead he turned and crossed the upper street and started up the slope of that street toward a still higher level.

Where he might be going, she couldn't guess. Terry could see him walking up there, getting smaller as he climbed higher. He followed the uphill curve of the street, disappeared for a time behind the brow of a leveled section, reappeared, and then disappeared again. She sat down on the stone ledge that lined the sidewalk, her hand shading her eyes from the sun, looking up. He was walking slowly, head down, as if he were thinking. Maybe that was it. He hadn't had time to think since he saw her pictures because she hadn't given him time. He had said he didn't know what he was going to do. Perhaps he wanted to be alone to try to figure it out.

She shivered, thinking about the fact that someone had been following them, maybe still was. The man could be watching her from some window of an empty building even now. Or watching Mike. This must have something to do with her drawings; how could it be anything else? Damn! They *were* after Mike already. But why just follow him around? If they knew where Mike was, and if he was a prison escapee, why didn't they just come after him, confront him?

The hotel was only a block away, but it was going to be the hardest block she had ever walked. She knew Mike was right about stopping the pictures but every step on the way to doing so was torture. How was she going to explain to her editor that she simply refused to draw any more of the strip? She'd have to think of a story to tell him, and she had only the walking distance of one block to think of one, and whatever it was, a lot of important people were going to be furious.

Her mind raced. And raced faster, while her feet were moving more and more slowly. An idea began to form, but it was not an idea that involved killing her story. Quite the contrary. Trying to still the anxiety in her pounding heart, she turned abruptly and headed back toward the Beyer House, needing time to think. The idea was risky and dangerous. But Mike was in danger already and so was she. What was a little more risk?

Little risk? she mocked herself. This plan was danger personified! Still, by the time she reached the house, Terry was convinced that her idea, for all its danger, was a good one. She had to find Mike at once to tell him.

The last she had seen of him he had been heading in the direction of the houses above the old church. Her whole body was trembling when she got into her car—a reaction to the scary aspects of her plan and to the emotional overload of the day.

Driving at a creeping pace up the steep, narrow road, she spotted Mike sitting on the porch steps of an enormous, obviously deserted house that sat high above the street. If she hadn't been specifically looking for him he would have been unnoticeable, for he sat in shadows of spreading elm trees, leaning against the top step, perfectly still, looking out to the valley.

She parked at the foot of the steep, weed-grown slope, got out of her car, and stood looking up at him. In the silence of the deserted street, the bang of her car door jarred his attention. He looked down.

She called, "I have to talk to you."

"I'm not in the mood. I've talked too much for one day."

"I'll talk. I have to tell you something."

His voice lowered so she had to strain to hear him. "I came up here because I need to be alone."

"It's important. It's very important. I'm coming up."

"The hell you are."

"Yes, I am. Mike, we have to talk."

He rose. "Don't try it. The slope is pretty steep. You could slip."

"Oh, come on! I'm not that helpless. There's a path."

His hands went to his hips first, then slid into his pockets as he watched her approach, moving slowly along the dusty, narrow path that coiled up the hillside from the street to the front porch. The path had been terraced once, and most of it still was, so that it was level to walk on, but it was necessarily long, snaking back and forth in defiance of gravity.

She climbed the short stairs and sat on the top step. Behind them the three-story house loomed like a great gray ghost, silent and empty, breezes sighing through broken window panes, windows like giant eyes staring down at them.

Reluctantly, he pulled his hands from his pockets and sat down beside her. "What now?"

"We have to talk."

"That's all we've been doing for the past hour."

"This is something else." Terry tried to ignore the rising prickles of fear within her. Something in her brain was sending out warning signals that what she was about to do, what she was about to say, was trouble with a capital T—the kind of trouble one can't disentangle from, maybe ever. The immediate risk was Mike's anger. But he was already as mad at her as any human being could be at another, and it hadn't killed her so far.

Sitting beside him in the shadows of the trees, Terry was aware of his size and of the hardness and warmth of his body, and of the subtle scent that was either soap or after-shave. Somehow, she felt protected by his size. It wasn't Mike she feared; it was the forces outside—his enemies. And his size loomed between her and those enemies, and whether it was realistic or not, she felt his strength could protect her.

He looked at his feet and not at her. "All this walking isn't doing your knee any good."

"The knee is much better. Better every day."

He seemed impatient, restless. "I don't know why you followed me up here. We've said everything there is to say about this whole mess."

She glared at him. "Do you know the man who was following us?"

"No. Do you?"

"No. But maybe he wasn't following both of us. I mean maybe he was only following me, for some reason."

"I doubt it."

She turned around and looked at the entrance, a heavy, weathered, sun-faded wooden door. There were splintered nail holes where the door had periodically been boarded shut, through the years. No board was nailed over it now; there was only a Keep Out sign painted with red paint and nailed to the bottom step of the porch. Terry said, with forced calm, "I've wanted to explore this big old house ever since I first saw it. Have you ever been in here?"

"I've got more pressing things on my mind than that. I told you, I came up here because I wanted to be alone."

"I know. There are pressing things on my mind too. I want to go inside and talk. Inside where that man can't see us from wherever he might be hiding. I feel like we're being watched out here. I *know* we're being watched out here."

"Terry, I really wish you'd just—"

She paid no attention to his protests. Instead she touched his arm as a summons and rose, looking up at the unbroken third-story windows. "Even this house is watching us," she said. "I hate the feeling of being watched and followed."

"Take my word for it. A person can get used to the feeling."

She looked back at him, wondering what his life had really been like. He'd lived with an inner hell while the peace of this mountain surrounded him. He could never have been sure when he woke in the morning that he would not be going to bed that night behind bars. Freedom was only a concept to him, a memory, but not a reality. Today, because of her, the echo of freedom sounded more distant; its existence was far more illusory than it had been yesterday.

"Please, can't we just go inside the door, where it's more private?"

With no further protest, he got to his feet and pushed open the door for her, then followed her inside.

They were in a wide hall. Stairs rose on one side, and on the other side a large arch opened into what must have once been the living room. The walls were pale blue, the stair bannister chipped white. Lighter circles and squares could be seen where pictures and mirrors once hung. The interior of the house was astonishingly eerie because the building wasn't in the state of decay Terry had expected. It looked as though someone had just walked out one day and closed the doors and the house had sat in silence ever since, gathering dust and echoing a thousand memories from its yellowing walls.

She stood in the archway looking up and down the long hall, toward the back of the house.

"I don't like it in here," Mike said, behind her. "I've never liked it."

"But it once must have been very pretty. Why don't you like it?"

"I can't say, exactly. Maybe I just don't like the vibes in here."

"Yet you did choose this particular house to come to be alone."

"I was outside, on the porch, where the air is fresh." He took the lead. "If you insist on being in here, come on this way."

She followed him into the living room. It was a sunny room, lighted by a bay window that looked out over the hillside and offered the usual breathtaking view of the valley. Three or four of the panes were still unbroken. The glass was so gray with age and dirt, it filtered out the sun. The pane-free windows seemed to breathe in the sun's rays and the fresh scent of orange blossoms. In spite of the turmoil in her head right now, Terry couldn't help but imagine a lady in a lace blouse sitting at this window once, looking down at this same view, surrounded by lovely dark furniture, cut flowers in vases, imported paintings on the walls.

Mike sat on the ledge of the window. "Hope you don't mind if I sit down. I'm feeling a little drained and not in the mood to be messing around in here. You should be home packing and I've got to think."

She sat on the dusty ledge beside him. All around them the building was wrapped in the musty silence of unshared memories. It was an uncomfortable sensation to be a pawn in the manipulative way that time changed everything. A few decades, a few days, an hour...

"Mike, I know you're understandably upset and angry. You have every right to be. I wouldn't blame you if you refused to even talk to me. But could I ask you a couple questions?"

"About what?"

"Well, the murder for one thing. Couldn't you have taken a lie detector test?"

"Polygraph tests aren't admissible in court. Howard's hotshot lawyer saw that rule was upheld. This isn't important now, Terry. There are more immediate problems to be concerned with."

"I know. I'm getting to that. You say this Boyce is well known now?"

"He comes from a prominent, wealthy family and he's into politics. Every bit of publicity or any vote-getting situation he can get himself into, he does."

"What about Gil, the other guy?"

"I told you, I don't know where Gil is. I think he fears Howard as much as he fears me, because outside of me, Gil is the only person who knows the illustrious young state legislator is a killer. Boyce hates anybody knowing that. I think he'd find a way to kill Gil. Maybe he's already killed him. But this doesn't concern you, any of it. What did your paper say about stopping the comic story?"

"I didn't call them."

"What?" He sat forward, and the anger had returned to his voice.

"I have to talk to you first. I have an alternative plan."

He held his head in despair. "Oh, God."

Addressing the top of his head, she insisted, "It's a good plan."

"I don't care how good it is. I don't want to hear it."

"Why not?"

"Because there is no way for you to grasp this situation."

"I wish you wouldn't underestimate me before you even listen to me."

He sat in silence. She could see his chest moving as he breathed. His breathing wasn't normal. He was even more upset than he tried to let on. But then, she thought, why wouldn't he be? For eight years he had clung to a single plan to get his revenge, and now he had almost no hope left.

She reached for his arm and shook it gently. "Will you just listen to me? I can draw the crime—the murder. I could draw it exactly as it really happened, in detail, with the caricatures of all of you, Gil and you and Howard. I can draw the whole frame-up and the trial afterward, the conviction of an innocent man, even your escape. I can draw it all in my comic strip!''

He had raised his head and was gazing at her with his brow creased in a frown and disbelief in his light eyes. "What on earth purpose would that serve?''

"Don't you see? It would establish his guilt. It would seriously hurt him. And if you want to bring your D.A. to Jerome in a hurry, that'll do it. You won't have to wonder whether he's stalking you or not. He'll have to be here fast to stop the story as quickly as possible. And he won't dare try to contact the newspapers about it without calling national attention to himself. We won't name him by name, of course. It'll only be the likeness of him, and of you. So he won't be able to call attention to it but he'll have to try to stop it. And then when we get him out here to Jerome, we can arrange for you to die suddenly and put your other plan back into operation."

He merely looked at her trying to absorb her logic.

Her voice became calmer. "You know, Mike, there's a strong possibility Boyce hasn't seen Rod Lightning yet. The strip has only been out about a week. There's no real reason to connect the man who was following me to this, is there?''

"I don't know, but I do know I can't let you do anything as crazy as what you're suggesting. You have no idea how dangerous this man is. He's a cold-blooded killer, and he's killed for far less reason than he'd have if you tried something like this."

"How could he kill me? Everyone would suspect him."

"Terry, for God's sake. Forget it!''

"No, I won't forget it. It's a good plan, much better than yours for getting Boyce out into the open. My plan would also get Gil out into the open, which yours probably wouldn't have done. Gil's guilt would be part of it too. Damn it, you know it's a good plan.''

"Dangerous plan."

"The danger is already there, according to you."

"No, Terry."

"I'm going to do it. Do you think I can live with knowing how I've cost you your chance for freedom? Do you expect me to go around living with that until I die? I have to make up for it, and this is the only way I can."

He fell into silence.

Finally she said, "The crux of this whole thing is Gil Spearow. It is, isn't it? Because he knows you're innocent."

"You're right about that. If he's alive, I've got at least a chance. But Boyce also knows this, and if I know Boyce he wants Gil out of the way. It has always haunted me the way Gil looked at me the day I escaped from jail and pointed the guard's gun at Gil's heart. I swear I saw some look of guilt or regret. But maybe it was just fear."

The hate in his voice, years of mounting hatred, unnerved her. She was beginning to understand more deeply what he had suffered because of two friends who had betrayed him. She said slowly, "My plan would almost have to bring Gil out of hiding. Maybe he's sorry for what he did."

"I'd give anything I own to be able to talk to Gil. But I'm not going to let you risk your life so I can do it. If I should get myself arrested or killed in the middle of this, there would be absolutely no one to protect you."

"If that should happen I'd go back to Los Angeles and tell the whole story to the police there. You have to let me do this, Mike. I refuse to be talked out of it. We can do it together. Please."

His voice held signs of weakening under her persistence. "You don't know what Boyce looks like."

"If he's in the newspapers, I can get a picture easily enough. With that and your description, I can do it."

"He was younger then."

"My specialty. Taking years on and off people is simple."

He sat, his arms resting on his knees and his head buried in his arms, deep in thought.

She said, "It's a chance to make your plan work, Mike. Maybe your only chance."

"I admit that. I hate to, but I admit it."

"Then we have a deal."

"All right," he agreed without looking up. "But you've got to promise to be careful."

"You too."

He raised his head and looked at her in a way he never had before. "Terry, you're as crazy as I am."

"Yes," she answered, meeting his look and slowly beginning to understand it.

To her astonishment, Mike smiled. It was not an enthusiastic smile, nor one of amusement, but she understood it, and now for the first time she was able to return it. His was a smile of trust, and so was hers. For whatever dangers it held for her, for whatever awful consequences if she was wrong, she believed him. His story was just too incredible not to be true, and his concern for her safety in the face of the hurt she'd done him was just too genuine.

So now, with the exchange of a simple smile, they were bonded in trust, and there was no going back. Terry was aware that she had set this up. Suddenly, he needed her. And she was there and she was going to stay.

SHE DEVISED a clever way to alter the gist of her story: flashback to the secret background of Rod Lightning. By the time readers were involved in the murder in the flashback, she figured, they'd forget the details of Rod's character and his present life. She could always devise a way to get out of the discrepancies when this was over.

The first thing Terry did was phone a close friend, an investigative journalist with an East Coast newspaper, and request an express mailing of newspaper file photos of Howard Boyce. They worked through that night, Terry drawing at her dining table, Mike pacing, drinking coffee, forcing himself to recall every small detail of the nightmare he had lived. Descriptions of homes, rooms, people, the murder site. It was going to be so accurate the two men who had been there would be jolted, horrified. Impatient to get the first of the panels out, Terry drew Howard Boyce from Mike's descriptions, using only the profile, waiting until she received the photographs to do a full-face drawing.

It took all night and part of the morning, but well ahead of noon the following day, the first batch of the "flashback" panels was on its way by special carrier to Terry's bewildered editor. Two days later Howard's look-alike character, and Gil Spearow's too, drawn from Mike's description, were introduced to America in forty newspapers around the country. In the comic strip, four college students were getting ready to spend the Thanksgiving holiday hunting pheasants on the huge estate where two of them lived. The character who resembled Howard Boyce was plotting to murder another—the cousin of whom he was jealous.

Morse Codes had become more than a comic strip: it was a testimony to murder. It was a trap. The trap was built and baited. The wait promised to be tense.

The days were still and quiet, like a calm before a storm. A week passed before either Mike or Terry caught a glimpse of the man in black leather again. It was evening, and they were walking on Main Street, strolling at a leisurely pace and eating ice-cream cones, winding down from the strain of several hours' work, when they spotted the man who had so far eluded Mike's pursuit. He was walking half a block ahead of them looking in shop windows while he headed in the direction of the saloon. In the evening shadows, he hadn't seen them; in fact, he acted like a man preoccupied with his own affairs. The light was not good, and they were too far away to get a look at his face. It was impossible even to tell his age.

"This time I'm going to catch him," Mike said.

Terry cautioned, "He's too far ahead not to get away if he sees you. And with all the people in the saloon, you're bound to create an awful lot of attention if you give chase now."

"He must be staying in town," Mike reasoned. "That means he'd almost have to be at one of the hotels. You're absolutely right, Terry, a smarter move would be to talk to Rosa before I create a royal scene in the street and start the whole town talking. Maybe I can find out who he is."

Terry took his arm, feeling a deepening affection for him. She knew what he'd been going through these past few days. There was pain in the unburdening of years of agony, frustration and hatred that had eaten at him from inside, coloring his view of the world and everyone in it.

His hand came over hers. As if he could read her thoughts, he said, "See how much effect you have on me? How calm I am with that fool just up the street and me letting him keep all his teeth?"

"I'm swelling with pride over your self-control but still wondering what it has to do with me."

"I dunno. It has something to do with you. I think it has been good for me to talk, to get all this stuff out that I've guarded for so long. I'd forgotten what truth is, Terry. I'd forgotten what sharing is. I'm starting to realize I'd completely forgotten what it feels like to be close to another human being, I mean be able to talk. It makes me feel more alive than I've felt in a long time."

"Then there is some good in all this."

"I don't know what there is in all this for sure, except danger. I feel as though we're sitting on a bomb."

"Is Boyce really as dangerous as you say? As desperate?"

"Believe it. He has a lot to lose because of us. He has everything to lose if he thinks there's any way I can prove my innocence, or even cause doubt about my guilt. He can't predict what I'm going to do."

"What are you going to do to lure him to a séance? Have you figured it out?"

"Not yet. There are too many unknowns. If Gil doesn't show up, I could pretend that he's dead and bring back his ghost. Or I might have to stage my own death, but that would be difficult. It's not as if I could get the cooperation of the police to pull this off. I'm not sure how I'll get Boyce into the house, but I'll figure out a way. If the press is alerted to the ghost's story and challenges it, Boyce wouldn't have the guts to publicly show his cowardice; he'd almost have to come to Jerome to save face. I think we'll have to wait and see what happens before I'll know just how to handle it." He scratched his head and scowled. "This whole scheme is like trying to get hold of a wet worm."

He took her hand and held it and his hand was warm. Mike had kept physically distant from her these past few days. He had been all business. And she hadn't thought a great deal about it, until now, walking in the moonlight on a spring night. He was attracted to her, that she knew. His eyes told her as they watched her sometimes when she wasn't supposed to know he was watching. But he had kept distant from her ever since he'd told her he was a convicted murderer. Did he think he'd frighten her if he touched her?

THE FOLLOWING DAY Rosa came to the Beyer House, but she did not venture inside. The women sat on the front porch drinking iced tea, Terry in jeans and a loose white T-shirt, Rosa in an ankle-length frock of light blue cotton with embroidery at the neck. For the first time Terry felt uncomfortable with her. The secrets made her uncomfortable. Rosa didn't know the past and she would never understand the present. Yet there was such wisdom in her dark eyes that Terry couldn't get over the feeling Rosa knew—always knew—far more than she let on.

Her question for example. "Do you and Mike talk much, Terry? Are you getting to be friends?"

"Uh, yes, I guess we are."

"Mike is lonely. Any woman could see that. But it would take a woman with great character and understanding to break through that shell of his, don't you think?"

"Provided," Terry said defensively, "she wanted to."

"Yes, provided that. The man guards deep secrets, but I feel people have a right to their secrets...."

"You have secrets, too."

Rosa gazed out at the view of the valley and sipped her tea. "Of a far different kind from Mike's I'm sure. They're not really secrets, dear, with me. Perhaps they were once but now they're only memories. When enough time has gone by no one cares."

"I care. I often wonder what your life has been."

"Do you?"

"Oh, yes. That's why I drew you as a young woman in the pictures. You saw the pictures."

The old woman gazed at her. "You made me beautiful."

"You are beautiful."

"No. I'm old. But once, yes, I was beautiful. Once many people thought so...."

"Why did you never marry?"

Rosa was silent for a moment or two, before she leaned forward and pointed to the mountain slope that stretched down below the town. "Do you see the house down there with the gabled roof? The one that's been restored? There used to be a grand house next to it. Well, I thought it was grand. The boy I loved lived in that house. He was a merchant's son. We went to school together."

Terry tried to picture a grand house on the now weed-grown hillside. "What happened to him?"

"He's dead now. Dead nearly twelve years." She leaned back in the chair and closed her eyes, a wistful smile on her mouth as she recalled days long vanished. "He married a girl who wanted only a big house and fine clothes to make her happy, but she did not ever make him happy, not ever. Except that she gave him a daughter and a son."

"He loved you?"

"Oh, yes. He always loved me."

"Then why didn't you marry?"

Rosa's eyes came open. She picked up the ice-wet glass and sipped slowly. "Oh, my dear. He was such a beautiful boy. He was blond, you see, and his father was a wealthy merchant. And I was a little dark girl from a miner's shack on Cleopatra Hill whose mother... well, my mother had a bad reputation. The boy couldn't have married me. But he always loved me."

Terry felt a small burn of tears at the back of her eyes but she fought the tears back. Rosa would not like to see her cry. "You knew when he died. Does that mean the two of you kept in touch?"

"Yes. Oh, not terribly often. Once, when his children were small, there were seven years that I didn't see him. But then, he came. He sometimes wrote to me, and always at Christmas there would be a rose."

Terry could not look at her. The tears were just too close to the surface. "You might have married, too," she whispered.

"No. Not without love. There was only one boy I ever loved."

She reached for the old woman's hand. "Rosa, what is love?"

"How strange your question is."

"Really, what is it? You loved so deeply, so long. Maybe you're the only one I've ever met who knows."

The aging eyes brightened as they gazed at her. "You ask such an age-old question of such a simple woman?"

"You're not a simple woman. You're anything but a simple woman."

"Why do you sound as though your question is so urgent, dear? Have you been thinking about love?"

"Yes, I can't help it, Rosa. I know I care for Mike in such a different way. I don't want anything bad to happen to him...."

"Do you think something will happen to him?"

"I don't know. I mean, my feelings are so confused. Rosa, please tell me, how can we tell if we really love someone?"

The older woman sighed heavily, closed her eyes for a moment, and then reached for Terry's hand. "You love someone when you'd rather be with him than anyone else in the world, no matter what the circumstances. It's very simple, I think. It is not a matter of wanting someone but of wanting to be with someone, and no one else."

"But if..." Terry paused, then stopped, for her attention had become riveted on the sloping garden at the side of the house where a man was climbing down from the street above. The man in black leather! He had seen them on the porch and he seemed bent on approaching them. Terry tensed and braced herself.

Rosa had seen him, too. "That man! Why is he coming here?"

Terry turned to look at Rosa. "Do you know who he is?"

"No."

"He's been hanging around here for several days," Terry answered.

"He's staying at the hotel. And I don't like him, Terry. I don't like him one little bit. He's very strange."

"Have you . . ." Terry began, and stopped, because there was no chance to talk. The man was descending the hill rapidly and with purpose, kicking up dust from the garden as his boot heels dug in for balance.

"Where is Mike?" Rosa asked softly, and from the urgency of her question, Terry knew Rosa's instincts were warning of some kind of danger.

"Mike's in town on an errand." Terry swallowed, trying not to show her fear to Rosa as the man reached level ground.

The old boards under them creaked and groaned as they yielded to the weight of a heavy man. He was already on the porch.

Chapter Eight

Close up, the man was even more frightening. Several days' growth of beard gave him a grizzled look, and his eyes were hidden behind the dark glasses. Shorter and heavier than Terry had thought, he was wearing a black T-shirt today without the leather jacket, and although his hair was very black, she noticed that the hair on his arms was light, almost blond. Sun bleached, perhaps.

Near panic, she thought he must have been watching them and he knew Mike was gone. So far he had done nothing but bolt from Mike, but he wasn't afraid of women.

Now he stopped in front of the table and looked down at the women seated there, taking the stance he had the first day Terry saw him in the doorway—legs wide apart as if he were deliberately trying to look tough, a thumb tucked in the top of a wide leather belt.

"G'morning, ladies," he said in a raspy voice Terry remembered.

Not wanting to have to look up at him, she rose to meet his gaze.

"What do you want?"

"Just a couple of answers to a couple of questions."

"I have nothing to say to you," Terry said, bracing herself vigorously against her own fear. She moved to position herself protectively between the intruder and Rosa.

His voice rose. "What kind of an attitude is that?"

"I don't like being followed."

"I was looking for you. Any crime in that?"

"I don't like being followed," she repeated, this time with more feeling. She glared at him. "You could have stayed and asked your couple of questions instead of running, but you ran, so obviously you have a problem of some kind."

"There was a madman after me."

She shook her head as though this didn't merit a comment.

"Who is he?" the intruder asked.

A glint of sunlight reflected from the frame of his sunglasses. While she was aware of Rosa taking a lace handkerchief from her skirt pocket and fanning herself with it nervously, Terry didn't take her eyes from the man; some inner voice was warning that she didn't dare.

"Who is he?" the stranger repeated, stepping closer, so close Terry could not help but back up. When she did take a step back, Rosa rose from her chair.

"His name? Is that what you came to ask me?"

"That's right. For starters."

She felt the wall at her back. "Ask *him* if you want to know."

"What I want—" he began but he didn't have a chance to finish before the unexpected assault came, from behind.

Because the man who was bearing down on her in such a threatening manner was between her and the street, Terry could not see past him. When he whirled around suddenly, she sucked in her breath in alarm. Mike had come back, come running full speed from down the block when he saw the encounter on the porch, and without warning had grabbed the man's shoulder from behind.

He pulled the intruder away from the two women, to the edge of the porch, and the stranger, not willing to be dragged around, fought back. Rosa let out a shriek when the first blow was exchanged. Mike ducked a swinging arm and came back with his fist against the side of his opponent's head, knocking the man nearly off balance.

Terry stood back in stunned horror, witnessing the first actual fistfight she had ever seen. Blood spattered. She closed her eyes, but the experience was no better with her eyes closed. The grunts and growls of fighting men, the sounds of fists connecting with flesh created a living nightmare for her.

Rosa's hand touched hers and she opened her eyes. Terry expected Rosa to be turning away as well, but instead she was watching intensely, wincing now and then, but never taking her eyes off Mike. Instinctively, Terry knew that this wasn't the first fight Rosa had ever seen. Sometime in her past there had been others.

With her hands over her ears, it was all Terry could do to endure it. The men had rolled off the side of the porch and were exchanging fierce blows in the dust of the yard near the edge of the street. Each was knocked to the ground time and again, only to get up repeatedly. They became more determined, more angry, more violent, until at last the stranger fell in the dust, groaned loudly, and lay on his back without moving.

Bleeding, his face smeared with dirt, Mike stood over the other man, staring down at him. The man stared back for a second or two, then closed his eyes. Mike got down on one knee, grabbed the man's hair roughly, and lifted his head.

When he looked back up at Terry, who was standing on the edge of the porch, something was in his eyes she hadn't seen before, something that frightened her.

He looked back at the man on the ground. "Get up!"

The only response was a groan.

"Terry, can you help me get him inside?"

She was stunned. "Inside where?"

"My apartment," he snapped with impatience.

"But . . ."

"Damn it! Just . . ." Forcibly he took control of himself. She saw him do it with a heave of his chest and a conscious relaxing of his shoulders as he wiped blood from his own mouth. His voice softened. "He's pretty banged up."

She stared at Mike, not understanding his abrupt mood swings except that they indicated a high degree of frustration. Rosa, who hadn't said a word since the stranger appeared, came now to the edge of the porch.

"I'm sorry about this, Rosa," Mike said.

"Why are you sorry? This man was starting to really annoy Terry and frighten me."

"Maybe I overreacted." Grunting, he urged the stranger to his feet.

"If you overreacted, so did he." Rosa stood back while Terry took the man's other arm and they guided and shuffled him toward the porch and through the building's entrance.

He protested going inside.

"We're going to talk," Mike said in a growl. He pulled his dirty, torn T-shirt over his head and shoved it at the other man. "Hold this over your nose. I don't want blood on my floor."

They lowered him onto Mike's living room couch; his head fell forward as if he didn't have the strength to hold it up. The shirt Mike had given him was already stained red with blood. Terry stood by curiously while Mike got water and a cloth from the kitchen, set the glass down on the coffee table and tossed the cloth roughly to the moaning man.

"The bleeding will stop faster if you put your head back. Just watch what you're bleeding on."

The other man caught the wet cloth awkwardly and began sopping at the blood that was still streaming from his nose.

"Your face looks awful, too, Mike," Terry said. "Is it your blood or his you're covered with?"

"Both, I guess." Mike's voice and eyes were filled with impatience and anger. His gaze was riveted on the man he'd just fought. "Terry, would you mind leaving us alone? I want to talk to this guy."

She felt a pang of fright. "What are you going to do?"

"Don't worry, I'm through pounding on him for the moment. My hands are sore. I just want to talk to him and find out what he's up to. But in my way, Terry."

"He really wasn't *doing* anything when you came. He just—"

"I said I won't start another fight. Please—"

"Okay. I'm going."

She looked back once, from the doorway, remembering the way Mike had looked at the man as he stood over him. His first real look at him without the sunglasses. As she closed the door of his apartment behind her, Terry realized what that look was about. *He recognized that man!* She was sure of it. And his taking the man into his living room added strength to the conviction. So did the fact that he wanted to talk to him without her present.

Rosa had sat down again at the table. Terry sat across from her, unable to voice the suspicion that Mike might know the man he'd just beat up and wondering what was going on in the house between the two of them.

Thinking about it, she couldn't sit still. After a short while, Rosa left to prepare for guests who had reservations at the hotel. Terry went to her own living room to pace. Through her open door she could see Mike's closed door. He might be innocent of murder up to now, she thought, but there was no reason to think he wasn't capable of it. Years of bitterness, years of paying for another man's crime, had hardened him. Revenge had become his power source. His eyes glistened with hate when he spoke of the men he called his enemies, deep, far-reaching hate for them. Even the most remote possibility that the man behind the door with Mike was someone from his past was enough to make her shiver.

MIKE SAT DOWN on a chair opposite the couch and crossed his arms. "I take it the dyed hair is for my benefit. How long did you expect to slink around Jerome and my house before I recognized you?"

The other man tried to straighten. He held the cloth over his nose. "I hoped you wouldn't recognize me at all. I knew if you did . . ." He rubbed his chin with his free hand, wincing in pain.

"You figured I might kill you."

"That's right."

"Gil, there's only one man I'd rather see dead than you. Obviously you found the caricature of me in Terry's comic strip. It looked that much like me, did it?"

"The scar . . ."

"Yeah, the damn scar. Another souvenir from our mutual friend. Did Howard send you?"

"Howard?" The voice was slow, raspy, but it strengthened as he began to talk. "Are you kidding? Boyce has been looking for me for years. I feel like a hunted animal. That bastard has tried to kill me half a dozen times. About three months after you disappeared, the lug bolts were loosened on one of the wheels of my car. I survived only through a miracle; I'd slowed down almost to a stop because of a freeway accident before the wheel came loose. I suspected him but tried to talk myself out of it. After that it happened a second time. I had left town and gone down to Kansas City when somebody took a potshot at me on a country road. I was jumping at every shadow. I knew I had to get away from him, and I finally did, but it wasn't easy. Hiding isn't easy; I found that out."

Mike eyed him with contempt. "If your story is true, which it may or may not be, I hope you don't expect any sympathy from me."

"No. Hell, no. I know you hate me for what I did. Boyce paid me a lot of money to lie for him and I had heavy debts at the time. Did you know he paid me?"

"Sure I knew. Why else would you have done it?"

"It wasn't just the money. There were other reasons, too. He—"

"I don't give a damn about your reasons now. Don't waste my time with your feeble explanations; I'm not interested."

Tasting blood, Mike rose and went to the kitchen. He rinsed his mouth with water and spit into the sink, then, wiping his lips impatiently with the back of his hand, returned to the almost immobile figure in the living room. Gil was sitting, head down, staring at the floor. His nosebleed had stopped. "If you're running from Howard," Mike said, wiping his hand on the seat of his jeans, "why the hell did you come to Jerome looking for me? Howard could be here, couldn't he? How do you know he didn't see the same comic strip you saw?"

"I'm in disguise. I'd have seen him first, if he was here. You didn't recognize me. Neither would he."

Mike's voice rose in anger. "Are you going to tell me why you're here or not? I'm in no mood to try to persuade you."

"Okay. No need to play tough. You proved you're tough. I thought I was in shape, thought I could . . . take you . . . if I had to. Colin, I've got to talk to you."

"Don't call me Colin! I don't answer to that name anymore."

"Mike Calhoun. That's what people call you. I couldn't get close enough to you to make sure you were Colin. I thought you were, but your hair is so gray now and you're heavier, and every time I saw you, your face was in shadow and I couldn't be sure about the scar. I figured, though, that cartoonist had to know you to draw you and if the cartoonist was in this town, you would be, too. Am I supposed to call you Mike now?''

"I don't care what you call me as long as it isn't Colin. As far as you're concerned, Colin MacKaine is dead.''

Gil Spearow found the courage to look directly at the other man and something was burning in Gil's hard, dark eyes. It was the first glimmer of life that had shown in his face. He said, "We've got to get Howard before he gets us!"

Mike sat back, ankle over knee, his eyes squinting with mistrust. Except for his chest moving more heavily than normal, he was a picture of steely control.

"If you want Howard so badly, go get him. You know where he is. Why involve me?''

Gil reacted with surprise. "Because nobody, even me, could want to get him more than you! I can't do it without you.''

"Why not?''

"You know damn well why not. He's too wary, and smart. Why haven't you gone after him?''

"Don't be an ass. I'm a wanted man.''

Gil Spearow fumbled in his T-shirt pocket for a cigarette. The packet and matchbook in the cellophane were crushed from the fight, and the cigarette he dug out was limp and bent. He lit it with shaking fingers.

"That day you escaped, when you had the gun pointed at my head, I saw hate in your eyes and you didn't even look like you, Colin...Mike...I thought you'd kill me. That's why I was afraid to approach you now. You've had seven years to build on that hate.''

"Eight.''

"Eight. And look at us now. And look at Howard with his bright and shining career and everybody respecting him. We're paying for the murder he committed and he's out there playing politics like the new young hope for the country."

"He couldn't have done it without your help."

"I know that. Don't you think that eats at me night and day? And now he doesn't want me alive because I'm the only person besides you who knows he's a murderer. He thinks the higher he gets the more likely I am to crawl out of the cracks."

"I don't know what you expect me to do about it. One cute move on my part and I could spend the rest of my life behind bars. Don't expect me to take any risks because Howard would like to get you shut up permanently."

"Look what he did to you!"

"Killing him isn't going to help me any. The only thing that would help me is to get a confession out of him."

"You've got my testimony."

"Howard had your testimony. Who the hell is going to listen to you now?"

"They'd have to listen, at least."

Mike leaned forward in his chair. "Gil, as far as I'm concerned, you're just blowing hot air. I wouldn't trust you with grocery money, let alone my life."

Gil could be telling the truth, Mike thought, but how could he be sure? What better plan could Howard cook up to get Mike quietly eliminated than to send Gil after him with a tale of woe like this—a tale Mike would know was likely true? What plans might the two of them have, if they were still in cahoots with each other? Gil would do whatever Howard told him to, and Howard was scheming enough to send Gil to do his dirty work. They'd have to kill him in a way that would cause no one to suspect murder, because if Colin MacKaine's identity was discovered after his death, and he'd been murdered, then diligent reporters would be led right back to Howard Boyce's connection with the case. That kind of publicity he'd avoid like poison.

Still, Mike reasoned, if Gil was telling the truth, he could make the difference between whether or not Mike was ever free again. Gil *was* the only person who knew the truth, and Mike needed him. Having him as an ally would change everything, give him a chance. Without Gil, even a taped confession out of Boyce, under the duress of a séance, might be too shaky to hold up.

Since Gil had been in Jerome for a week, he couldn't know about Terry's latest scheme to reenact the crime in the comic strip, unless he'd somehow seen a Phoenix paper. Or unless he was in contact with Howard. Whether he was acting alone or with Howard, each day that went by—with Terry's pictures revealing more of the true story—each day would become more tense. Howard's desperation would intensify, if he was watching the story develop in the strip.

Gil was looking around for an ashtray. Mike rose and went to the kitchen, brought one out and stood watching the other man crush out the half-smoked cigarette and immediately reach into his pocket for another. The shaking had not subsided much. Bruises were already beginning to form around his eyes and on his cheek. Mike felt no emotion but contempt.

He said, "I could kill you and have nothing to lose for doing it."

Gil looked up. "Kill me? What would you have to gain by doing that?"

"Satisfaction."

"Come on! You need me. I'm the only one besides Howard who knows you're innocent."

"What good does that do me?"

"I'll help you! We'll figure out a plan to get him."

While the smoke of Gil's cigarette formed a ring like a halo around his dark head, Mike made the decision to pretend to trust Gil, to feign interest in whatever plan he had concocted about eliminating their common "enemy." Pretending to trust him would give Mike time to work out his own revenge. He wanted to keep Gil in town. And if Gil *was* telling the truth, then Mike could only gain by having him on his side.

"Okay," Mike said. "Okay, we'll talk about it."

"You believe me, then?"

"Believe Howard wants you dead? Yeah, I believe that. I've tried to find you for years so I figured you'd been in hiding."

"I've been in California working backstage in a movie studio. I had big plans for my life once."

"So did I."

"We're going to get him. Now, the two of us. We'll figure out—"

There was a knock at the door. Mike knew who it had to be before he opened it. Terry stood in the doorway looking from one man to the other curiously.

"I'm sorry to interrupt, but I was worried. It was so quiet in here. For all I knew one of you had killed the other. Mike, my lord, you're a mess! Look at your face, still covered with blood."

He closed the door behind her. "Terry, I'd like you to meet Gil Spearow."

She stared at the other man, whose face was also streaked with blood and dirt and beginning to swell badly around the eyes and on one cheek. "You're Gil Spearow?"

He was instantly alert. "You know who I am?"

"Mike told me about you."

This seemed to both surprise and annoy him. "What else did he tell you?"

"Quite a lot." She noticed Mike touching a gash on his forehead and wincing. "I'm going to get something to wash your face with, Mike; I can't stand to look at blood."

"I'll do it."

"Never mind. Sit down and be a casualty."

She found a small towel in the bathroom, soaked it in cold water, and proceeded to wash Mike's face, kneeling beside him while he sat in an overstuffed chair, allowing himself the luxury of closing his eyes while the cloth smoothed over his eyelids. Mike wasn't worried about Gil Spearow leaving, Terry thought, and she couldn't figure out why. The spirited animosity between them during the fight seemed to have dissolved.

"What'd you tell her about me?" Gil asked.

Mike didn't open his eyes. "The truth."

"She knows about you?"

"That I'm an escaped convict?"

Gil was silent a moment, then said with what sounded like contempt, "So that's how it is, then?"

"What is?"

"The two of you . . ."

Mike opened his eyes. He flinched as Terry dabbed gently at the cut on his forehead. "Don't push your way into my personal business. Don't push me even a little, about anything. I feel like I'm walking a narrow ledge getting mixed up with you and I'm skittish as hell. It's really important for you to remember how tense I am."

Gil made a nervous, shuffling sound with his boots. "Why did you, Terry, draw the character that looks like Mike?"

"Never mind why," Mike answered. "Look, I want to do some thinking, about what we discussed. Maybe you do too. We don't have time to mess around, Gil. Anything that's going to happen has got to happen soon. Give me some time to think and come back later this afternoon. Oh, if anybody asks, tell them you ran into a wall." He sat back in the chair while Gil rose from the couch, testing his legs and wincing. "Or better yet, tell them you've been inside the Beyer House today."

Gil turned. "What's that supposed to mean?"

"Didn't you know this house is haunted? Everybody in Jerome knows about the ghosts of the Beyer House."

"Very funny." Gil was favoring one leg slightly while he made his way out the door.

When they were alone, Terry looked at Mike inquisitively.

He said, "I don't blame you if you're confused, Terry. I'm confused myself, as to whether or not I'm doing the right thing or falling into a trap. I'm letting Gil think we're combining efforts to get even with Howard Boyce."

"Why?"

"Because he says he wants to. And because if he's telling the truth, I need him."

"And if he's not?"

"I'll try to keep one step ahead of him. Terry, I don't think you should stay here in the house. It's too dangerous."

"I have to stay here. I don't have any place else to go."

"Maybe you ought to leave Jerome. Things could get—"

"We've been through that," she interrupted. "I can't finish the sketches without your help and you know it. And I can't stay at the hotel because of the stairs, and even if I could, I . . . I wouldn't want to. I want to stay here."

He touched her shoulder gently and his voice was husky. "I don't want anything to happen to you."

"I don't want anything to happen to you, either. Mike, what if it's all a trick—Gil's story? Could it be a trick?"

"It sure could."

"You're taking an awful chance."

"It's a chance either way. But if the two of them are working together, then Gil is as great a threat to you as Howard is. Stopping the story in your comic strip is as important to them as getting me; in fact, probably more important. I don't want you out of my sight."

"In that case, I'd better stay in the House, hadn't I?"

"I can't sleep unless you leave town."

"You'd better. You need your sleep."

He heaved an enormous sigh. "I don't know what to do about you."

She rose from her knees, then bent over and kissed his forehead.

He pulled her toward him and kissed her lightly on the lips, and repeated, "I just don't know what to do about you, Terry."

"I don't know what to do about you either." Terry's voice had become a whisper as his lips touched hers again. The kiss, light as it was, sent shivers through her. *It's just a kiss of friendship,* she tried to tell herself. No, it was more. His lips had come softly against hers and lingered only seconds, both times. Yet she felt the touch all through her body, electric and full of the wildest kinds of sensations. His was a caring kiss, a wondering kiss. But not a kiss of promise; it stopped short of that.

He touched her face with the back of his hand and stroked it lightly. "I had no right to get you involved in my life."

"Your memory isn't functioning, Mike. You didn't get me involved; I got myself involved and you in trouble, if you recall."

His eyes were sad, troubled. "But *this*...this is dangerous."

"I knew that before I decided to stay."

"You don't realize how dangerous."

"Well then, if you're in danger, maybe I can help."

"Oh, Terry..." His voice dropped away and he shook his head despairingly.

She stroked his arm and asked in a soft, careful voice, "What are you and Gil going to do?"

"I don't know yet. I have to think. Whatever we decide, I've got to figure out a way to cover myself if he double-crosses me. It could get tricky."

"I'll leave you to think, then. I've got work to do if I'm going to make my deadline."

"Do you need help with it?"

"No, not with the panels I'm doing now. I've got what I need."

He kissed her forehead at the door. "Promise me you won't leave your apartment without telling me. I have to know where you are every minute that Gil is in this town."

TERRY WAS AWARE, in late afternoon, that Gil Spearow and Mike were holed up in Mike's apartment again, talking, scheming. Her instincts were tuned to danger so finely that she worried Mike's life was threatened by just being alone with his longtime enemy. When Gil left, well after nine o'clock, she hoped Mike would knock on her door, maybe confide some of what they'd talked about. But he didn't come by. And she kept busy, drawing ideas for future panels and making notes of any special information she might need later from Mike.

It was nearly ten o'clock when the knock finally came. Terry's spirits soared and her heart beat more heavily in anticipation of seeing him. Her strong feelings about Mike worried her when he was not present, but when he was, she immersed herself in the luxurious feelings of warmth and the joy of just looking at him, and now of anticipating his touch.

Opening the door, she jumped. It was not Mike, but a stranger who stood there, a middle-aged man wearing a baseball cap. "Are you Terry Morse?"

"Yes."

"I was told I'd find you here." He held an envelope out before her. "Telegram."

She stared at it. By the time the messenger had left, her hands were sweating. She tore open the envelope, and reading the message, her knees grew weak and all the color drained from her face.

Chapter Nine

MORSE CODES IS TREADING DANGEROUS GROUND STOP ADVISE CEASING STORY LINE IMMEDIATELY STOP FAILURE TO DO SO WILL RESULT IN ACTION AGAINST YOU STOP CONSIDER SERIOUSLY STOP LAST WARNING

Terry read the telegram through several times. There was no question who had sent it. Howard Boyce had discovered the comic strip and recognized the story line and the cast of characters, and he was threatening her. The message was chilling in its simplicity. And the man who was threatening her was a murderer.

Light was shining from under Mike's door, evidence that he hadn't gone to bed. Clutching the yellow paper, she crossed the shadowed hallway and knocked on his door. There was no answer.

In spite of the fact that she knew the ghosts upstairs were frauds, Terry felt uneasy in the darkened hall. The old house creaked and groaned around her, and the longer she waited, the more fidgety she became. He was so concerned that *she* not leave the house without telling him. Now, where was he?

Had something happened with Gil? Could Mike have been hurt? She had heard Gil leave over half an hour ago, and there had been the footsteps of only one man in the hall and on the steps. Could Mike be upstairs? If he was up there, surely she'd have heard him moving around because there was no insulation between the two stories. She knocked again, harder, becoming genuinely frightened. *Where was he?*

She tried the door. It was unlocked. It was usually unlocked, yet one would think Mike would begin locking it now that his old enemies knew where he lived.

The living room light was on. There was music playing on the stereo, but no sign of Mike.

Almost immediately he appeared, walking out of the open bathroom door, drying his hair vigorously with a towel, droplets of water shining on his wet, naked body.

Terry, reaching in desperation for the handle behind her, backed into the door so hard it slammed shut. He looked up, startled.

"Oh, I'm sorry!" she breathed. "I knocked and pounded and when you didn't answer, I got worried. I'm...sorry..."

She expected him to cover himself immediately with the towel, but he didn't. He said, "I was in the shower."

"Yes...I realize that." Terry averted her eyes, looking at everything in the room but him.

"Second shower since the fight. Being around Spearow makes me feel dirty, like I can't get clean." Unhurriedly, he drew the white towel over his waist and fastened it loosely, unbothered by the fact that she had seen him. "Why were you knocking? Is something wrong?"

For a few rattled seconds she had completely forgotten the frightening telegram. Now, at his question, reality rushed back, but it wasn't the same as before, and her shaking had not the same cause as before. Naked, Mike was beautiful; his body was perfectly formed. He was huskier than she'd have thought, and more tanned, except where shorts or a swim suit had stopped the sun's rays from touching him.

Terry was visibly shaken, first from the shock of the threat on her life, and then from embarrassment, and not a little from some new emotion far less easy to define. She held out the paper to him as he walked toward her, his hair damp and mussed and falling over his forehead, his shoulders and chest still wet.

"What is it?"

She didn't answer, only looked at him.

He read the telegram, combing his hair away from his forehead roughly with his fingers. "Damn!"

She found her voice again. "Well, at least we know that Howard Boyce reads the comic page."

"This is serious."

"I know."

"Obviously he figures there's no point in being subtle because you already know who he is and what he did, or you wouldn't be able to draw the story so accurately."

"How did he find me so fast?"

He looked up, surprised. "The same way Gil did. You've set the story of the comic strip in Jerome so that's the first place they'd look for the artist. It's obvious you know me if you're drawing me here."

"Or Gil Spearow could have told him."

He sat down on the couch. "Possibly. But I don't think the two are in touch. All that really matters is that Boyce did find you. Now can we talk about you getting out of town?"

"No, we can't. Anyway, I wouldn't be safer anywhere else and you know it."

He crumpled the paper in his fist.

She sat next to him, facing him, her feet curled under her, her eyes involuntarily moving to his bare thighs. "Mike, what did you and Gil talk about for hours?"

"About Howard mostly."

"Not about how to kill him, I hope."

"Killing him would only make my situation worse. We talked about getting him to confess to murder. It's the only thing I'm willing to discuss with Gil."

"You didn't tell him about your original plan—about the ghosts, did you?"

"Yes."

She shifted her body and her eyes. "But isn't that terribly risky? He could tell Howard and then everything would be for nothing!"

"He won't tell him."

"How do you know?"

"I have to trust him. It's the only way I can do this."

He moved his hand to her knee, and when he turned toward her, the loose knot on the towel began to give. If Mike noticed it, he gave no sign of it, but Terry tensed and felt her heart begin to jump around. She was aware of his bare chest so touchably close, and, sitting next to him, she had begun to ache to touch his skin.

Her voice was higher than normal when she spoke. "Your trusting Gil is very scary."

"I had to come up with something—my ghost plot—because Gil's ideas are so damned violent. He believes Howard has tried to kill him half a dozen times, and he's lived in terror of him—and of me—for years. I think it's affected his mind. He wants revenge as much as I do."

"You can believe what he says?"

Mike shrugged. "Gil admits that my plan, crazy as it is, has a chance of working, because he knows about Howard's phobia. Nobody would believe it if they hadn't actually seen Boyce when he thinks there's a spirit around. He's terrified. I think something must have happened in his life long before the cemetery incident that scared the pants off him and he never got over it. And I've thought sometimes that maybe Howard's phobia is what drew me to this house, subconsciously, because when I bought it, I knew its reputation for being haunted." He was caressing her shoulder in tiny circles with the tips of his fingers as he talked. His voice was calm, and the calm worried Terry.

She said, "Why am I more frightened now that I know you've told Gil about the ghosts?"

"You don't like my trusting him. But I have to." His touch deepened. "Honey, we talked for a long time. I'm not going to pretend I have any feelings but bitterness and contempt for the guy, or ever will have. But in a sense, I know him very well, and he knows me. We grew up together."

"He betrayed you once."

"I'm not about to forget it."

Terry was feeling a liquid fire fill her body. Mike was quietly driving her crazy, sitting so close and so relaxed in his state of undress, as though it were the most natural thing in the world. He was taking the familiarity of touching her for granted. And if he was aware that he had called her "honey" for the first time, he gave no sign of that, either. It all seemed so natural, sitting here with him, and so easy, and so right.

Yet fire burned in his fingers when he touched her, and when he looked directly at her, his pale eyes were lit with the same fire, and when she took a deep breath, the fire flamed in her chest. And the damned towel that was knotted around his waist was coming loose.

It was difficult to continue their conversation, but Terry tried, attempting to pretend they were not becoming engulfed in the flames, because she thought she had to. She was afraid for Mike, because his fate was so uncertain. And she was afraid for herself because she knew she was falling in love with him.

"Will you tell Gil about the telegram?"

"Sure. It's proof Howard is reading the story. Gil didn't know about your murder story until I told him, and when I did, he hyperventilated. He couldn't believe we'd pull a stunt like that, ask for that kind of trouble. It proved to him how desperate I am. It also scared him. And it's just as well he is scared of me. I had to convince him I'm calling the shots. It's that or nothing.''

Involuntarily, she shivered. "It's all so terrifying."

"Remember," he assured her, "I know both these guys. I know them really well." His arm encircled her. "Don't be afraid, honey, I won't let anything happen to you."

With the hardness of his chest against hers, she became conscious of his breathing and of her own, and of his heartbeat and of her own. He felt so strong—his body, his breathing, his heartbeats—so strong. And it came to her that she relied on his strength, that without it she couldn't be taking the risks she was. His was a different kind of strength from her own, physical strength she stood in awe of. But Mike had another kind of strength that caused her to trust him—the strength of his own principles, his own kind of morality that kept him sane when the rest of his world had gone mad.

"It feels so good," she said softly, "when you hold me."

"Do you want me to hold you?"

"Yes."

She was pulled gently, deeply into his arms, and she closed her eyes and luxuriated in the strength and the warmth of him.

His lips moved over her forehead and her cheek slowly at first, and then rapidly, until a certain moment when they both knew there was no going back in time—not from that moment. Their lips came together solidly in a kiss built on silent yearning that had risen, day by day, to heights that seemed unreachable. They were reaching toward those heights now by silent, mutual consent.

He sighed deeply and his voice was very soft. "I've come to think of myself as a very disciplined man. I've not allowed myself to feel, because I couldn't. But with you,

Terry, with you my senses come alive and I feel, whether I like it or not, I feel so many things."

"Tell me what things."

"Curiosity about you. Fascination with you. My thoughts wander to you when I least expect it, and my thoughts want to stay. And more, I burn inside. I want you. I ache and burn with wanting you. Does it scare you when I say that?"

"It makes me tremble all over when you say that."

"I don't want you to be afraid of me."

She hugged him tighter. "You're sitting here almost naked and expecting me to act normal? It isn't fear that makes me tremble. You know that. Not fear of you." She drew away and met the misty gaze of his blue eyes. "I'm not afraid of being close to you. I want to be close to you. This close, even closer..."

"Honey, right now, if we were any closer..."

"Yes," she said in a breath, barely voiced, feeling his heartbeat next to hers. "Yes."

He bent to kiss her again, while his hands moved over her shoulders and under the neckline of her blouse, caressing her skin softly. She slid her fingers over the length of his bare back. At just the slightest touch at his waist, the loose knot gave and the towel fell away, and he let it fall. He was caught up completely in sensations of the deepening kiss.

His body was against hers, tight and hard, until she felt herself being swept up from the couch and into his arms. With the same ease that he had lifted her the night they met, he lifted her now, and carried her through the living room and into his bedroom, where he lay her on the bed and stood over her, his body silhouetted by light shining through the open doorway.

She gazed up at him, wanting to tell him how beautiful he was unclothed and not knowing how to say it. He seemed to have no need for modesty, and she wondered if he was always that way, or only now, with her. Her heart was pounding so wildly she imagined she could actually hear the sound of it.

He said huskily, "I'm going to lock up your apartment so no one can get in there. An ounce of precaution, as they say. I'll lock my door, too. We don't want to be disturbed tonight."

She watched him walk back out of the shadows of his bedroom, and she heard him in the front hallway of the building. There were certain advantages to living in deserted, haunted buildings; there was the privacy to walk around in the nude, she thought as she kicked off her shoes and wriggled out of her tight jeans. When he returned, she was propped up against the pillows in her underwear.

He paused in the doorway muttering praises to her beauty—praises she barely heard over the sound of her pounding heart. She opened her arms to him.

Amidst the rain of kisses he poured on her, he muttered, "You don't know how much I want you."

"Maybe I do," she whispered, feeling the strength of him against the softness of her belly.

"Yeah, maybe you do...no, honey, you don't. It's not just my body that wants you; the longing is far deeper than that. I've tried to fight it, but some things a man just can't fight."

"Or a woman."

"I felt...felt your feelings."

"I felt yours too."

Kissing the swell of her breasts around white lace, he loosened her bra and let it fall away. His hands were warm and gentle. His lips were warm, less gentle. His kisses a silky blur rustling with slowly heightening boldness over her quivering flesh.

Her fingers clutched his shoulders, then moved over his back to the taut muscles of his hips. He shifted, allowing her access to his body, without lifting his warmth from her.

Accepting, receiving. Taking, giving. They were the same with no division between them. Night and morning, too, became one with the other, for Terry felt sensations of a sunrise in his touch—shimmering new beginnings, blaze of promise...exploding colors of love engulfing her. Dawn of a different morning streaming from a midnight sky. And there was no going back; there was only forward from here. The dawn was surrender. The dawn was joy.

In the silver-yellow light that filtered in from the doorway Mike's face was in shadow as he looked at her, but his eyes caught the light so she could see into them and through them. She witnessed need replacing sadness, passion replacing caution. Desire was overpowering him. Terry, lost to the febrile force of his power over her, realized her power over him was every bit as fervid. And she let go, let herself slide body and soul into the fiery dawn.

He whispered, "Your skin tastes so sweet. It makes me think of dew on rose petals."

"Dew is part of the dawn," she breathed.

"Hmm?"

Terry closed her eyes, unable to answer. While she yielded to his kisses and his searching hands, a small cry of pleasure came from her lips.

In turn, her hands took possession of him, savoring first touches of intimacy, until he moaned and turned toward her, leaning hard into the softness of her body.

He whispered huskily, "Terry..."

"Yes..." she responded in breathy rasps. "Yes..."

"I wanted to wait...to..." he groaned and shifted. "But when you do that..."

"I want you," she managed to whisper against the beating wings of her passion.

His warmth entered and filled her and his heartbeat became hers and his breath became hers and the rhythms of his body were the rhythms of hers. Their bodies blended, became one. Terry lost all awareness of herself; she was aware only of him and of being part of him.

A breath-filled groan came from deep inside Mike. His body shuddered. He clutched tightly to her hand and she squeezed back as if his grasp were the only link to the reality of earth. Hands clasped, bodies clasped, each to the other. He went weak, with the shuddering spasm, and Terry clung to the magic and to him, wanting the moment to last forever. Knowing it would last forever, in the lens of her memory.

IN THE AFTERGLOW, with Terry lying on his arm, he stirred. His free hand began to move in gentle circles over her breasts.

His voice was still husky, different from his usual voice. "I'd forgotten...actually forgotten...or maybe I never knew."

"Surely," she said, "in these eight years you've had girl-friends."

"It's not the same."

Terry closed her eyes and welcomed the sensations of his caressing fingers and the sweet murmurings of his voice telling her she was special.

"I tried to resist you," he said softly.

"I know."

"I have no right to involve you in my life, Terry."

"I involved myself."

"Not to this degree. I don't want to cause you unhappiness."

She noted his frown and knew it was because of guilt. Touching his bare shoulder, she said, "Mike, we were already bound together by danger, thanks to me. Danger has a way of heightening emotions and of creating a sense of immediacy or even urgency. I tried to resist you, too. The conditions for resistance just weren't right."

He smiled, but the smile was sad. "At this moment, I have no future, none at all."

"Are you discounting our intricate plan for turning everything around?"

A heavy sigh heaved in his chest. "No. I'm impractical and desperate enough to keep faith in the plan, but at the same time my intellect is realistic enough to recognize how chancy it is."

"Don't think that way. Just keep convincing yourself it's going to work."

"Damn, it *has* to work."

"Yes, it has to."

With his head resting against her shoulder and one large hand covering her breast, Mike closed his eyes. In the silence that ensued, she stroked his thick gray hair and listened to his breathing as it changed. Soon he was breathing quietly, evenly, in the comfort of sleep.

Terry thought, *We are bonded by more than danger now.* There was no longer a doubt in her mind that she loved him. Future or not, she loved him. And knowing instinctively that it had been a very long time since he had fallen asleep like this against the softness of a woman's body, the aching need within him satisfied, Terry lay wide-awake with tears of overflowing emotion brimming her eyes.

BECAUSE OF BOYCE'S threatening telegram, Terry spent the following nights with Mike. Twice during the day, while she was working on the sketches in her dining room, Gil came to see Mike, and they talked behind the closed door of his apartment. They had little to say to her about those sequestered discussions. Terry could not shake off an uneasiness about Gil. Mike seemed to trust him, and this was dangerous and it bothered her. Gil had turned on Mike once, and he could do it again.

At night shadows seemed to come to life. Each day that went by caused her to get more and more nervous about the threat in the telegram. Mike was sure it wasn't an idle threat and refused to let her spend a night alone.

Terry was near her window in the morning when a uniformed police officer parked in front of the house and knocked on Mike's door. For an agonizing ten minutes she waited. Could Boyce or Gil have decided to give Mike's real identity to the police? To her relief, the officer left alone. She met Mike in the hallway.

"What did he want?"

Mike looked slightly uneasy. "Two things, actually. Some neighbor reported what looked like a vagrant hanging around this house for the last two nights."

She paled. "You don't think it could be Boyce?"

"Anything's possible."

"Or Gil."

"I don't know."

"I'm getting so jittery, Mike. When I saw the officer, I was afraid they knew who you were. Haven't you worried about that these past years? About your identity being discovered?"

"Sure, that's always a worry, even more so when the police officers are your friends and you know how sharp they are. But they've never had reason to suspect me of any crime. If there was ever a wanted poster out on me I never saw it. Boyce might have stopped it somehow; he wouldn't have wanted me to be caught still insisting on his guilt. I have good false ID and a reputation for minding my own business around here. But that doesn't mean some unexpected thing from outside couldn't alert the police sometime. The life of a fugitive isn't exactly relaxing."

Terry cringed. "Did he say they'd keep a lookout for whoever is hanging around the house?"

"Oh yeah. And they will."

"What else did he want? You said there were two things."

Mike's expression changed to one of frustration. "There's a hiker lost in the area of the big cliffs and they suspect he may be seriously injured. Since I'm their most qualified and experienced volunteer, they want my help for search and rescue, but I'm hesitant to leave right now."

"Because of me."

"Yes. Although the search may not take very long, and it's daylight."

"You really want to go, don't you?"

"I like to feel useful to society. It's the main thing that's kept me going these years of hiding—the fact that I can put some of my experience to good use."

"I'll be all right in daylight, Mike. And if you're not back by tonight, I can lock myself in tight, or I could even stay with Rosa. I'll be okay. This is important to you. I think you should go."

"It is important to me. This hiker—I don't know him personally but I know his brother, who lives in Cottonwood, and he's specifically asked for my help." Mike rubbed his chin. "What I could do is ask Gil to keep an eye on you for the few hours I'm gone."

"I don't need Gil."

"Terry, I wish you were a little more trusting of him. He's on our side."

"Is he?"

"He is. And he doesn't have a damn thing better to do today than make sure you are guarded. You don't have to have anything to do with him, or even talk to him. But I'll alert him, and I can feel pretty secure about your safety as long as he's right here."

"I'll be okay. I'd planned to have lunch with Rosa today. I'll spend some time in town with her."

"You and Rosa are quite a pair, I've noticed."

"I like her a lot."

"And she likes you. She's told me so."

Terry marveled once again that Mike's best friend in Jerome was an old woman. Perhaps she was like a mother to him, like part of the family he had lost because of Howard Boyce.

She said, "You need to get started, don't you?"

"If I'm going, I do. Gil should be at the hotel. I won't leave unless I talk to him about guarding you. Did you plan to be in town all afternoon?"

"No, actually I planned to go up to the old hospital and do some sketches for my files because as soon as this story is finished, I'm going to work on my original Jerome one. I need to keep working. I feel so much better when I'm working; there's less time for worrying."

"The hospital is kept locked."

"I know, but I'm making friends around here. I was able to borrow a key to a side door. I've wanted to explore it but there are so many stairs. I can do it now if I go slowly; my knee is so much better."

Mike frowned. "I don't think you ought to go up to the hospital alone."

"No one else can get in."

"People often break in there. The building is so big, they find ways. The police are always arresting trespassers."

"I thought Gil was going to be protecting me," she said teasingly.

"If you knew what that building was like inside, you wouldn't be so anxious to wander around there alone."

"Now I'm more intrigued than ever. People say the hospital is haunted. What could be in there besides a few old ghosts?"

"Probably nothing. I just don't want you taking any chances."

"Boyce isn't in Jerome. He couldn't be here without our knowing, could he? Or are you afraid the vagrant hanging around here could be Boyce?"

"I doubt it. It's not his style. But Howard is a desperate man. So who knows what he might do?"

"You really think he'll come here?"

"I think he'll have to. What Howard hates more than anything else is having to trust anybody with secrets about himself. That's why he's tried to kill Gil and why he doesn't want me found and arrested again. He believes any person is capable of turning on another, and with that kind of mentality, I doubt if he could completely trust his own mother. Howard's style is to always do things himself so there's nobody to talk afterward. A man with high political ambitions can't afford to have people pop out of his past. I think it's only a matter of time, Terry. He'll be here to take care of this problem himself, and he can't dare to wait too long, with the comic story unfolding more every day."

Terry shuddered. "What do you think he'll do?"

"Whatever he thinks he has to do to stop us."

"Would he actually try to kill us?"

"Honey, he's a murderer. He had a lot less reason to murder his cousin than he has for getting rid of you and me."

"Aren't you frightened?"

"You're damn right I am. What I'm afraid of is that he might try sniping, just shooting at us. He wouldn't try it in the daytime in this small town because the police would be down on him in three seconds. But at night he might have a better chance. Don't venture one toe outside at night."

"But if I was killed, wouldn't that look pretty bad when reporters figure out what I'm doing with the story? I'm dropping a lot of clues."

"Yes, that would be dangerous for him, unless he made it look like an accident. Howard has a challenge here, but he

thinks he can rise to any occasion. He'll try *some*thing. He
has to. You've left him no choice.''

ON HIS WAY out of town, Mike dropped her off at the hotel,
where Rosa was waiting for her. While he hunted down Gil
Spearow, Terry and Rosa walked to a small restaurant for a
brunch of tea and freshly baked biscuits. Terry found some
comfort in the knowledge that Mike would not leave town
until he found Gil, but along with the comfort came trepidation, too, for there was something about Gil that she intensely disliked. Even the slightest possibility of having to
place her life in his hands left her feeling weak in the knees.
  Perhaps, she told herself, it was only because of what he'd
done to Mike long ago that she had such bad vibes about
him. Maybe she should rely on Mike's judgement. But
still . . .
  Conversation with Rosa was difficult on this day, because Terry was trying to conceal the worry and fear that
weighed so heavily on her. Restless, Terry wanted only to
escape from the pressure of having to make friendly conversation, to escape thinking about the danger Howard
Boyce represented in the best way she knew how—by working on her drawings.
  Mike had admitted there was little danger of anything
happening in the daytime. In such a small town, with many
tourists on the streets, nothing could happen without being
noticed. Terry walked back to her car, which was parked
outside the Beyer House. There were sketch pads in the
trunk. She drove up the steeply winding streets toward the
hospital.
  The building and its surroundings were familiar to her
now; she had driven up several times to see it. There was the
decaying house just down the hill and No Trespassing signs
were posted everywhere. At the top of a steep, high stairway, the hospital entrance appeared to be boarded shut.

Terry parked on the side of the road, fumbled in her hand-bag for the key loaned to her by a police officer, and un-locked the padlock and chain on the side door, which once must have provided access to an ambulance entry.

She stepped into a broad, hollow chamber of dead silence and billowing darkness, the hospital basement. Clutching a flashlight in one hand and her sketch pad in the other, Terry searched for a stairway, and it was there, not far in front of her. She climbed slowly, giving all her weight to her strong leg. The stairway was short. At the top there was light from the first floor windows.

The wide corridor was filled with shadows. Walking around, searching the empty rooms, it was impossible for Terry not to think of stories about the history of the building. It had been locked up since the early fifties when the mine closed and everyone left town. Just left. Their memories were locked in here. Memories of epidemics, of mine casualties and fire casualties, of suicides, of shootings, birth and death and pain. A thousand echoes seemed to lurk within the shadows of the empty rooms.

She made her way up to the second floor. In the hallway a wide, round metal-lined laundry chute with the door torn off its copper hinges opened through to the basement. Doors lined the walls of the corridor, and each summoned the explorer. In fascination, Terry wandered through wards with ceiling lights spaced above where each bed would be, through staff meeting rooms and examining rooms. One flight above held the surgery wing, with the many hospital fixtures still intact. An operating table stood under an enormous light fixture. Blue-tiled walls. Broad windows facing north, toward Cleopatra hill, allowed the sun's light to stream into the room. Caught up completely in the intrigue of the silent, deserted building, Terry spent several minutes sketching these surgical rooms.

Leaving this wing, she entered shadows again, determined to find her way to the wide third-floor balcony that overlooked the city below and the Verde Valley beyond. In the hallway, just as she passed an old fire hose mounted on the wall, a sudden sound chilled her—a sound of slow-moving, muted footsteps. She remembered she hadn't closed the door behind her at the basement entrance because it had been so dark. Someone could have come in after her.

She listened, heard nothing, and told herself it was only her imagination working overtime in the spooky atmosphere of the old building. But her intuition was keenly tuned, too. She felt she was no longer alone. The sounds were all too real.

It must be Gil, following her as Mike had asked him to do. But Gil would call out to her, wouldn't he? With trepidation, Terry began to move toward the stairway in the center of the corridor. Wanting to get out, wishing she didn't have the dark basement between her and the outside, she made her way down to the second floor.

Turning at the landing, scanning the deepening shadows, Terry's heart leaped into her throat and began to pound wildly. One of the shadows had moved. Someone *was* here, watching her.

"Who's there?" she called in a trembling voice, shining her light into the shadows.

The figure of a man emerged abruptly, startling her. The beam of her flashlight caught a pair of dark, staring eyes, the meanest eyes she had ever seen. Terry stood stunned. Baring his teeth in a strange kind of snarl, the man began to move toward her.

Chapter Ten

Gasping, Terry backed up, only to find herself against a wall. Who was he? Someone exploring the hospital? This desperate hope was dispelled the moment she heard her name come exploding from his curling lips. Danger became real, and terrifying. He knew who she was! The man was not Howard Boyce; Terry, having drawn that face so often, knew Boyce's face.

With scarcely a second's hesitation, Terry ducked into a doorway. The room she entered, like so many others, opened through a bathroom to the room on the other side. Terry ran through several connected rooms and bathrooms until there were no more inside doors, and nowhere to go but back into the main corridor. Her heart was in her throat. The man called her name one more time. She couldn't see him, but she was certain he was chasing her through the empty rooms. Could Howard Boyce have sent this man? Making good his threat?

Gil was supposed to be protecting her, she remembered. Where was he? But Gil wouldn't know she had come up here to the hospital. He'd assume she was still in town or home working. Besides, Gil wasn't to be trusted. Flashes of fear bombarded her mind as she turned back to the sound of heavy footsteps behind her. Gil was good at disguises! *Could he even be this man?*

Terry was forced out to the main corridor again, but it was empty. Darting across the hall and through another room, she found a very narrow archway that had no door and led into a space that looked pitch-black inside, like a closet. It might serve as a hiding place. Ducking in, she bumped immediately into a wall, then hit another. This was a small maze! What could it be? Feeling her way through, too far inside the maze now for the light to come in from the corridor, she flicked on her flashlight. The walls were painted black, and at the end was a wide counter. It could only be a darkroom for developing X rays. Turning the flashlight off, she crouched against the metal countertop in total blackness, aware that if her pursuer happened to come in here, there would be no hope for escape; she would be cornered. Yet if she came out now, he would probably see her.

With heart pounding, like that of an animal in a trap, Terry jumped when she heard a man's wild shout. The cry was followed immediately by another. Then through the hollow hallway came more sounds, grunts and slams, the sound of two men fighting. The awful, savage sounds carried through the empty shadows and echoed from the walls.

This could be her only chance to get out. Cautiously, Terry slid along the black wall of the darkroom. There was no way out except through the main hallway, where the fight was taking place. She had to dash through there, and she was sure to be seen, unless the men were too wrapped up in their fistfight to look up. It was a chance she had to take.

There wasn't time for anything but a swift glance in their direction as she darted into the hall and ran toward the stairs. Neither of the men's faces was visible as they fought, but she did get a glimpse of the second man's shock of blond hair. Any wild hope she'd had that he might be Gil, come to help her, quickly dissolved. One of the men had been chasing her. The other was fighting him for reasons of his own. All she could think about was getting out.

A loud shout followed her; she had been seen. Praying her knee wouldn't give out, Terry raced for the stairs. She had barely started down when the thudding crash of a man's body hitting the floor filled the empty hallways. Then there was silence. The fight was over.

Terry listened for footsteps. She thought she heard a few, but then they were gone. Silence came down on the huge old building.

Puzzled, she didn't dare slow down. The men were a good forty feet from the stairway, which would give her a fair lead if her knee wasn't weak. She had a chance with that much of a head start—at least a chance—if the man who was still on his feet came after her.

But there were no sounds of footsteps, or even of creaking stairs behind her. This small encouragement enabled her to consider her knee and force caution upon herself. As nearly as she could tell, the threat was over; no one seemed to be behind her.

Moving steadily down the wide stairway, Terry's mind kept flashing on sunshine, on the bright day outside these darkened, aging halls. The noise of the fight was like some hideous nightmare, still pulsing in her brain. The stare of the man who had startled her, and the threatening sound of his voice, were still too close. She wanted to get out, wanted to be free of the sounds and the shadows and the threats of this place. There was terror here. Mike had warned her not to come; if only she had listened.

From somewhere in the building came an odd noise like someone kicking a tin barrel. It seemed far away. Silence had fallen again by the time she reached the bottom floor, the basement, which was not underground but had very few windows. The door she had entered through was closed now. Obviously this was how the men came in. How could she have been stupid enough to leave it open? But she had been too frightened to close that door behind her and enter the darkened passages. It was almost pitch-black in this chamber. She shone her light, looking for the door.

Into the beam of her flashlight came a face—a horrible face! Terry jumped and shrieked. It was the man who had been chasing her upstairs. Behind him was the round, open, tin-lined hole of the laundry chute. He had slid down the laundry chute in order to reach the basement before she did.

Her heart nearly stopped. Ducking back, knowing there wasn't time to try to get the door open, Terry ran across the room, shining the beam of her flashlight ahead of her under some pipes, into the boiler room. Three huge furnaces were partitioned off by a railing over a floor drop of several feet. Below her an old drain hole was filled with murky, green water. Dodging the huge equipment, she found herself facing another sheer drop of five feet—the floor of the elevator shaft. From the bottom, giant springs poked up out of solid concrete; weights were hanging down from the cables.

Eager to get away from the frightening elevator shaft, Terry beamed her light along the wall, doubling back. She entered a small room that contained a giant metal box, possibly an old ice box, but actually large enough for a morgue. A good hiding place, she thought at first, and then she thought, no, a better coffin. Sweating, weak-kneed, heart pounding, Terry forced herself to keep on moving.

The man's footsteps were not steady. They would halt for a time and then they would begin again. Her only hope was to get back to the entrance before he did, but it was a slim hope; if he was smart, he'd have already thought of that.

Yet the slim hope was her only hope. Passing by what looked like a garage part of the basement, trying to keep her directions straight, Terry crept back. Her shoes made no sound at all, but her flashlight beam could be seen. She tried to cover it except for the light around her feet.

Silence ensued again, but this time there was no reassurance in it, only horror. Coming out into the entrance room again, Terry stopped dead still. The man was standing in front of the doorway. This time her light flashed on something shining silver in his hand. He raised a large knife into the air.

His voice echoed through the hollow chamber, chilling her like a rain of ice. "I'm a dead shot at knife throwing. If you try to run from me again, you won't get two feet."

She stared at the knife, her hand shaking so violently the flashlight beam trembled. There was blood on the blade. He had stabbed the man he had fought with. She was face to face with a possible murderer!

Terry stood frozen with fear as he approached her.

She managed to mumble, "What do you want?"

"We have some business to attend to. A comic strip story that needs to be changed."

"Who...are you?"

He continued to approach her. "Is that important?"

"You're not..." Her shaking voice faltered and stopped.

"Not who?" He asked the question as if he dared her to answer.

She didn't answer, standing frozen to the concrete floor, in the dark.

He moved in behind her so that she was between him and the door. "Let's go. We're driving back to your house in your car, and don't try anything because this knife will be about five inches from you the whole way."

When he reached around her to open the door, Terry caught the scent of heavy perspiration, and remembered the fistfight. His hand was bloody. *Had he just killed another man? Who was that other man?*

Roughly shoving at her shoulder, he guided her into the car.

Terry hesitated with the keys rattling in her hand. "I'm shaking so much I can't drive."

"I'm not giving you a choice. Only an order. Start the car."

While she drove, jerkily, with her knee aching, Terry found herself looking out frantically for a sign of Gil Spearow. He was nowhere to be seen. *Some guard he is,* she thought. *Some friend. He has betrayed Mike again.* Why couldn't Mike have foreseen it? Mike was so careful about everything else. Why was he so blind when it came to trusting a man who had already proved himself his enemy?

From the sound of her captor's demands, he intended for her to change the comic strip whether she wanted to or not. Boyce must have decided that to stop it abruptly would be unwise. Changing it would serve him much better; in fact, changing it was really his only hope of never having to answer to curious inquirers who saw the likenesses and remembered Mike's trial. So obvious. Why hadn't this occurred to her before?

The drive down to the Beyer House took less than two minutes, not enough time to try to sort out anything, with the knife blade only inches away.

Shifting the knife without flashing it in view of anyone who might be around, he forced her out of the car and into her apartment. This end of the street, as usual, was deserted in the growing heat of midday. There was no wind, not a sound of a human voice anywhere—only the singing of birds and the dull hum of automobiles around the town's business section.

Terry now understood that her life wasn't in immediate danger. As long as the man needed her to change the drawings he wasn't going to kill her. He had to be an employee of Boyce's. Mike had been wrong when he had predicted

Boyce wasn't going to hire a thug to take care of this "problem" for him. He'd hired a thug, all right; one who might have already committed a murder in Jerome. But *who* was the man he had stabbed?

In the bright light of her apartment, Terry allowed herself to look at her kidnapper for the first time. He was big, unshaven, with sandy, curly hair and dark eyes that frightened her. His features were large and blunt, his jaw very broad and heavy. A wrestler type or a heavyweight boxer, maybe. A man who looked as if there weren't a sensitive bone in his huge body. A typical hired thug.

He closed the door behind them and turned the bolt, locking them in. Then he walked directly to the table that held her drawings and studied them hurriedly without bending over, moving papers about with the tip of his knife blade.

"I don't know what you want," she said, watching him.

"Like hell you don't. You've just shown a murder here. And it's not correct. The wrong guy committed the murder."

She had to stall. Terry knew that stalling was the only thing that was going to keep her alive. "This is a comic strip! Why should you care which character did what?"

"Don't act so innocent, lady. There's no sense pretending, is there? You've copied an actual murder her. Ain't that illegal?"

"An actual murder? Are you sure?"

The big mouth turned down at the corners in anger. He said, "I don't like games. And I don't enjoy conversation. You're going to change these drawings so the guy with the scar is the murderer, not the law student."

"I can't do that. The murder has already been shown."

His eyes turned on her in fury. "Change it anyway. Draw it so the guy with the scar was planning to make it look like the other guy did it—like he was thinking this plan, and then show him actually holding the gun and pulling the trigger. And show him arrested and the law student grieving for the murdered cousin.''

Terry hesitated, becoming more frightened. ''I...can't do that.''

''You can, and you will. And hurry up. You're wasting time.''

''And if I don't? What will you do about it?''

He said nothing, only looked meaningfully at the knife.

''If I was murdered, don't think there wouldn't be plenty of investigation into the reasons why. It would look very bad for the man who hired you, wouldn't it? Starting with my newspaper editors, a lot of people would be asking questions. Could he—your employer—take that kind of publicity?''

He glared. ''There's your friend to consider. The guy who calls himself Calhoun, whose real name is Colin MacKaine, and who is an escaped convict.''

Colin MacKaine. Terry was distracted for the moment by the sound of Mike's real name. He'd never told her. It was difficult to think of him as someone else. *Colin MacKaine.* A strong name. It suited him.

She muttered, ''Mike is in as much danger whether I change any drawings or not. That we both know.''

He glared, his impatience showing in the clenching and unclenching of his fist. ''That may be so. I've been in town several hours, lady. It's a damn small town and I've been inquiring around about you. Seems you've made friends with the old lady who runs the hotel, Mrs. Gonzales. It sure would be a bad thing if something were to happen to her. Be a damn shame, wouldn't it?''

Terry went ice cold. Mike had tried to warn her about the caliber of men she was baiting with her pictures. But she hadn't comprehended. This sort of thing happened only in movies, not in real life. The man was not bluffing. He could threaten to harm an elderly woman as easily as most men could order a whiskey.

Her voice trembled. "What sort of man are you?"

"I just do my job, kid, any way I have to do it. Now, let's get on with this. You know what to do."

Still urgently trying to stall, she asked, "How can I draw when my hands are shaking so much?"

"I strongly suggest you figure out how."

Wringing her hands, Terry sat down at the table and began to arrange papers.

"Hurry it up."

"I'm thinking, damn it! I have to think how to do this."

"I told you how. Now just do it."

She worked as slowly and painstakingly as possible. This man had no way of knowing how fast she could do the drawings once the character was already established and she had drawn him several dozen times. She set about making subtle changes hoping he wouldn't notice—clues to her editor that something was terribly wrong, in case this strip did go through. Deception came more easily as she worked, boldly changing a character's name to the name of the publisher of one of the major papers that carried her strip. A cry for help, although if it came to that, it might be too late to help her. She put some age on the character of Howard Boyce so he would be more recognizable as his present self.

In order to distract the thug from these deceptions, Terry began talking about the haunted house he was standing in. And how for decades people had heard strange voices coming from this house, how she has heard them too, hideous howling and growling sounds. And how she saw a ghost appear on the hall ceiling. The thug was only amused at first, then impatient again, knowing she was trying to distract him and stall for time. The man was not as stupid as his looks led her to believe. He studied the drawings over her shoulder, and turned red in the face.

Terry shrank from his rising anger. At that moment ghoulish moans cracked the silence of the big old house. The man jumped and looked up at the ceiling from where the sounds seemed to be originating; his eyes were wide.

Terry welcomed the sounds of the Beyer House ghosts. Relief flooded her. *Mike must be back!* How else could the stereo equipment be turned on? Gil? *Where was Gil?* she wondered for the thousandth time.

The growling, screeching noise continued.

"What the hell is that?" the man asked, his mouth open, his eyes wide, staring at the ceiling.

"I told you. The house is haunted. Those are the spirits that live here."

He looked at her incredulously.

"Oh, it's true," she said. "Sometimes you can see one of the ghosts moving around."

The distraction of the noise allowed the master key to turn unnoticed in the lock, but Mike's entry was not swift enough. As the door was flung open, the thug made a grab for Terry. She shrieked in startled fright.

Mike had returned to his apartment only long enough to get the gun he had purchased years ago when he was on the run—a gun he had never had cause to carry, until now.

Terry felt herself being roughly jerked out of her chair with the cold steel of the knife held against her throat. So tight was the man's grip she could scarcely breathe. Mike muttered a terrible oath.

"Drop the gun!" the man demanded, pulling Terry so tight she gasped. "Drop the gun right there and back away. Now!"

Without hesitation Mike did as he was told. "Let go of her, damn you! Your boss wants *me*, not her!"

The thug forced Terry toward the gun, and released his hold on her only after he had retrieved the weapon from the floor. He directed Mike to stand beside her and held the gun on them both.

"We have a little unfinished work to do here with the drawings," he growled with rising impatience cracking his voice.

"Don't do it, Terry," Mike said. "Once you've done what he asks..."

She answered, "I know. I know..." just as the noises upstairs started again. Terry's eyes met Mike's for a moment, but there was no answer for her in his eyes. She had no idea whether Mike had set the machines to work or whether Gil was in the house.

The thug's discomfort was impossible for him to hide. His eyes darted around wildly.

"The ghosts are out early today, long before dark," Mike said. "It's not often they show up in the daytime like this. Something is riling them up."

"Shut up! You're talking like a fool!"

Mike met the other man's eyes and said with sinister seriousness, "It's your presence in the house that's triggering this. If you knew what was good for you, you'd get out of here."

"I'm getting out of here, all right," the man muttered in the wake of another ghoulish shriek that would make a hyena howl sound like a kitten's purr. "Both of you are coming with me."

Mike's jaw muscles were tensed. He was angry at himself for miscalculating the possibility of a hired hit man showing up. It just wasn't Howard's style to employ somebody like this. But then, he hadn't seen Howard in many years; people change. Still, Howard was a man who trusted no one. But Mike was almost certain that this hoodlum was the only one they'd have to confront, since it was highly unlikely that Howard had sent more than one man to do this job. The job, he calculated with icy coldness, was to murder both him and Terry in order to stop them from talking about the truth of David's murder.

Still, Mike was very surprised Howard wasn't here to oversee this operation himself, to make sure the job got done. It just wasn't like Howard to leave everything to this Neanderthal who was showing nervous signs of succumbing to real fear as the ghosts of the Beyer House continued their macabre ragings. Mike strongly suspected that the man's connection with Howard probably went no deeper than the few thousand dollars he'd been paid. His restless and anxious eyes hinted that there was a limit to what Boyce's money would buy. This place was more than haunted; angry spirits in this house were raising hell!

Sweating profusely, Mike tried to find a way to deflect the danger from Terry, if only to start enough trouble to give her the chance to run. The burden of guilt for getting her into this situation was heavy on him and only added to his fear for her life.

Terry understood the danger. The minute the hired killer had what he wanted from her with the drawings, neither her life nor Mike's was of any use to him. Noting his understandably nervous reaction to the sounds of the ghosts, Terry rubbed her arms and began to shiver. "I can't stand it!" she wailed in a voice edging on hysterics. "Those ghosts! They've never been this noisy before." She glared at the big man. "It's you. You that's causing this. I want out of here! People die mysteriously in this house. It's evil! It's horrible! We have to get out of here!"

Mike jumped in. "She's right. The ghosts have never been this noisy. They're mad as hell about something." He squinted at the man who wielded the knife. "It *is* you!"

"Something terrible happened in the hospital," Terry said in a quivering voice, trying to get a chance to move closer to Mike. "There was a fight. I don't know who the other man was or how badly he was hurt, but I think he might be dead.'' She looked at the thug with fearful eyes. "Who was the man you fought with?"

Staring at the ceiling, his Adam's apple moving as the rattle of chains echoed through the house, he appeared not to hear her question. Mike looked at Terry, confused, questioning.

"I don't know who he was," she repeated to Mike in a half whisper. "I got only the slightest glimpse of him, but I'm sure I never saw him before. There was blood on the knife so he must have been stabbed."

"Shut up!" the thug commanded in a high-pitched, out-of-control voice. "Both of you—shut up!"

Mike's face grew pale with concern. He cursed himself. What a fool he'd been to leave. Now Terry's life was in danger along with his. If they were murdered here, in the isolated Beyer House, the killer would probably have time to get away before the police discovered a crime had been committed.

The taped sounds of the ghosts were well-timed, well-spaced. Another wail sounded from the rooftops. Terry shrieked in pretended terror. Mike backed toward the door.

It was now or never, Mike realized. The guy was most vulnerable right now. "We're getting out of here!" Mike said, pulling on Terry's sleeve. With force Mike pulled her toward him and swung around in front of her, putting himself between the knife and her, actually leaning over her to protect her should the blade come flying. If it had, he'd have caught it squarely in the back.

He rasped, "If I get stopped, run and keep running!"

The thug recovered his balance easily and dashed toward them. He held the knife inches from Mike's heart. His sweat-soaked shirt was heaving up and down as he breathed. "We're all getting out of here! Don't try anything, Mac-Kaine, or I'll go after her, not you."

With a powerful grip, he seized Terry by the collar and guided her outside with the knife touching her ribs. Mike was helpless to attack as long as Terry was in that predicament, and all three of them knew it. But he hung back stubbornly.

"Get over here! Get in front of me!" The hit man jabbed Terry with the knife point hard enough to draw blood and cause her to gasp. He raised Mike's gun and cocked it. "I said get over here!"

Once they were on the front porch, Mike found the gun aimed at his head.

"Get in the car, both of you!" He gave Terry a small shove but never let go of her collar while he held the gun on Mike. "You drive."

"Drive where?"

"Up the hill. The hospital."

Mike's stomach knotted. No answer could have been worse. Once they were in the hospital, anything could happen. Even a gunshot from deep inside that huge building might not be heard outside. He was helpless to protest anything as long as the knife was in Terry's ribs. There was no choice but to do as he was told.

His hope lay in Gil. But he had begun to worry. Gil should have been back at the house when Mike had gone up to set his timed sound effects machines, and there had been no sign of him. *Something must have happened to Gil! Had Gil been killed?*

Terry had said there was a fight at the hospital. Did Gil try to keep this thug away from Terry and get himself killed? But Terry would have recognized Gil. Surely she would have! She was certain someone had died, though. Who the devil had been there? Mike felt sick to his stomach. It must have been Gil, protecting Terry. And if it was, then Gil was probably dead.

Without Gil it would take a miracle to get out of this predicament alive. Mike knew the layout of the hospital well, but that advantage probably wasn't going to be of much use to him. He wanted to try to reassure Terry, but he couldn't. Terry was smart enough to comprehend what serious trouble they were in.

Her keys were in the ignition. Sweating, Mike started the car. He felt Terry's trembling thigh against his. The thug had crowded into the passenger seat of the small sports car, forcing Terry to sit on his lap. The two large men and Terry were so cramped in the car that the odor of the thug's perspiration quickly became overpowering.

Terry felt like vomiting, but she wouldn't. *I got myself into this,* she was thinking. With eyes wide open, she'd ignored Mike's warnings and walked right into this. Maybe in the back of her mind the belief had always prevailed that Mike could protect her. He couldn't protect her now. There was nothing he could do to save her, or himself.

She glanced over at him as he pulled the car around and shifted gears against her leg. Perspiration dotted his forehead. His jaw was tight. *I love him,* she thought out of the mist of unreality that settled over her. *I don't want him to die.*

Chapter Eleven

The door to the side entrance of the hospital stood open, just as they had left it. *If I had only listened to Mike and not come up here,* Terry thought, *this door wouldn't have been open!* Yet she had been told by the police that arrests were constantly being made when people broke into the building, mostly curiosity seekers. A criminal like this hired thug could get in if he wanted to, without her cooperation. But in this case, he'd had her unwitting cooperation: the open door.

As they were being forced out of the car, she was shaking with fear. There was no question now that their captor had been sent to get rid of them and his earlier signs of impatience—the jerking of his mouth, the darting eyes—were in evidence again. He was in a hurry now; they were running out of time. The man pulled her out of the car and walked her into the building while he held the gun on Mike. Terry's knee was hurting from the earlier flight down the stairs. When she went limp against the brute strength pushing her, it angered him.

She caught sight of Mike's eyes. Never had they been so filled with fury. His gaze was trained hard on the other man like a cat ready to spring. Terry realized he *was* ready to spring at the first opportunity, and this frightened her even more. Trying anything now could get him killed. How long did it take for a finger to press a trigger? She tugged against the restraint of the thug's grip, but escape from him was physically impossible.

Cool afternoon sun streamed in through the open door to light the dark chamber inside. They were forced up the stairs, away from the entrance, into the echoing depths of the hospital. By this time, Terry was certain Mike was planning to do something as soon as the least opportunity arose. He wouldn't bolt and leave her alone to face a half-crazed criminal, even if he had the opportunity. But neither would he stand by and be shot or stabbed without putting up a violent protest. Yet, what *could* he do?

The thug led them past the landing of the first floor, pushing and rushing Terry, causing her knee to protest more with each awkward step. Mike had become deathly silent. The shadows of the old building closed in around them like lurking ghosts of souls long dead.

"Where... are you taking us?" she choked.

"Up where there's some light."

This made no sense, but she didn't ask, for they had reached the landing of the second floor, the floor where the fight had taken place two hours ago. Terry tried to look behind her at the darkened corridor to see if the body of a man was lying there, but she couldn't turn her head without touching the knife blade.

If Mike saw anything, he didn't comment. His silence alarmed her more as each second dragged by. He walked with the barrel of the gun jammed in his back so that it was impossible for him to get too close to her, while their captor had to remain absolutely alert, holding the knife at Terry's throat and the gun in Mike's back at the same time. Under these conditions, either of them might have found the opportunity to pull away, except that to do so could mean instant death for the other. Their tormentor counted on this. He was experienced at his job.

He had a definite destination in mind, for on the third floor, without hesitation, he guided them down the hallway toward the far north end, the surgery wing. Here was the light he'd mentioned, under the wide wall of windows. It was a cold light, shining in on the steel frame of the operating table that stood in the center of the room. How, Terry wondered, had the man had time to learn about this room? Had he been following her earlier while she had wandered around exploring the hospital? Had he been behind her all the time? He must have been, or how would he have known about the laundry chute that opened from the center of each hallway?

The thug said to her, "I don't know what the hell was going on in that weird house and I don't care—as long as we're out of there. Anybody who could stay in that place..." His voice dropped and his shoulders jerked in an involuntary shudder.

"What are we doing here?" Terry asked.

The fact that he hadn't controlled the shudder had angered him, and now his voice came harder, louder, while he challenged her with his eyes. "I picked up the corrected drawings from your table. They're in my pocket. I want the names changed back like they were, and that law student's character drawn like it was before—and I want to see the gun smoking in the killer's hand. I'm not stupid. Did you think I haven't studied this story carefully just in case you tried something cute? Pull the paper out of my pocket and fix it right now, right here. Any more stalling or tricks and you get to watch your boyfriend die."

Terry was stunned. She hadn't seen him pick up the pages, and if Mike had, he hadn't said anything.

Mike broke his silence with a sharp turn. "Don't do it, Terry."

"Do you want to see your boyfriend's blood spattered all over this room?"

Her eyes moved toward Mike, horrified. He repeated, "Don't do it! He's going to kill me anyway. If you change the story as he wants you to, he'll have no reason not to kill you too. It's what he came for."

"My back pocket," the would-be killer growled with gritted teeth. "Take the papers and pencil out of my pocket, and do it now! I'm tired of all this stalling!"

For the first time since they'd left the apartment, the knife was drawn away from her neck, not far, but far enough for her to reach around to his pocket. In that split second Mike's eyes met hers. He was trying to convey some message to her with his eyes. She could interpret it only as a signal that the time for a move was now.

As she reached for the large, folded papers that were sticking out of his back pocket, Terry held her breath wondering if there was anything she dared do, with Mike in danger of getting shot in the back.

The hollow room suddenly rang out with Mike's shout. "Shove him! Now!"

Mike ducked and lunged in so swift a move Terry didn't really see how he did it. But, so alert she was tingling, she gave the man a shove forward at almost the same instant. Mike had managed to hit the man's arm so that the gun flew out of his hand. The blade of the knife flashed. Mike grabbed his enemy's wrist in time to stop the blade from piercing his chest. A hard struggle ensued. Terry tried to pick up the gun but the men were rolling on it and she couldn't get close.

Her heart was pounding so hard it seemed to cut off her breath. Adrenaline was pumping into her system as never before in her life and with it came strength she hadn't known she possessed. When she'd shoved the thug he had nearly lost his balance. Now she tried again and again to reach the gun, but each time, the struggling men would roll forward over it, both aware that it was there and trying to prevent the other from getting it.

Sounds of the struggle filled the entire floor of the hospital. In spite of the would-be slayer's size, Mike, who was nearly as big, was the better coordinated, better in control of his body. He was able to render two very hard blows to the side of his opponent's face, momentarily dazing the man each time.

The struggle ended in terror. The men rolled out of the surgery room and into the adjoining room. Terry scrambled for the gun and was able to pick it up, but her shouts went unheard and it was impossible for her to fire into the tangle of male arms and legs without the risk of hitting Mike. They were moving so fast, changing positions quicker than her eye could follow. It did no good to have the gun! All she could do was shout for attention, but if they heard her, neither slowed down his attempt to kill the other with his fists. They fought like madmen. And gradually they were moving closer to the French doors that opened onto a little balcony with low, decorative wrought iron bars edging it. The balcony extended only about two feet out. It looked toward the distant valley and straight down over the steep hillside that plunged to the city below.

Half of the panes of glass in the French doors were broken out, but the other half remained intact, reflecting the rays of the sun. The men struggled, grunting, to their feet once again. Blood glistened in the sunlight, blood gushing from their noses and their mouths. The fight was more savage than anything Terry had ever seen or imagined; Mike was fighting for his life—and hers.

He hit a powerful blow to the thug's neck, knocking him completely off his feet. The man staggered back, arms flailing, trying desperately, uselessly, to keep his balance. He hit the glass doors with a tremendous crash. His wriggling body bounced onto the balcony bars, but they were too low to hold him. He sailed over backward, howling with fright.

Terry dropped the gun and covered her eyes, wanting to erase forever the sight of a man's terrified eyes in the last seconds of his life. Mike leaned over the balcony, staring down three stories to the rocks of the hill slope below, where the body lay limp, unmoving.

As he stood looking down, he said in a soft, unreal voice, "So this is how it feels to kill a man."

"Mike..." she protested weakly. "It was an accident...self-defense. It was you or him."

He stood for several seconds more, his back to her, looking down at the body, wiping blood from his face with the back of his hand. Even from behind him, Terry could see that his hands were shaking. She wanted to go to him, but couldn't just now—not until he came away from that balcony.

Suddenly, with no warning whatever, a form descended upon her from behind. Terry gasped with fright.

The man, wearing black, had entered without a sound. Before Terry realized what was happening, he had stooped to pick up the gun she had dropped, and holding it, along with one in his right hand, he stood behind Mike, hesitating a second or two before he called out, "Colin!"

Mike whirled around. His body went completely rigid. His eyes told Terry what she already knew. The man was Howard Boyce.

He was wearing a brimmed hat that shadowed his face, and several days' growth of beard, trying not to look like himself. But Terry was startled at how much he looked like her drawings of him, even then. He had a face that was easy to re-create in caricature because of eyes that were set so close together and an unusually long chin and thick lips.

Mike squinted, looking not at the guns, but at his enemy's face. His voice came huskily through the heavy dust of silence. "You haven't changed much since the last time I saw you with a gun in your hand, Howard."

Boyce smiled without humor. Evidently encumbered with two guns, he flung the one he'd picked up from the floor out over the balcony before he turned his full attention on Mike. "*You've* changed, kid. Is that gray hair the real thing?"

With the light at his back, Mike walked into the room. His voice, in the face of his enemy, steadied and hardened. "Your hired killer is dead on the rocks down there."

"I guess if you want a job done, you have to do it yourself."

"Someone in town might have seen him fall," Mike said.

"If they had, we'd be hearing sirens by now."

Terry stood back listening to this conversation in complete disbelief. Their voices were so hideously calm, both of them. Their eyes were riveted on each other's, their bodies stiff. But their voices sounded as calm as if they were discussing last week's baseball game. It was as if she were witnessing some kind of ritual that only the two of them understood. Perhaps it was because this encounter had been so long in coming. But, calm as it sounded on the surface, the ritual was deadly.

Boyce, with the gun, had the upper hand, total control over Mike's life, and her own, and Mike knew it. Yet he stared at his enemy's eyes with challenge rather than fear.

"You're right though," Boyce said. "Someone might have seen a man fall over the balcony, so I'd better get this over with and get out of here. I never had a damn thing against you, Colin. It wasn't personal before. But then when you started this cockeyed scheme with the comic strip—hell, I couldn't let you get away with that. You knew I couldn't."

"Sure, I knew."

Mike brushed his fingers through his hair. His face was streaked with blood, his lower lip bleeding badly. "Terry," he said without taking his eyes from Boyce. "Terry, for

God's sake, will you run? He can't shoot both of us at the same time. Will you try to get the hell out of here! At least you'd have some chance."

"Stay right there!" Boyce commanded.

"Go!" Mike shouted. "Try, Terry, try! There's nothing to lose now!"

We're both going to die, that's what Mike is telling me! Terry went numb all over. She couldn't move, couldn't leave him, yet he was telling her not to try to stay. He didn't want her to see him die. Didn't want to prolong this. A horrible sob filled her, nearly choked her.

Mike moved forward to divert Boyce's attention from Terry.

Knowing he was in danger of being jumped if he didn't fire, Boyce's arm tensed. Mike could see it. It was what he wanted. "Terry, run!" he yelled once again.

She started to turn when a shot rang out. Mike doubled over, clutching his thigh. Her heart nearly stopped. Her voice was completely gone. Her legs trembled too much to move. She wanted to run to him, not away from him, but to run to him would be to run into a barrage of bullets. What did it matter about the barrage of bullets now? she thought, crazed with panic and grief. Mike knew. *It was too late!*

The instant Mike doubled over with blood seeping through his jeans from the wound on his leg, a shout rose from the hallway. Gil Spearow stood at the room's entrance, gun in hand, blood on his head, blood soaking his arm, his eyes wild. He was not the Gil Terry knew. No more black leather. This man was plain looking, wearing brown corduroy slacks and a wool shirt. His clothes were dirty and torn and he was bleeding.

Terry felt tremendous relief at the sight of him. But he didn't even look at her. His gaze was turned on Howard Boyce, who was standing paralyzed, staring down the barrel of Gil's gun. His own gun still aimed at Mike, Boyce couldn't seem to move.

Groaning, trembling with pain, Mike dropped helplessly to his knees.

Gil glared at Howard Boyce. "So! I got you! I finally got you! You've threatened my life for the last time, Howard!"

"What are you talking about?" Boyce asked, his voice shaking.

"As if you don't know! You've tried to kill me to shut me up. You've made my life hell. I've had no life at all, because of you. Now I'm going to get even. I'm not going to live like that anymore!"

Boyce took a step backward, looking around desperately for an escape. There was none. Gil's finger was steady on the trigger of his gun and Boyce's head was the target.

"Drop your gun!" Gil demanded. "You can't shift and fire before you're dead. Drop it or I blow your head off."

"That's not necessary, is it, Gil?" Boyce's voice came out surprisingly reassured all of a sudden, even strong, as he fought for control of the situation, his only chance to get the upper hand. "Look, I don't blame you for being upset, but I never tried to kill you. You imagined that."

"Yeah, sure I did!"

Mike made an attempt to get up. Boyce, wide-eyed, steadied the gun on him threateningly.

"I'm talking to you, Howard!" Gil screamed like a madman. "I'm gonna kill you! Have you got that?"

Startled at the tone of Spearow's voice, Boyce turned back to him, for the moment forgetting the wounded man who was immobilized and therefore no immediate threat to either of them. Terry stood by helplessly, staring at the guns and at Mike.

He was holding his leg and perspiration covered his face. Whenever he tried to move, he'd fall back, forced down by pain that seemed more than he could tolerate. Terry tried to cross the room to get to him. Gil stopped her, threatening her life if she took one step.

"Get back where you were, Terry, or you're going to find yourself in a line of bullets!"

This demand was a shock. Why would Gil refuse to let her get near Mike unless he didn't trust her? Did he expect Boyce to fire at Mike again?

She tried to ignore his command. Moving forward, she called, "Mike, can I help you?"

"Get back...." was all Mike managed to say, his voice no stronger than a fierce whisper. Fighting back tears, Terry looked from one man to another, two holding guns, the third felled by a gunshot wound, and outside on the hillside lay the body of another. Madness surrounded her. Madness and death. And it was far from over. She ached to go to Mike to try to help him, but he didn't want her to. With his last ounce of strength, he'd told her not to get near him.

Boyce was ignoring her altogether. His concern was the man who had just threatened to kill him. "We can talk about this," he was saying to Gil. "We worked something out before. Hell, you need money? How much do you need?"

"I'm not going through that again!"

"Don't be a fool," Boyce said, his pleading tone once again beginning to turn authoritative. "You tell me how much you want, it's yours. We've got to stick together. Otherwise, we're both ruined."

Howard Boyce stood pleading for his life while Terry stood by watching Mike try unsuccessfully to get up. His wound was bleeding heavily. The frustration was burning in his eyes, and he moaned again. The bullet must have hit the bone, Terry thought. Possibly even shattered it. Boyce had fired at close range.

Mike seemed to be swearing under his breath, although Terry couldn't tell what he was muttering. It was becoming

obvious that Gil was weakening under the pressure of
Howard's glittering bribes, just as he had done once before, eight years ago when Boyce needed an alibi for murder. Now the offer was three hundred thousand dollars to
spare Boyce's life.

As she began to realize Gil was giving in to the temptation of the fortune Boyce was offering in exchange for his
life—and help in eliminating those who threatened his future—Terry felt a wave of disgust. Her instincts had told her
not to trust Gil Spearow. Her instincts were right, and this
time, Mike's were wrong.

"We're wasting time," Boyce said. "That gunshot has me
worried. What if it was heard by somebody? Even kids
playing around on the slope? Come on, Gil. Think about a
quarter of a million dollars. Let's just get this done and get
out while we still have a chance to get away."

"Okay. Okay," Gil agreed. "But I'm warning you,
Howard, I intend to collect that money personally. If anything goes wrong with the deal, you're a dead man. I promise you that."

"What can go wrong? We both have the same thing to
lose, and the same secret to protect."

Gil nodded. "You go on, then. I'll take care of these
two."

Boyce squinted with his brow wrinkled. His mouth curled
up at the corners. He turned toward Mike. "No. I want the
satisfaction of finishing this. Colin is trying to ruin me with
his scheme. Nobody does that to me and gets away with it!"

The same bright spark of hatred that Terry had seen the
first time he fired and hit Mike had returned to Boyce's eyes.
She yelled as she saw him lift the gun toward Mike again.

That instant Gil's voice rang out, "Get out of my way,
Boyce! I'm doing this! I got my own reasons to want Colin
MacKaine dead!"

Gil's voice cracked like a popping firecracker—cracked with madness. His eyes grew large and utterly wild, the way a cornered cat's eyes glaze. Like a frightened rabbit, Boyce loosened his fingers on the trigger and he lowered the gun just in time to duck from the hail of gunfire that filled the room. Gil's trigger squeezed again and again, every shot fired directly into Mike's body.

In disbelief, Terry screamed and watched Mike fall after the first bullet. But Gil kept firing like a madman, making sure there was no chance left on earth that Mike was still alive.

Reality left her. Reality was too much to cope with, too painful, too filled with grief and horror. In those seconds, the only reality that still existed was the sound of Mike's last words to her. *"Run!"* he had begged her. *"Try, Terry, try!"*

His last request of her: *try to make it, Terry, try to live.*

Mike's bullet-riddled body was crumpled on the floor and absolutely still. Yet his voice seemed so alive to her, coming through the sudden awful silence. His voice... She couldn't stay with him now. Mike was not here now. Mike was gone....

Blinded by tears, Terry had the presence of mind to realize the two men were momentarily occupied with each other. A few seconds was all she had. A few seconds was probably not enough. She needed a miracle to save herself, but Mike had begged her, *try!*

She turned and bolted through a room lined with lockers, a room that once had held surgeons' gowns and medical instruments designed for saving lives. Behind her she could hear Gil Spearow's voice telling Howard Boyce that all those gunshots were sure to have been heard by now by someone. There were so many windows here on this wing of the third floor, that it was probably true. The shots might have been, *must* have been heard!

"We have to get the hell out of here, and fast!" she heard Gil shout.

Boyce said, "That girl can't be allowed to get away!"

Their voices were fading as she put distance between herself and the men, and then they got louder again. One of them, she was sure it was Gil, shouted something about going after her. Of course, he had to come after her. She had just seen him commit murder!

"Mike..." she cried over and over as she ran into the dark caverns of the hospital. "Mike... this can't be true. It can't be real... Mike..."

Some heretofore unrecognized energy force propelled her. Through the incredible weakness and grief came a strength Terry had never known she possessed. Strength born of a will to survive. To live. To see the men hang who had taken Mike's life. Suddenly, even with her severe loss, Terry was determined not to die.

She had the advantage of knowing that the small rooms with the adjoining bathrooms opened from one to another. Discovering this had saved her once before—that short time ago only hours ago and a century ago. When Mike was still alive and down in the valley trying to save an injured hiker. Could it have been only today when he kissed her goodbye and told her to be careful?

Her tennis shoes made no sound on the cement floor as she slipped from one room to another as fast as she could. She'd always been fast, but now she was hampered by her knee. It hurt badly, but she ignored the pain, determined that the knee wasn't going to slow her down. Every second mattered.

Her hope was to find a place to hide. Within the walls of this enormous building were a thousand places to hide, most of them darkened by shadows. If they were right about the gunshots being heard, then Mike's murderers didn't have time to waste looking for her. The police station was just down the hill, in the center of town. The police could be here in less than three minutes.

If the shots were heard. They must have been, Terry thought as she ran, panting, through the rooms, to get as far from her pursuers as possible. In this sleepy little town on the mountainside, there were few sounds except for automobiles along Main Street, and not many of those. Howard had fired one shot and Gil had fired four or five. She hadn't been able to count Gil's shots because everything had gone black before her eyes the minute Mike fell, fatally wounded. Now Terry calculated that here in the wing, directly overlooking the town, with most of the windows broken out, the shots had to have been heard.

If she could just hide long enough for the police to start investigating, she'd have a chance.

The old elevator stood with its door open like a gaping mouth, evidently stuck for decades on this, the third floor. When she'd been exploring earlier, she'd been afraid to step into it for fear the cables wouldn't hold. Behind the elevator she'd seen a permanent ladder that led up to the top of the elevator shaft. From what she'd seen with her light, there appeared to be an actual room up there. A possible hiding place. But could her knee hold out? That runged ladder, built against the wall, would be very difficult to climb.

The rungs began several feet from the floor. Using all the strength she had in her arms, she pulled herself up and tried to climb, but the full weight she had to exert on her injured knee forced her back down, trying to suppress a cry of pain. The room above the elevator shaft wasn't going to work after all, and she had lost precious time. Time was a matter of life and death.

There were footsteps in the hallway—rushing footsteps. But not the steps of two men, only one. Gil and Howard seemed to have separated and one of them was trying to get to her.

In desperation, she began to descend the stairway in the center of the corridor, knowing even as she did so that it might be a grave mistake to keep running instead of ducking into some place to hide. But her breathing would give her away. She was breathing so hard every breath hurt.

The rushing footsteps behind her were getting nearer. In the distance came the sound of sirens. Constant sirens. The police would get there in seconds. But capturing the murderers in this hospital would not be a quick or easy task. It was probably an impossible one. There were too many nooks and crannies, and too many ways to get out if one was motivated enough.

Coming out onto the second floor, Terry remembered the laundry chute. If she could just remember where in the corridor it was located, she might be able to slide down as Boyce's hit man had done earlier that day. If it was large enough for him, she should be able to do it easily enough.

The knee was slowing her down now; her pursuer was catching up. The footsteps were getting louder. He had already reached the middle of the stairway, and he was fast. Very fast.

She reached the laundry chute—a gaping round hole in the east wall of the corridor. The door had been removed. Inside, the chute was lined with metal. It was dark and steep. She could kill herself doing this, she realized, but it seemed a small risk compared to what was going to happen to her if she got caught by either Gil or Howard Boyce. Gil had at least one bullet left, maybe two, and Howard had all but one of his.

The sirens were growing louder as she paused to try to lower herself into the dark, round cylinder. Now there were voices in the building, the shouts of men. The police were on the first floor.

Her slim body was halfway into the chute when the leg of her jeans caught on one of the raw edges of the lining. Her leg was badly scratched, and she had to struggle to remove the denim material from the sharp edge.

She wasn't fast enough. Tugging frantically at her pant leg, Terry felt an arm around her throat while a hand came over her mouth to keep her from screaming.

Barely able to breathe, from fear and from the smothering male hand, her only thought in defeat was: *I didn't make it, Mike, but I tried. I really tried.*

Chapter Twelve

It was Gil who had caught her. With his hand held tightly over her mouth, he pulled her out of the laundry chute. Terry struggled and kicked wildly. Even knowing how useless it was against his strength, she still fought with every last ounce of energy in her body.

"Stop it, Terry," he whispered fiercely. "Damn it, stop!"

"Go burn in hell!" she breathed the second his hand slipped; she was trying with all her will to kick him.

"Stop it!" he repeated as if she should do as he told her. "The police are in the building. I have to get out of here."

She tried to scream, but his hand was firmly over her mouth once again to keep her from doing just that.

"Terry, for God's sake! Don't you understand? Mike isn't dead! You've got to get back up there!"

She heard only three of the words he said. *Mike isn't dead!* Her body went completely limp. She ceased all the struggling. Gil released his hand. "I thought you knew my gun was loaded with blanks. I had to catch you so Boyce wouldn't, and to tell you to go back."

She stared, barely comprehending, still thinking, *Mike isn't dead.* "But . . . but . . . Boyce was . . ."

"I had to move fast to fire before he did."

"Oh, my God, if you had been one second later . . ."

"Terry, listen! We screwed up. Mike's hurt. I'm not sure he's still conscious; he's so good at playing dead, he even had me convinced. Look . . ." His voice was a frantic, hurried whisper. "Mike sometimes works with a valley ambulance crew, knows those people well. When they get here, you've got to make sure no one releases any information about him being alive, if Mike isn't able to explain that himself. Same thing with the police. Describe Boyce to them as the man who tried to kill Mike. Blame the death of Howard's hired killer on Boyce, too. Don't name him. You don't know anything except what you saw. That way, Howard won't be able to get out of town and the police won't be looking for me. That's important. Now, hurry! There are police all over this building. I've got to find a place to hide."

The dim light and shadows emphasized every line of Gil's face, making him appear much older than she knew him to be. He had saved Mike's life by his quick action, firing the blanks split seconds before Howard Boyce could pull the trigger of his gun for the second time. *He had saved Mike's life!* And she had thought . . .

"Gil!" she whispered as he was moving away in one direction and she was backing away in the opposite direction.

He turned back, without stopping.

"I'm so sorry . . ."

His shoulders heaved in a hurried shrug. It was impossible for her to tell whether the shrug meant he understood, or whether it meant he didn't know what she was talking about. There wasn't time to communicate any further, or even to think about it. Gil immediately ducked into the shadows and through a doorway, moving swiftly and silently, like a cat.

Terry's knee throbbed as she climbed the stairs, but this time she was able to cope easily with the worsening pain. Her mind was elsewhere—back at the surgery wing—and the same phrase echoed through her whirling brain with every hurried step. *Mike is alive!*

He was hurt and she'd left him, but Mike hadn't told her about his crazy plan so that there would be nothing she could do to give the pretense away. And of course, Mike wouldn't have expected her to be there when he and Gil perpetrated their hoax. They must have had it all planned out, and she had messed it up by getting captured by a hired gunman. Mike hadn't expected that gunman. He'd expected Boyce to come alone and that miscalculation had almost cost him his life.

Was it Gil who had fought the thug earlier in the hospital? Gil protecting her? Is that how he got so beat up? All these whirring thoughts were skidding through her brain as she rushed, limping badly, along the wide, hollow corridor toward the surgery wing of the third floor.

Sirens were all around the hospital and voices and shouts of men sounded from below, on the second story, and also from the surgery rooms at the bright end of the hall. They had already found Mike. How had they been so fast? The broken window and the body below would have told them immediately and exactly where the trouble was. It seemed only seconds ago that Mike had been shot. Seconds ago and hours ago. Time had become immeasurable to her.

She paused for a second or two in the doorway of the room. Two young men in jeans, one wearing a T-shirt, the other bare chested, were kneeling over Mike. A third man, in a uniform, his gun drawn, was standing at the window signaling to someone below and talking through his portable phone. Shards of glass gleamed in pale sunlight on the floor. Echoes of a police radio reverberated through the silent mountain air from the parking area on the side of the building.

Howard Boyce must still be in the hospital somewhere, she thought. *Should I tell them that? Will they automati-*

cally realize that? If they went on a heavy search for Boyce, they might find Gil. They might find Boyce and arrest him, and then Mike's plan to trick a confession out of him would be for nothing. Well, obviously, the police *would* search the building from the inside out. No doubt the search had already begun. Mike's was such a crazy scheme to start with. How could such a crazy scheme have any chance of working? He had known the danger and the risks, though, and had been willing to take them, because he had had to. His future was worth nothing to him without his freedom.

These thoughts raced through Terry's mind in the seconds she stood facing the policemen, the seconds before either of them saw her, the seconds before she summoned the courage to rush between them and go to Mike, knowing how grueling their questions were going to be as soon as they saw her. She was desperate to know how Mike was, but her intellect told her that a shot in the leg wasn't going to be fatal. The most important thing right now was for her to take control of her emotions—to do what she had to do, for Mike's sake, and not make a simpering fool of herself if Mike was still suffering as much as he seemed to be right after he was shot.

Terry squared her shoulders, tried to ignore a shooting pain in her knee, and limped into the room. Her pant leg was torn and dirty, her shirt tail was hanging out, her light hair was in her face. A smear of blood from Gil's arm was streaked on her cheek, and she was breathing hard.

Both men kneeling on the floor looked up at once. Terry said nothing, but walked straight to Mike and dropped to her knees beside him.

Mike lay on his back. His eyes were so tightly closed that the creases of a wince furrowed his forehead and temples. His breathing was fast and shallow. They had wrapped what looked like a T-shirt—no doubt one that had been worn by the bare-chested man—around Mike's thigh. Blood was seeping through the soft white fabric of that shirt.

They said nothing to her at first, but she felt their eyes on her as she touched his forehead and called Mike's name.

His response was a gruntlike moan. He moved his good leg restlessly.

The uniformed policeman at the window turned and approached them. He stood tall and straight above them, looking down as he returned his gun to its holster. One needed only to glance at Terry to realize she knew what had happened in this room.

"Were you here?" the officer asked.

Terry nodded, head lowered so that her hair hung down around her face, hiding her face. She could not take her gaze from Mike. He appeared to be conscious, but in too much pain to care what was happening around him.

The deep male voice above her seemed to fill the room and echo from the walls. His voice was authoritative and loud, but also kind, if edged with impatience. He asked, "Who are we looking for?"

"He's wearing dark clothes," Terry recited in a monotone, shuddering as she pictured Boyce with gun drawn and Mike doubling over at the sound of the shot. "Dark slacks and a plain maroon long-sleeved shirt. Some kind of black boots, low-heeled boots. Unshaven for a week or so. Short dark hair and very dark eyes. Narrow eyes, close together, and a long face with a sort of curve at the base of his chin." Describing Howard Boyce was second nature to her; she had drawn his caricature a hundred times.

As she gave the description, the officer was repeating it word-for-word into his radio device.

When Terry paused, he asked, "Did you see the actual shooting?" His voice was calm now, deliberately so. Even Terry was aware that he was trying to make it as easy as possible for her. But it was vital for him to get as much information as he could as quickly as possible. Details could come later.

"Yes, I saw everything," she answered. "I ran because I thought he would shoot me too."

"Why? What was it about?"

"I...don't know." She shook her head. She couldn't look at him. It was not easy to lie to a police officer.

"You don't know?"

A slight shaking of her head. Terry was close to tears and she knew the officer knew it. Her hand was stroking Mike's forehead and cheeks, and at her touch he was responding by moving his head. His breathing was uneven, shallow for a while, and then it became deeper. He was not lying still; his body was jerking around. He seemed to be fighting the pain.

"He...the man I described...tried to kill Mike," she said, her voice edged still with disbelief. "And then he ran. I don't even know which door he ran out of because I ran out first. I thought he would chase me, but he didn't for long, probably because of the sirens. I didn't see him again."

"Our report said there were several shots. The men below tell me the man who fell from the window has no gunshot wound, and Mike has only one."

"He was just firing wildly. He's a madman." It wasn't exactly a lie, she rationalized.

"Who is the man outside? I've never seen him in Jerome."

"I don't know."

"He's dead."

She nodded, not wanting to talk to anyone but Mike, and wishing desperately that Mike would talk to her. A word, anything...

"Did you see the man fall from that window?"

"Yes. There was a fight...."

The officer waited for her to say more. She didn't. He prodded, "Yeah?"

"He went...through the window." Terry could not force herself to answer the questions anymore. A sob broke loose and her eyes filled with tears.

She felt the man's hand on her shoulder, comforting, understanding. "Okay," he said gently. "Okay. You've been a great help. We've got our men already searching for the man you described."

Crying, Terry said Mike's name again, louder this time, while she touched his chest. His eyes blinked open and for some seconds he merely stared up at her. With this response, the police officer knelt on one knee and studied the wounded man carefully.

"Terry..." Mike mumbled. "Thank God you're all right...."

She sighed a silent prayer of thanks. "Mike, I was terrified. I was sure you'd been killed."

His eyes closed again. He whispered, "For a while I thought we might not make it...."

"There's an ambulance on the way," the officer said.

Mike looked up at him. "Karl, can you keep reporters away from me? I don't want...I don't..."

"He's trying to ask you a favor," Terry said. "He wants the man who shot him to think he's dead."

The officer frowned. "Mike, do you know this guy?" When he got no response but a small nod, he looked up at Terry. "Does he know the name of the man who shot him?"

"I...don't know. Will you do it? Just not say anything to anybody yet? About Mike being alive? It's very important to him."

While Terry was talking she was carefully studying Mike, trying to decide if he was only pretending to be unable to answer any questions about the shooting. One miscalculated word might serve to bring down suspicion on himself. Guarding his real identity had become second nature to him in his eight years of being a fugitive from justice. He wasn't faking pain; that was real. But his state of semiconsciousness could be an act.

The uniformed officer, his badge gleaming in light beams from the window, gazed at her. "You're Terry Morse, aren't you? You're the woman who's staying in the Beyer House? I think you'd better tell me what you know about all this."

"I just recently met Mike," she hedged. "All I can tell you is, that madman with a gun was determined to kill him."

"Mike's been in a hell of a fight, from the looks of him. Was he fighting with the guy that shot him?"

Terry felt cornered, frightened of the truth. There would have to be an investigation of the thug's death, and Mike had been fighting with him when he fell. Would that constitute manslaughter? Gil had told her to blame everything on Boyce, yet Mike was bruised and cut from a fistfight, and the corpse on the hillside would be cut and bruised with signs of having been in a fight too. Or could they tell, after a fall of three stories?

She shuddered visibly. "They were all fighting. They were ganging up on Mike. I don't know why. I only know it was horrible and they tried to kill him and if the man who shot him thinks Mike's alive, he'll come after him again."

"What makes you think so?"

"He...threatened him."

"Over what?"

"I...don't know. But that's why Mike wants the guy to think he died, I'm sure. Obviously Mike isn't going to be walking for days. He won't be able to protect himself if the man comes after him again. Until you catch him, can't we just keep quiet about Mike surviving the shooting?"

The police officer was frowning. Some message was squawking over his radio which he ignored. She looked at the officer's soft hazel eyes. "You've known Mike for a long time, I'll bet. You're friends, aren't you? The public doesn't have to know all the details of this, does it?''

"No. It's police business. *I* want to know all the details though. People don't try to murder a guy without a reason. Mike obviously knows, and the sooner he tells me, the sooner we can—''

Frightened by the tone of the lawman's voice, Terry interrupted, ''If Mike knows, he'll tell you who the man is as soon as he can.'' She looked at the bleeding leg. ''He's bleeding terribly! Isn't there something we can do?''

"The medics are on the way. He shows no signs of shock as far as I can tell. It's better left to the paramedics, who know exactly what they're doing.'' He lifted the soaked cloth to examine the wound without touching Mike's leg. "The bleeding is stopping. Not all wounds cause this much pain, but some do. It depends on the type of bullet, on the angle, on a lot of things.''

The officer, Mike's friend of several years, pressed his shoulder reassuringly. "Take it easy, Mike. You'll get the proper help right away. I can hear ambulance sirens out there now. Sounds as if they're just turning up the hill.'' He turned to Terry. ''I've got work to do.''

The two young men who had been kneeling over Mike when Terry came into the room had been standing by, one of them watching the activity on the hillside from the window, the other sitting on the floor, arms on his knees, taking in the conversation between Terry and the lawman. The officer whom Mike had called Karl glanced at them now, and then back at Terry. He said, ''These two men are part of our volunteer force. They'll help you if you need help. Are you okay?''

She nodded, but she knew the affirmation was not very convincing, for she was shaking badly, much more than she had been when she came into the room. The more time that went by, the more she shook, as the reality became sharper and she comprehended more vividly what had taken place in this empty hospital. She had seen the terrified eyes of a man falling to his death. She had watched Mike shot—not once but several times—with no way of knowing Gil had not really killed him. She had run for her life and believed she, too, was going to die. It wasn't real, but it was becoming real, more so with each passing second. Leaning over Mike, trembling violently, Terry began to feel faint.

Moments later she felt hands on her shoulders gently lifting her away from Mike. More people were in the room, and they had brought a stretcher. Two paramedics knelt over Mike while a man who seemed to be a third paramedic questioned her softly, to determine her physical condition.

"I'm all right," she insisted. "Just dazed. Scared. I can't stop shaking...."

There was noise in the room now, voices and the echoing hum of a two-way radio, as the medics reported their findings to the hospital and waited for instructions. *Why was everything taking so long?* she kept wondering. She tried to follow what they were talking about, and couldn't, except she was aware that Mike was given an injection for pain.

Once he was on the stretcher, he was quiet, if not asleep, at least not suffering from the jogging and lifting.

"I want to go with him," she said.

"The police have ordered us to take you along to the hospital," the paramedic said. "They don't want you coming back to Jerome because you're in too much danger from whoever shot Mike."

Terry hadn't thought of that. She *was* in serious danger as long as Howard Boyce was out there running loose. There were no guarantees that Gil would protect her. Thank God the police were ready to take responsibility for her safety. They all knew Mike personally—the police and the paramedics. For years they'd been friends with an escapee, convicted of murder, and never once suspected. Everything about Mike's life was so very unreal.

Her knees would barely hold her. The injured leg had no strength at all; it ached when she wasn't standing on it and throbbed when she was. And her good leg was numb; the day's terror had taken its toll.

A strong arm supported her while she tried to walk. Seconds later there was another. Two men assisted her, all but carrying her, lifting her down the steps and finally out of the side door where the ambulance, its lights flashing, was parked. Mike's stretcher had already been lifted inside.

There were police cars and guards keeping people away from the area around the door. On the slope of the hill people were gathering near the spot where the body of Boyce's hit man had been found.

They lifted her into the ambulance where a paramedic was attending to Mike, and she sat back, feeling cold and weak, wanting desperately to take him in her arms and to hold him, just hold him, and feel his heart beating strong and alive against hers.

If only this could be the end of it, she thought as the vehicle started down over the steep, rough road. If only Boyce could be arrested and Mike could be freed and it would all be over.

But it couldn't. Mike had been convicted of murder. All that could come out of police involvement now was his return to prison. Even with Gil's help, it could be months or even years before anything changed. *If*, in fact, Gil was willing to confess to perjury and take the consequences of that. When push came to shove, Gil might be of no use at all, with or without his confession. Mike had been convicted of murder. And nothing short of proof of Boyce's guilt was going to overturn that conviction. Boyce would probably die before he confessed to anything.

"Please, God," Terry prayed silently. "Don't let the police find Boyce...please...not yet."

In the jogging ambulance, heading down the steep mountain to a hospital in the valley, Terry thought, *It's going to take a miracle to help Mike now, especially since he's been incapacitated with a bullet wound.* Boyce was crouching somewhere in the shadows of a ghost town hiding from the police, and Gil was slinking around with him, making sure he didn't try to leave. But what was going to come of it all? What other horrible things were going to manifest themselves before this was over?

One thing was for sure, she decided. The story was going to continue in the newspapers. The drawings already submitted were several days ahead. The convicted killer, Rod Lightning, was about to escape from prison on the day of his trial. No doubt Boyce wanted to prevent a reenactment of the escape being printed, because too many people would remember it.

The drama of Rod Lightning's past was going to be played out all the way no matter what. Terry was more determined to accomplish this than anything else she'd ever done—to expose a false murder conviction. To draw the escape of a framed man. It was a story of lies, of fear, of revenge, and of an eventual clash with the real killer, an ambitious state legislator who looked exactly like Howard Boyce. Yes, the story was going to unfold in pictures before America—all the way until the end. No one was going to stop her. She and Mike had come this far with the daring plan; they were going to carry it through, no matter what happened in the next few days.

If Mike had only been pretending that he could barely talk, once he was given the injection he didn't even try. The drug knocked him out. Terry made no attempt to communicate with him in the ambulance, because the medics were working on him. He was in good hands; that was the only thing that mattered for the moment.

She did want to convey to him that she was there with him, and she couldn't, but surely he knew. He must know she wouldn't leave him.

Once inside the small hospital, one of two in the valley, she stood numbly by, clutching the arm of a tall male attendant for support while she watched Mike being wheeled through the doors of the emergency room.

A nurse took charge of her, questioning her about her limp. Terry reassured her there was no emergency with the knee, that what she wanted most was to shower and lie down.

With the promise that a doctor would look in on her later to examine her knee, the nurse led Terry to a small, private room with an adjoining bathroom.

"You don't look very good," the woman in the white uniform said. "You're trembling. Will you be all right?"

"I'm just shaken up. I'll be okay."

"I'll look in on you to be sure you're all right. The doctor can prescribe a mild tranquilizer if you need one. Meantime, let me go find a robe for you. It won't be glamorous, but it'll do."

"Thanks," Terry said, unbuttoning her shirt. The thought of the warm water, cleansing water, was calming her a little already.

Soon, Terry felt the water washing away the dust of the old Jerome hospital and the blood streaks from Gil Spearow's hands and the sweat of fear. Warmth penetrated through her pores to the numbness in her bones.

Her knee was swollen, but not as badly as she had expected it to be; that meant that in spite of the strain she had put on it today, the knee was in the process of healing. Her leg had been cut by the sharp edge on the lining of the laundry chute, but the cut was small. She had been lucky.

The doctor who examined her knee was optimistic and cheerful, not concerned about any complications. He prescribed only rest and gave her a small green tranquilizer to help her sleep, and the nurse brought her a cup of herb tea.

She crawled in under crisp white sheets, wearing a long, light blue hospital robe, and sipped the tea and thought about the man she loved until she felt the effects of the pill. Then she slept, soundlessly, dreamlessly, in welcome, drug-induced peace.

WAKING WAS SLOW. In the background she heard a Dr. Wilcox being addressed on a loudspeaker; that summons was followed by words that chilled her, even in her sleepiness. "Code Blue." Then silence again. Unfamiliar sounds, unfamiliar smells, unfamiliar sensations surrounded her in the groggy moments of trying to push away the weight of sleep. Even when she managed to open her heavy eyelids, she was unsure at first where she was. Darkness engulfed her. Through an open doorway was light from a wide hall. The light shone in on shadowy white walls. Night. She sensed it was very deep night.

Gradually she remembered. Stiff, unmoving, she lay in the high hospital bed and listened to the sounds outside the open door. The building was eerily silent, except for the faint echo of voices far away, down the hallway. The voices lasted a few moments, then disappeared, and she heard nothing. She must have been asleep for hours.

Forcing herself out of the bed, Terry fastened the wrinkled cotton robe tighter around her waist and tried to smooth it. Her thoughts were of Mike, only of Mike. Was he all right? It had been hours. She had to see him.

The floor felt cold against her bare feet. Her knee was better; the pain was minimal when she put her weight on it. The tranquilizer or the heavy sleep had left her a little groggy. And she hadn't eaten since breakfast with Rosa, many hours ago.

The lighted corridor was deserted. Terry made her way toward one end, where she remembered seeing the nurses' station when she came in. No one was behind the desk. A wall clock said three-twenty. Three-twenty in the morning? She *had* slept for hours!

She paced a short way in each direction. It was such a small hospital, it shouldn't be hard to find someone to tell her where Mike was. There had been an emergency earlier; she'd heard the "code blue" message just as she was waking. The emergency might be the reason no one was here.

Farther down the hall, in a small waiting room, she found a candy machine and a coffee machine side by side, but she had no money. Yes, she did, she remembered. There was a little change in the pocket of her jeans.

Barefoot, combing her fingers through her tangled hair, Terry made her way back to the room, found her clothes in a closet where she had hung them earlier, and hurried back to the coin machines, eager to fill the hollowness in her stomach.

Fifteen minutes later she felt better, but there was still no one at the nurses' station to tell her where Mike's room was. The information must be on a chart there; she ought to be able to find it, Terry thought. It was either that or start looking in rooms until she found him. With each minute that passed she became more restless, more desperate to see him, if only to stand and watch him sleep. Just to be near him, to know he was all right. The awful fright from yesterday, thinking he had been killed, had not completely worn off.

She reasoned that the room numbers would have to be kept in the most obvious place so that they could be referred to easily. A chart was next to the telephone with patients' names and room numbers. This was so easy, Terry was disgusted with herself for not thinking of it sooner. She'd been too groggy then. It took a little coffee to bring her to her senses.

Mike's name was there on the chart, and the number of a room. One-twenty-one. That would have to be on the far end of this floor. He'd be asleep, of course—everybody in this silent place had to be asleep—but that was fine. He'd be asleep and she could sit beside his bed for a little while and no one would ever know she was in there.

Counting room numbers as she passed through the quiet hall, Terry found herself hurrying, almost running. One-sixteen. One-eighteen. One-twenty.

The door to room one-twenty-one was open, and to Terry's surprise, a light was burning brightly from inside. Did that mean Mike was awake? Or that something was wrong? A ripple of fear went through her but she fought it down. It was only because there had been so much fear, she told herself. Since Mike had come into her life feeling fear had almost gotten to be a habit.

Halting at the open doorway, she gasped. Two beds were in this room, and both were empty. One bed was made up, the other was being stripped by a woman in a nurse's aide's uniform. At once the adrenaline began pumping. Fear.

The young woman looked at her quizzically.

Terry said in a high-pitched, frightened voice, "I'm looking for a patient that is supposed to be in this room."

Glancing at her watch, the woman answered, "It's after three-thirty in the morning. Shouldn't you be in bed?"

"I'm not...not...oh, never mind about me! Where is the patient who was here?"

"I wouldn't know that. I'm just told to strip off the beds and wash them down between patients."

"Between patients? He's not here anymore?"

The young woman frowned as she gathered the sheets into a pile on the floor. "No. He's not here anymore."

Chapter Thirteen

Terry's heart felt as if it were in her throat. For a second she could barely breathe.

"Where is he?"

"I have no idea," the woman said. "I'm only an aide here."

Her voice rose. "Why are you changing sheets in the middle of the night?"

"I work this shift. When it's quiet, I do whatever needs to be done. And they need this bed for morning."

Terry looked up and down the corridor frantically. "Where is everybody?"

"It's always this quiet at night."

"I can't find *anybody*."

The aide went back to her work. "The staff is busy with some emergency. There was a code blue an hour or so ago."

"Was it this patient?"

"I'm sure I don't know."

"I have to find him! Can't you help me find him? I checked the room chart at the nurses' station, and it listed this room." Terry double-checked the number on the door. She fell back against the wall. "Oh, God! Where is he? What's happened?"

The woman finally left her work and approached Terry. "Are you all right?"

"No! No. We came in at the same time. We were in an accident. I just woke up and wanted to see him, and he...he's not here! Something has gone wrong! What is this emergency?"

"Please," the young woman said, touching Terry's arm. "Don't get hysterical. I'll try to find out something. All right?"

"I'm not hysterical. I'm frightened."

The woman gently led her a distance down the hall, to where there was a bench. "Wait here. I'll check and see what I can find out."

Terry leaned back and closed her eyes. All she could see in her mind's eye was the empty bed—the shock of the empty bed being stripped. It was almost impossible to make herself just sit and wait, but there was nothing else she could do. A staff member could find out about Mike faster than she could. She hated the awful silence, hated the disinfectant smell that permeated the halls of the hospital, hated the fact that Mike had been shot, hated Howard Boyce, hated how slowly time moved when she was afraid and forced to wait.

Eventually the aide returned and touched her shoulder. "Come with me," she said.

Terry jumped. "Where?"

"Just down the hall. Mr. Calhoun was moved to another room. The nurse at the desk hadn't had a chance to record the change before she was called to help with an emergency."

Terry allowed herself a full breath for the first time since she had seen the empty bed. "Oh, thank God! Why was he moved?"

"I believe he requested the move. He wanted a private room."

Of course, Terry thought. A man who wanted to be thought of as dead wouldn't like sharing a room.

"Here it is. Room one-twelve. The patient is asleep, I'm sure."

"I won't wake him. I just want to look in on him." Terry managed a weak smile. "Thanks for your help. I'm sorry I was difficult."

Her smile was returned. "I understand. You were scared. I'd have been scared too."

Relieved that the aide had turned back, Terry entered the room alone. It was not dark. A pale white light was burning on the far side of the small room, throwing a soft glow over the sheets and the metal rails over the bed, and on Mike's face.

He lay on his back, eyes closed, his hair mussed and curling over his forehead. A blanket was pulled over his legs to his waist, and above that a thin white short-sleeved jacket was all that covered his chest. He looked pale and his lips were bruised and there was a gash on his forehead, but he was sleeping peacefully. It took all the self-discipline Terry could muster to keep from bending down and kissing his cheek. A kiss might wake him, though, and he needed the sleep.

Damn, you scared me again! she thought, tears forming in her eyes. *Mike, when are you going to stop scaring me? When am I going to be sure you're safe? Will you ever be safe? Ever again?*

For some minutes she stood next to his bed, watching his chest move evenly, watching his fingers twitch now and then. He did not lie still. His body moved slightly from time to time, but she noticed he did not move his right leg even a little. His upper arm was bruised, perhaps from a needle. His neck was bruised rather badly, but his face had come through the fight with the thug much better than the fight he'd had with Gil, even though this fight was so savage. *Lord,* she thought, *why do men always manage to get into fights?*

Terry shuddered. She didn't want to think about the battle of fists that had ended in a man's death, yet she couldn't help recalling vividly the look on Mike's face as he stood at the railing looking down at the body of the man who had fallen, knowing he was responsible for the man's death.

Standing so near his hospital bed, Terry could no longer keep herself from touching the man she loved so deeply, the man whose safety meant more to her than her own. She drew closer and bent over him, closing her hand over his, touching her lips to his forehead, then his cheek, and finally his lips so feather-lightly she was sure it wouldn't wake him.

But he stirred. His eyelids fluttered open. He saw her with the cold white light behind her filtering through the edges of her ash-blond hair, like a halo, her face pale without makeup, her skin clear and soft. Her eyes misting.

And he smiled and said her name.

"Oh, Mike, I woke you."

"Did you?"

"Yes. I'm sorry. I didn't mean to."

"Why not?" His voice was husky and very sleepy. His eyes closed and then opened again.

She touched his hard chest with both hands. "Are you all right?"

"No. But I guess it could have been worse. That flying bullet could have caught me anywhere. I was getting real nervous before Gil showed up. I was afraid Howard was going to kill you."

"*You* were afraid? Mike, do you know what it was like watching Gil firing at you? I thought he killed you!"

"Boyce was convinced?"

"Anyone would have been! The way you fell and just lay there."

"Gil fired barely in time." Mike reached for her hand and squeezed it. His voice was weak. "I can't believe what I'm putting you through, honey."

She chose to ignore this. "How bad is your leg?"

"They tell me the wound was pretty clean. The bullet just barely grazed the bone. It hurt like hell, I'll tell you. Still does. The way it was hurting I expected it to be a lot worse than it is."

"You look and sound so much better."

"Miraculous how much difference a little codeine can make. What about you, honey? What the devil are you wearing?"

"Like it? It's something glamorous they found for me at the hospital. I came in the ambulance with you, did you know that?"

"I was aware of you talking to Karl. It was easier to let you try to explain; I just couldn't think straight. You did great, from what I remember."

"Your cop friend, Karl, insisted I stay here for tonight at least, because he wasn't sure I'd be safe from Boyce. For that I was grateful. I had a shower and climbed into one of these awful hospital beds and didn't wake up until just a little while ago."

"How do you feel? You weren't hurt?"

"No."

"Your knee?"

"It's okay. It gives me a bit of a bad time, but it's healing. You're the one with the leg problem. I wonder how long you'll have to be here."

"A few days, they tell me. Damn, have we got a few days?"

"I don't know what's going on, except that Gil is going to keep Boyce from trying to leave Jerome and from getting rooted out of his hiding place by police."

Mike shifted his head on the pillow. "Howard can't get out of Jerome. There's only one road in from the valley, one from Prescott, and one rough one over the mountains north. All are narrow roads easy for the police to block. He's trapped up on that mountain like a treed cat."

"And thinking Gil is helping him."

"Yeah."

"I was wrong about Gil," she said. "I didn't trust him."

"I know."

"Why did you trust him?"

"He told me something that convinced me he was on my side."

"What?"

Mike's eyes closed. "I'll tell you about it, but not now. I don't feel like talking about Gil and Howard now."

Her voice softened. "Oh, I'm disturbing you in the middle of the night, and you're doing all this talking and you sound so sleepy and you need to sleep."

"Who says I need to sleep? Did somebody say that?"

"Well, I . . . said that."

"What I needed tonight more than anything was to know for sure you're all right."

This was not enough to assuage her guilt over waking him. "But you're sick."

"Hell, I'm not sick. I've got a sore leg."

She lay her hand on his forehead. "And a little bit of fever."

"I always have fever when you're around."

"Not this kind. Do you want anything?"

"Yes, but with our luck, we'd get caught."

Terry smiled, "You talk big. You're just trying to make me think you feel better than you do. I can tell by looking at your eyes that you are sleepy."

"Maybe a little. Stay with me."

"I'm not going anywhere. I'll sit right here by your bed until they kick me out."

His voice was weaker than it had been a few minutes earlier, but his grip on her hand was strong and warm. "You won't be comfortable sitting in a chair the rest of the night. Come up here on the bed with me." He started to shift to one side, grunting slightly. "Here. Crawl in."

"Mike! I can't do that!"

"Why not?"

"What if they... what will they think?"

"Who cares?" He continued scooting, with effort, wincing when he moved his sore leg. "There's only one pillow. We'll share the pillow. Come on, Terry. I can sleep better with you wrapped in my arms. I want to hold you."

"Well... I guess I wouldn't take up much room."

"Hardly any."

She boosted herself up onto the bed in a sitting position, then lay back, adjusting the thin cotton robe against her legs while Mike pulled the blanket over her.

"I'll try not to touch your leg."

"You can touch whatever you want."

His hand caressing her arm and shoulder felt so good, so reassuring. Terry snuggled down into the warmth of him, trying to pretend that the peace she felt in those moments was going to last forever.

Mike kissed her tenderly and there was more love in that soft kiss than in any kiss he had ever given her. He said, "I love you."

Her heart swelled. "I love you too."

A long silence ensued. "Do you love me enough to leave me?"

"What?"

"If things don't work out as we plan and I have to go back to prison, I want you to leave me."

"I'll never leave you."

"You'll have to, Terry, if I'm in prison. I've wrecked your life enough as it is and almost got you killed. I won't ruin your life by allowing you to be tied to a convict."

"You won't be in prison, Mike. I can't picture you in prison. It just can't happen. Boyce is going to prison instead of you, remember? Mike, he can't get out of the shooting. He shot you!"

"He shot a convicted murderer. He can use self-defense, any number of legal tricks, and he knows them all. I'll end up trying to do all the explaining, if it comes to that. The séance has just got to work, that's all. It's a stab in the dark, but it's got to work."

"It will. You've planned it so carefully."

"But if it doesn't . . ."

"We're not going to talk about if it doesn't. Can you carry this off without being able to walk?"

"I don't know how much trouble the leg is going to give me. It could complicate things. I've been trying to think, figure it out, but it's hard to think with your head full of painkillers."

"Mike, I believe in you and in us. You just said you love me. Do you know what that means to me?"

"You already knew it."

"I hoped you loved me. But your saying it makes it true."

His voice was getting more sleepy. "Maybe we'll make it," he mumbled.

She hugged him carefully, not wanting to jar his leg. "Can you go back to sleep now?"

"Yeah. Can you?"

"I think so."

Tonight she found love and warmth in Mike's arms. But Terry dreaded the light of the coming mornings. Mike had asked her to leave him if anything went wrong, and about that he was deadly serious. If his ghosts failed them, she was going to lose him, probably forever.

TWO HOURS LATER Terry woke. She lay for a few minutes watching Mike sleep, then tried to get out of the bed without waking him. Once again, he proved to be a very light sleeper; he reached out for her.

"Where are you going?"

"I have to find somebody I can pay to take my clothes to a Laundromat. I don't have anything to wear."

"Is it morning?"

"Yes. It's getting light."

Mike sighed heavily and shifted his body. "You're not going to leave me to the mercy of the nurses, are you?"

"For a while, yes. Do you need something?"

"I need to go to the bathroom and I don't think I can get out of bed."

"You could lean on me, but maybe they don't want you to get up."

"It's my leg, not theirs. And my bladder that's about to burst. Please don't jiggle the bed any more than you have to."

"Oh, Mike!" Terry slid from the bed and opened the door of the cabinet at the side of the bed. "Here's what you need."

"Never!"

"How long do you think it's going to take you to get from the bed over to the bathroom? Half an hour or so? Can you wait that long—while you're hopping on one leg?"

He scowled and swore.

"I'll just leave this where you can reach it and I'll ring for your nurse. It's her field of expertise—this problem—not mine."

"Don't do this to me, Terry. This is humiliating."

She had no opportunity to answer. At that instant a nurse entered the room, and couldn't hide her surprise at seeing Terry there, her hair tangled and in her eyes, her thin hospital robe crumpled.

Terry decided the best strategy was to speak first. "Is he able to get out of bed?"

The woman eyed her strangely but there was the hint of a smile in her eyes. "Not until the doctor has examined him this morning."

Terry looked at Mike and shrugged. "You'll survive this. I'll come back later, when I have something besides this hideous sack to wear and have found a toothbrush and a hairbrush." On her way out, she turned to the nurse. "Hold the jokes. Don't make him laugh right now."

GIL SHOWED UP at the hospital room in mid-morning. When Terry was sitting beside Mike's bed, dressed in her freshly laundered, slightly torn jeans and pale blue shirt, he came bursting in breathlessly. "Here you are! I got the wrong hospital. Can you believe I got the wrong hospital first and then I came over here and they wouldn't tell me whether you were here or not. I've been walking up and down the halls looking in doors."

Mike watched his former enemy pull up a chair beside the bed and sit down, exhaling a breath of exasperation. "You forget, I'm supposed to be dead."

"The gossip all over Jerome is that you're dead. How'd you manage to get the police and the hospital to cooperate with that?"

"They're my friends here. People I've worked with in the rescues. I didn't ask them to lie, only to not give out any information about me."

"Well, they didn't. I can't get over the fact that you're buddies with the cops! And you an escaped convict!"

"Not so loud. I'm not a criminal. There's no more reason they should suspect me of being a wanted man than anybody else. It's a small town. They know everything about me except where I came from."

Wearing brown slacks and a white shirt, Gil looked nothing like the sleazy man in leather clothes that Terry had first seen following her home. The bruises were still on his face from the fight he'd had, protecting her. He had risked his life to protect her; he had been injured protecting her.

Gil leaned forward now and lifted the blanket and sheet from Mike's legs, exposing his bandaged thigh. Stains of red disinfectant colored his skin around the edges of the thick gauze. "How bad is the gunshot wound?"

"Not as bad as it could be," Mike answered, frowning at his own bandaged leg as if it might belong to someone else. "The doctor tells me I can get out of here in three days."

"Three days? But can you walk in three days?"

"Probably not without crutches."

"Great. Just great. We're going to have a ghost on crutches."

"I'll figure it out," Mike said mildly. "Ghosts don't have to walk, necessarily."

"It makes it tough, you getting shot. The way we had this planned, it was going to be just between the three of us, no police. Now police are combing that town and I have to keep that idiot Howard in hiding for three more days. He has to keep moving around just ahead of the law. He's driving me nuts. I've got the hard part, Colin. All you have to do is lie here and talk to pretty women while I have to put up with him. Sneaking food to him and pretending I give the slightest damn whether he starves or not. Pretending I'm drooling for his money."

Gil snickered happily. "Actually, it's a miracle both of us got out of the hospital yesterday. We both headed for the top floor and got out on the roof before the police got up that far. I found him just in time, or they'd have had him. Howie's as afraid of heights as he is of ghosts. You should've seen him climbing on this narrow ledge shaking like an olive in a blender. It was just great! It's no trouble keeping him in town because he thinks he can't leave without stopping Terry from drawing any more little pictures for the paper. He's convinced that comic strip is going to ruin him.''

"It is," Terry said. "He's right about that."

Gil's smile was one of satisfaction. ''I've got him convinced that we'll get away with your murder Mike, if he can stop Terry. He actually bought the story that Terry hasn't given the police his name because she doesn't want to spoil the impact of revealing it through her comic strip, that she plans a big sensational exposé in the paper and wants the exclusive—and wants it even more now that she can claim Boyce shot Colin MacKaine. Man, I had to do some talking! For a smart lawyer, the guy is stupid as hell.''

"He has a total blind spot when it comes to his own schemes," Mike said. "We've always known that."

"Yeah. He's absolutely convinced you're dead, Mike. Who wouldn't be after seeing you die? So he thinks Terry doesn't have your protection anymore. Terry, you've got to be careful. Don't come back to Jerome. I can't guarantee I can control everything that maniac does. He's slinking around up there like a serpent, just waiting for you.''

Chapter Fourteen

"I have to go to Jerome today!" Terry said. "I've already arranged to hitch a ride up the mountain with a delivery truck this afternoon. I must talk to Rosa Gonzales. I phoned her to try to explain that Mike was alive, but I didn't dare say much on the phone and of course she couldn't understand."

Gil looked from her to Mike. "I didn't know somebody else was going to be in on this."

"I couldn't have Rosa thinking I was killed," Mike said. "Besides, we can use Rosa's help now. She can cover for me when I try to get back into Jerome. Don't worry. Rosa's absolutely trustworthy." Mike turned to Terry. "But I don't like the idea of you going back up. Do you know what it feels like lying here helpless, knowing you're in danger? I don't want you going back up there yet."

"Boyce can't get at me in the open. I'll stay in the open, with the police in plain sight. He's not going to risk that, and you know it. His only chance to get me is inside your house." Terry smoothed the wrinkled sheet over his legs. "Actually, it's perfect. Without me there, how would you possibly lure Howard into your haunted house?"

"She's right," Gil said.

Before Mike could protest again, Terry added, "I can also start getting set up for the séance. We have to—"

"Terry," Mike cut in forcefully. "You're taking too many chances!"

Gil interrupted him. "She doesn't have to get the house ready. I can do that. I can move around Jerome easily because nobody is looking for me. I don't even have to bother with disguises anymore."

"Speaking of disguises," Terry said, leaning forward. "Was it you who fought Howard's hired thug off in the hospital yesterday morning? When he was after me?"

"Sure. Who else would it have been? He got the better of me by pulling a knife." Gil rolled up his shirt sleeve to show them a heavily bandaged arm. "Look at this. He sliced me but good."

She said, "I couldn't tell it was you. Why were you wearing the disguise?"

"Because I thought Howard was probably in Jerome and I didn't want him to know I was there. If he'd have seen me and recognized me, we'd have lost the surprise element we needed for the big confrontation when I shot Mike with the blanks. Or he might have just simply found a way to snipe me from the trees."

"I can't keep ahead of the two of you," Terry said. "All this intricate planning."

"You have to know Howard to understand," Mike said. "Knowing so much about him is our ace in the hole. I just hope we'll have time before the police figure out I'm lying to them."

Gil's eyebrows raised. "You talked to the police?"

"I had no choice. Karl was here this morning. No doubt he'll be back, too. I had to convince him I didn't know why this guy was after me, that I was sure my would-be killer thought I was somebody else. I said Terry and I were at the abandoned hospital because she wanted material for her cartoons. I think he almost believed me because we're friends and because I've become an expert in the art of lying. But I also think Karl is uneasy and he suspects he's not getting all the facts and won't be satisfied until he does. So we don't have any time to waste."

Gil took a small knife from his pocket and began to clean his fingernails as he sat ankle over knee, leaning back in the chair, as if he were discussing the weather or the latest town gossip. "Okay. I'd better not stay here too long. We've got to plan. What's happening with the comic strip?"

Terry answered, "Rod Lightning is escaping from prison. Then I'll show him in Jerome and Boyce's character getting on with his illustrious political career. If I can get something out by express carrier in the next couple of hours, I think I can talk them into inserting a new set of panels by the day after tomorrow—that'll be our deadline date, the last day we'll have before the séance. I'll skip over the eight years with a quick reference to the years, make the characters eight years older and show Howard's character murdering Rod at the Jerome hospital. Your character won't be in the confrontation at all, Gil. It'll be Howard shooting Mike. My editor has been cooperative with all these sudden changes because I've convinced him something interesting is going on here in Jerome, a real-life drama, which I promised to reveal in the comics. He's been super, really, and I think he'll do this insert for me. It's not difficult."

Mike was propped up in bed with a pillow at his back, wearing a fresh hospital gown, his hair brushed back and his face cleanly shaven. He said, "Even if it doesn't get into the paper in time, the important thing is that Howard thinks you killed me, and everyone is going to start seeing the resemblance between Terry's drawings and Boyce, especially after the eight years, now that she's actually seen how he looks. Meantime, we can talk to Rosa about getting some Phoenix papers up to Jerome so Howard can keep on reading the story. Rosa can make a phone call and get the papers delivered to the hotel on the same day they come out.

Gil, you've got the finest task of all, getting to deliver those papers to Howard and watching his reaction. I envy you that."

Gil chuckled viciously. "Howard told everybody back home he was going to Arizona on vacation. He's sure having a super time on his vacation." He folded the knife blade back into its shield. "I can work in your house with no problem while Howard is holed up with the spiders and mice in some old ruin. What do I do?"

"First move everything into the north apartment—the one above mine. Then check the lock I just installed on that apartment door to be sure you can work it. Take down the board barrier from the stairway. Upstairs you'll find a sheet of safety glass on a sliding frame. Install that with the glass pushed aside so the staircase is open. It's all ready to go up; the outside frame is installed. You just need to get it set. Then I'll pull the glass across the stairs after you and Howard have gone up. I need the glass for ghost effects, and also it'll prevent Howard from escaping if he decides to bolt."

"You'll have time to do that? How can you if you can't walk?"

"Terry might have to do it, but it'll only take seconds. You'll be distracting Howard while I start the electronic switches and Terry blocks the stairs."

Terry's heart began beating with apprehension. She said, "This is a brilliant politician we're dealing with, you guys! How can this crazy stuff possibly work?"

"Hardly brilliant," Mike said. "We've been all through school with Howard—kindergarten through college. He never took an exam he didn't cheat on. And he never did a lick of work he couldn't pay somebody to do for him. And he's a simpering coward, scared of everything that goes bump in the night. Brilliant, ha!"

Gil grinned in agreement. "His money has always been his source of power. He's got no inner strength at all, except that his political ambitions are so strong he'll stop at nothing to get what he wants—whatever he has to do to get it, even murder. He's got his blind spots, all right, and we know what they are."

"Gil," Terry said carefully. "If all this does work the way you plan it, what happens to you? Won't you have to face perjury charges?"

His eyes clouded. "Yeah. And I'm willing to. It hasn't been easy living with what I did to Colin. But he says we may be able to minimize the charges by my helping him now, and by bringing out that Howard was blackmailing me. I don't know how it works. Right now, I don't care. I'm not thinking about that. One hurdle at a time is enough."

Blackmail. So there was more, Terry realized, among the three of them, but she couldn't ask now. What Gil had told Mike in confidence had convinced Mike he could trust Gil in spite of the past. It concerned blackmail.

She looked from one man to the other and wondered how fate had gotten her into the middle of something like this. Her fate was Mike Calhoun—or Colin MacKaine—of whose life, really, she knew so little. Whoever he was, she loved him, enough to risk her own life for him. She wanted him desperately, and she wanted him free.

TERRY AND ROSA DROVE down from Mingus Mountain at eleven o'clock at night in a borrowed car. Terry had managed to escape the sheriff's deputy outside her house by prying off the boards from an upstairs window and then replacing them loosely after she had climbed out onto the upper porch. Since the upstairs of the Beyer House had been boarded up for so many years, it would not occur to the guard that Terry could escape from upstairs or that anyone could get in from up there. From the window, she crept along the upstairs porch in the dark shadows, and out onto the high street, where she met Rosa in the borrowed car they had parked there two days earlier.

Rosa was as steady as steel, loving the adventure, like adventures in the old days of her youth, and glad, at last, to know Mike Calhoun's secret. She had known he was a fugitive from the law, she told Terry; there were just too many indications of it. That was why she'd never asked. Part of her didn't want to know and part of her burned with curiosity. But murder? That she hadn't thought of. It would have been impossible to think of Mike as convicted of murder. Now Rosa welcomed the opportunity to help him try to clear himself. And she had laughed aloud at the secret of the ghosts. All the rumors and the sounds from the old Beyer House—nothing more than Mike's playing around!

Mike was wearing the dark slacks and dark shirt Terry had brought down for him the day before. For three days he had been practicing on the crutches. He was doing well, except that so much exertion caused pain, and he couldn't function without his prescription of codeine pills.

When Terry pulled the car up to the hospital entrance, he was sitting on a bench outside, the crutches propped next to him, and a bottle of pills in his hand. They got out to assist him, but he managed the walking fairly well, handing the bottle of pills to Rosa while he prepared to lower himself into the back seat of the car. She dropped the bottle into her purse and gave him a hello peck on the cheek. It was the first time she had seen him since three nights ago when she had heard the rumblings all over Jerome that he had been shot and killed.

"Gil is giving us until one o'clock to get you back into the house," Terry said as she pulled out of the drive. "I'm a little worried about the guard."

"We can take care of the guard," Rosa reassured them.

Mike could not help but laugh. "Rosa, you sound like a seasoned pro."

"I am a seasoned pro. When I was young and forbidden to see my boyfriend, we learned everything there is to know about tricking people who were always watching us. Anyway, the police have been so busy these past three days, they've had to get volunteers to help. That guard is a volunteer. What we really have to worry about are the police all over Jerome with their dragnet. They know their fugitive can't keep out of their reach much longer if he's still in town, which they think he is. What they don't know is that somebody's helping him, but they're beginning to suspect it. I'm glad you didn't have to be hospitalized any longer, Mike."

"So am I. I left before I was supposed to, even at that. This damn leg is giving me some trouble. It hurts like hell. One more score to settle with Howard. It's going to take self-control to fight the temptation to let the ghost hobble over and slowly strangle him to death."

The ride up the hill took thirteen minutes. Entering the dark, silent ghost town, Mike crouched down in the back seat. It was unnecessary; the streets were deserted. Terry turned right before entering Main Street and drove to the street above, and, with her lights out, pulled up a safe distance away from the upper story of the Beyer House so the guard below wouldn't see or hear anything. There would be no worry about Boyce until one o'clock; Gil was making sure he didn't come out of his hole before then. Gil was going to pretend to Boyce that he planned to knock the guard unconscious to gain entry to the house, but the conspirators, all four of them, knew that if all went according to plan, the guard wouldn't be there at all.

The two women slipped out into the darkness and onto the upper porch, and climbed in through the window that Terry had rigged with loose boards. Mike had to wait. Trying to maneuver the crutches would be awkward and noisy.

They slid down the secret stairs into Mike's apartment and across the hall into Terry's, where Terry quickly changed into the clothes she had laid out, Rosa's clothes, almost identical to the dress Rosa was wearing. She donned a gray wig, slid a black knitted shawl over her shoulders, and stepped onto the front porch where the guard was tilted back in a chair, petting a cat that he had befriended during his long vigil.

Terry paused and started down the steps. The guard stood. "Hey, Rosa! What are you doing walking around here in the middle of the night?"

Terry turned toward the light of the street lamp and paused and smiled.

"I thought you were Rosa Gonzales," the young guard said, pushing his cap back on his head.

"That's what you were supposed to think. Pretty convincing disguise, huh?"

"Yeah, real convincing, Terry. Do you know it's nearly midnight? What are you doing out here?"

"I can't stand being cooped up in that house any longer. I'm going over to the hotel and stay with Rosa and I'm afraid to go out at night in case that . . . that man might see me." She raised a hand toward him. "Oh, it's not that I don't have confidence in you guarding me! But I've seen how crazy he is and I can't be sure he might not be up in some window somewhere with a rifle ready to just fire at me. In fact, that's probably what he would do, if he could. You yourself told me to stay down and hidden at night. But he wouldn't fire at Rosa, would he? He only wants me."

"I still think you should wait till morning to go walking on Main Street."

"Rosa often takes late walks. It will be the same as if it were Rosa. Besides, you'll be behind me. You'll follow me, back a safe enough distance so as not to be seen and then you'll guard the hotel all the time I'm inside, won't you?"

"Naturally, I'll be right behind you. I'm not going to let you out of my sight."

"Good, then it'll be fine. Just don't get close enough for anyone to suspect I'm not Rosa."

"I know how to do my job, Terry."

"Yes, you do. I'm sorry. It's just that I'm a little nervous, you know. I'll spend the night at the hotel. That's where I'll be."

"If I could, I'd stop you from going now."

"You can't stop me. I'm not a prisoner."

"Yeah, I know." He fingered his gun. "Just be careful."

"I'll just be Rosa." She smiled. "Give me a second to lock my door and get a little distance ahead of you before you follow me."

Rosa was at the inside doorway. Terry quickly pulled off the shawl and threw it over Rosa's shoulders, and in fifteen seconds Rosa was descending the stairs, not looking back. The switch was fast and completely convincing. From the window, Terry watched the guard disappear into the shadows, following Rosa.

"Damn, we're good!" she said aloud. "Boy, are we good!" And rushing to Mike's apartment and up the secret stairs, she crawled out of the window and ran back to the car.

"Damn, we're good!" she repeated to him when she opened the car door.

"It worked?"

"To perfection. The guard will be at the hotel all night. Now you can clomp around the house to your heart's content."

He struggled out of the car awkwardly, and even more awkwardly climbed into the house through the upper porch window, trying not to put his weight on his sore leg. Terry replaced the boards loosely. They had had to revise their original plans so that Terry could take over some of the responsibilities Mike couldn't manage on the crutches. They'd had no chance for an actual rehearsal, as Mike had hoped, but at the hospital, with Gil, they'd gone over the plan in careful detail. Everything had been covered. Gil had been in the house several times in the past three days and readied everything. The biggest concern was that Gil wouldn't be successful in getting Boyce to come in without a gun. He would try, but they knew this might be impossible.

Mike went to work without delay, setting up his equipment. There were three false walls in the room, behind which he had installed stereo speakers and a continuously playing tape machine. While she watched him, Terry asked, "Where on earth did you get a tape of these unearthly noises?"

"I made it up myself. With the proper pauses between. Took me months to get it like I wanted it."

"But the *sounds*. Where did they come from?"

"I invented some of them myself, the rattling chains and some of the squeaks. But most of the sound effects came from movies. I got them off video cassettes of horror movies, recorded them, and then rerecorded them in the places where I wanted to put them on the tape."

"That's clever."

"It's a way to spend long winter evenings."

Terry was busy moving wires out of the way while Mike was involved with some films. She asked, "And the ghost on the wall? How did you get that?"

"It's here, behind the false wall; I was about to get it out. I made the thing myself out of a store mannequin that I bought in Phoenix. Painted his eyes and hair to look like mine, worked for days with a mirror and laundry markers trying to get a likeness of my scar on the mannequin's face. Dressed him in black and then draped this white gauzy material over him and made the material flutter with a fan. Using strobe lights and doing a lot of experimenting with other lights and deep shadow, I filmed it with an eight millimeter movie camera. Plain black-and-white film. With ghosts you don't have to worry about color. It took about a hundred tries to get it right, but photography has always been a hobby of mine so I had fun with it. Learned the special effects by trial and error."

Terry watched as he began moving equipment out of a cabinet that was so well-concealed she hadn't known it was there. The mannequin, wrapped in its gauze, gave her a start. At first glance, it *did* bear a strange resemblance to Mike. She helped him move it into the center of the room. "You said we'd better rehearse transferring from the projected ghost to you. Are you ready to try it?" Terry moved closer to him. "You're sweating, Mike. Are you okay?"

"No. My leg is hurting. Did Rosa give you my pain pills?"

Terry went weak. "No! Oh, heavens, does she still have them?"

"If she didn't give them to you, she does." He wiped perspiration from his face with his sleeve. "Damn, Terry. I'm in trouble without those pills."

"Oh, no! What will we do? I'll have to go get them."

"How can you get them? I'll have to manage without..." His voice trailed away and Terry realized why. Mike knew that with the worsening pain, he wouldn't be able to pull this off. He needed every bit of his strength and alertness. And without the codeine, the pain was going to incapacitate him.

"I'll try," she said.

"No. Howard and Gil are going to be on the street out of hiding very soon. And on top of that, how would you get past the guard at the hotel where you stationed him?"

"The guard...damn..." Terry pushed back her hair nervously. "Well, I'll just have to, that's all. It's either get the pills or blow this one chance."

Without waiting for a reply, she started for the stairs. "I have to hurry."

Rushing to her apartment, Terry tucked her blond hair into a dark cap, changed to dark shoes, and in her jeans and a navy blue sweater rushed out of the door and into the street.

The night was deathly still, no sign of a breeze. A quarter moon shed some light onto the mountainside. Terry's mind was racing. If Rosa had bolted the hotel door, it meant big trouble. And probably she had locked up. No, Rosa had said something about leaving the door open tonight in case she was needed for anything. And she had insisted she wouldn't be able to sleep until she knew the outcome of the night's séance. Thank heavens for that much: Rosa would be awake.

The guard would not be expecting any trouble on Main Street, or expecting Terry's life to be threatened as long as she was in the hotel, so he wouldn't be on full alert. Maybe she could sneak by him. It was a big maybe! If he saw her, she'd have to come up with a whale of a story, and then he'd accompany her back to the Beyer House, and everything would be ruined. Worse, the young guard was in danger of getting hurt or even killed by Boyce. Every minute she wasted meant Gil and Boyce were that much closer to entering the house, and Mike's pain was intensifying.

Rushing down the street, trying to keep back in the shadows, Terry felt her knee start to protest. She swore silently and ignored it. The knee *was* better, much better. If it could survive the ordeal at the abandoned hospital, it could survive tonight. But it was imperative that it didn't slow her down too much. She needed every second. Her mind was obsessed with how she was going to get past the guard and get into the hotel. There was a bench on the sidewalk outside the hotel; that's where he'd be—stationed right by the door on that bench. There wouldn't be a chance of getting past him.

Terry was near panic. Slowing as she neared the hotel, she saw that there were two people standing by the bench under the streetlight, talking. Rosa and the guard! Now, past midnight, what was Rosa doing out here visiting? She hadn't been exaggerating about not being able to sleep.

The young man was nearest Terry as she approached; Rosa was on the other side of him. If she could just get Rosa's attention without the guard seeing her.

Terry pulled back into the shadows, ducking under the awning of the adjacent store to wait and pray that by some miracle Rosa would glance in her direction. The "miracle" came almost at once. Rosa looked up as if she'd been expecting something. An instant later, the old woman convulsed with coughing.

Her frail, choking voice came through the night air. "Oh, please, rush inside and get me some water, will you?"

The guard did as he was asked. He hurried into the hotel kitchen.

To prevent Terry from coming out of hiding, Rosa hurried toward the shadows.

"I just remembered the pills," she whispered frantically, pushing a small silk purse into Terry's hands. "I was on my way back to the house to try to get them to Mike, but Johnny was making it impossible."

There was no time to answer. Terry stood stunned, watching Rosa rush back and sag onto the bench, resuming her choking. Feeling the shape of the pill bottle through the silk of the purse, she blinked and began to move back through the shadows soundlessly, knowing time was running out. Gil and Boyce were out somewhere—on their way to the House—like coyotes hunting prey. And she was the prey. If Boyce saw her, there might be nothing Gil could do to save her life. And if they caught her, Boyce wouldn't enter the house; he'd have no reason to.

The street was dark. It had been pure luck that she'd made it to the hotel without tripping. She was depending on extended luck to get her safely back. The half-moon's glow and her eyes getting used to the darkness helped. She could follow the curve of the street easily. Now and then a sharp pain shot through her knee, and she couldn't keep from limping, but determination kept her from slowing down or stopping.

The light from her apartment shone through the closed curtains. Leaving the lights on had been deliberate, so Boyce would think she was in there. Only another hundred yards through the darkness separated her from the front porch.

When she started up the three short steps, suddenly at the side of the house the shadows moved, and two men stepped out into the gray moonlight. They were here! Terry clutched at the silk purse and paused in a swift daze of terror. So close, so damn close, and she hadn't made it!

Her heart lurched and began pounding wildly. One thought overpowered all others: she had to get inside the house or everything was going to be lost—including her life. Boyce might have a gun. If only it weren't too dark to see Gil's face, she might be able to get some clue from him as to what to do. Her natural instinct told her it was best to try to dash past them, up onto the porch and into the house. If only she could depend on her knee to allow her to get enough speed. And if only she could depend on not getting caught or shot, in the space of that short dash.

The shapes of the two men, both dressed in dark clothes, were shadows at the edge of the porch. They, too, had paused a few seconds, perhaps only to determine whether or not there was a guard behind Terry, but it hadn't taken long to satisfy themselves that there was nobody else on the dark street.

Howard moved forward. As he did, Terry froze. He was holding a gun.

Chapter Fifteen

A second after Howard Boyce raised his arm in the shadows along the side of the front porch, a dim flash of light, barely visible, streaked down the darkness behind him. The streak was followed by a startling thud. With their backs to the source of the sound, the two men couldn't see what Terry could see—that something heavy had been tossed from the balcony above. The object had landed in the dirt about five feet behind Boyce.

Terry breathed without a voice, "Mike!" Her quick thinking gave her the seconds she needed, time for a dash to the door while Gil was pushing Howard down onto the ground screaming at him to take cover. The teamwork—Mike's and Gil's—was spontaneous and effective.

She nearly tripped on the top of the three short steps of the wooden porch, but Terry was able to keep her balance, open the front door and rush, limping, up the stairs before any heavy footsteps sounded behind her.

Panting for breath, she entered the north apartment as Mike was replacing the boards over the window he had just crawled through to get back inside from the high porch—the boards Terry had loosened earlier. The sight of him startled her, because he had been busy with his makeup while she was gone. He was a ghost now! His face was pasty white, except for the skin directly around the scar. Heavy lines surrounded his eyes, with shadows underneath. He had powdered his hair and eyebrows white. As she came in, he was trying to balance on the crutches while he finished with the window boards. His hands were shaking and perspiration dampened his face. Wiping his sleeve across his eyes, he looked up and saw her.

She rushed to him. "I have the pills. Mike, you're in terrible pain, aren't you?"

"It's pretty bad—especially with all I have to do. How did you get these? Are you okay?"

"Yes, thanks to your fast thinking on the porch."

He struggled with the bottle cap until Terry took it from him and found the lineup of little arrows in the light of the candle that burned behind him. She poured out two capsules into his palm.

He swallowed them quickly and slid two more pills into his pocket. "I was worried about you being out so close to zero hour. Climbed out on the balcony and watched you come back down the street. I didn't see Gil and Howard though until they were already here. They must have come down the slope from the upper street. Are they in the house?"

"Yes, I'm sure they are. Gil will have led the way into my apartment first, as we planned. Gil will stall all he can, but they'll be on the stairs in no time. I've got to get moving. How soon will the pills work?"

His answer came on a groan. "I don't know. They'd better be fast or I'm in trouble." Hobbling back to his hiding place behind the false wall, he asked, "Will you help me with this gauze before you go down?"

While she held it for him, he slid the filmy white material over his head and down over the upper part of his body, over his black shirt. "You look so authentic you're scaring *me,*" Terry whispered, carrying the candle for him to the place behind the wall. Darkness descended behind them, filling the hollow room with its thickness.

Men's voices could be heard on the stairs. Mike closed himself off from view. It would take a few minutes for Gil, having convinced Howard that Terry had to have come upstairs, to lead him on a futile tour through the empty south apartment before they entered the north one, the trap.

With the help of a small flashlight, Terry made her way down the secret back stairway and into Mike's apartment. A tiny sliver of light from the street lamp shone in through his living room window. As quietly as possible, she unlocked his front door and entered the cold hallway. From above she could hear the voices of the men in the rooms over her apartment.

She slipped quietly through the hall and pulled the glass across the bottom of the stairway. It slid easily, almost noiselessly, on the runners Gil had installed. Howard couldn't run back down now, no matter what he encountered upstairs, without hitting smack into an invisible wall.

But Mike had taken extra precautions to ensure that Howard wouldn't run, by projecting a photo of his mannequin ghost onto the glass from a camera installed in the ceiling. The same ghost Terry had seen that first night, it wasn't clear enough for immediate identification with a likeness of Mike. Recognizing the ghost wasn't important at this point; Boyce wasn't going to run down a stairway that had a writhing ghost hovering over the bottom landing.

In moments Terry was back upstairs behind the false wall, peering out of the view slits in the boards with Mike beside her.

She whispered, "Are the pills working?"

"Not much yet. They will."

"I don't see how you're going to—" Terry's voice halted. They could hear the creak of the opening door and see the gleam of Gil's flashlight—the flashlight that had been left on Terry's kitchen cabinet for him to spot and pick up before leading the way upstairs. Gil had walked through the scenario yesterday and had thought of everything, or so they hoped.

Gil's voice came in hushed tones through the empty room. "She has to be up here. All the windows and doors are boarded shut upstairs. There's no way she could get out of the house."

"I don't like this place," Howard said.

"Hell, neither do I. I'm the one who killed Colin and this is his house, and everybody in Jerome says this house is haunted. That doesn't make me feel real good about being in here."

"Haunted?" Boyce's voice rose. "This house?"

"That's what people say. In fact they say strange sounds come from here at night. They say ghosts just love this place. They say—"

"Shut up!" Howard growled. "I'm getting out of here!" He turned back.

Gil stopped him by grabbing his arm. "Don't expect me to stay here by myself and take care of your business for you, because I'm not staying in this place alone!"

Mike pressed a power level on his electronic soundboard. A low moan rolled from the dark recesses of the room, becoming louder, then softer until it was gone.

Terry and Mike could see the flashlight beam darting wildly and they could hear the sounds of a small struggle. No doubt Gil was trying to keep Howard from running. Mike released the pause button, which in turn released a hideous growl that swept down from the ceiling.

With a shriek, fighting frantically to free himself from Gil's grip, Howard darted for the front door of the crumbling apartment and the stairway to safety.

He was stopped dead. The stairway was blocked by a living, moving ghost, that hovered just a few feet from the steps near the bottom landing. It was oddly transparent; only its weaving, outline, was visible against the darkness of the far wall. Shards of light moved out from the edges of the form.

Gil yelled and pulled Boyce back inside, slamming the door behind them. He feigned terror, but by this time, Howard wasn't paying much attention to anyone's terror but his own. He slid down the door onto the floor because his legs would no longer hold him up.

To get a better look at what was going on, Mike flicked on one of his "ghost lights"—a white glow through a patterned cardboard screen that made eerie shapes on the wall and lighted the room enough for them to see.

With the sudden light, Howard covered his eyes and shook.

"It was him!" Gil breathed.

"What? Who?"

"The ghost. It looked like Colin." Gil began to pace. "You killed him as much as I did, Howard. You shot him first."

"I didn't kill him."

"You were going to. You planned to. And don't think Colin didn't know that. He heard everything. It's him, I tell you. We've got to get out of here, Howard!"

Gil pretended to struggle with the door. Actually he was triggering the lock Mike had installed. This ensured that there was no way for them to get out once the ghost appeared inside the apartment. The fly was stuck fast in the spider's web now.

"I can't get this door open." Gil grunted, tugging frantically, trying to pull it against the other man's back.

With difficulty, on shaking legs, Howard rose from his crouched position in front of the door and began pulling at the door himself.

"Something's going on here," Gil said. "And I don't like it. This is your fault. You weren't satisfied with killing Colin. You had to come after that girl. We could've left town but you had to come after the girl who's living in Colin's house."

Behind the false wall Mike had lit more candles to see by when he had switched on the light in the room. What small light shone through their peepholes was no longer noticeable from the other side. Listening and watching, Terry glanced at Mike and smiled. Gil was a convincing actor. Gil was enjoying this. And judging from the smile that crossed Mike's white, ghostlike face, he was enjoying it too. He released the pause button of the stereo player again. The room filled with a ghostly howl.

Then a groan, from the farthest, dark corner. On a signal from Mike, Terry moved along the inside wall toward that dark corner and pulled a wire that raised a black curtain on the other side. The effect in the room was startling, for suddenly, out of the darkness, the ghost was there.

A fan from above moved the gauze draped over the dark clothes of the mannequin so that the figure itself appeared to be moving. It stood for a moment in deathly silence. A childlike moan came from the throat of Howard Boyce.

Terry dropped the black curtain again so that in the shadowy light, the illusion was of the ghost's sudden disappearance. Originally, Mike had planned to be on the other side of the room working another curtain, but because he couldn't move swiftly or quietly without crutches, the task fell to Terry now. She crept back and raised a black curtain that was placed opposite the mannequin. Behind this curtain was a mirror. Mike dimmed the lights, blackening the room until Terry had time to lift the curtain above the mannequin once more. When Mike lit up the mirror, it appeared that the ghost had moved to the other side of the room. They repeated this procedure once again with a mirror placed near the back of the room, allowing the ghost to appear three times in three different places, but not letting it stay visible long enough for close scrutiny.

Gil was feigning hysterics. Mike had done a good job on the mannequin. The macabre lighting effects he had come up with made the thing appear both dead and alive at the same time. And because of the contrast of the scar to the whiteness of the face, there could be no question as to whose ghost it was.

Howard Boyce had fallen into a catatonic silence. He stood as if paralyzed and would respond to nothing Gil was saying. Finally, suddenly, he jumped to life with a screech. Emitting a long series of whimpers, he ran to one of the windows and began tearing at the boards with his hands, trying to loosen them, trying to escape.

Mike recognized his perfect opportunity. While his victim was distracted by his futile escape attempt, he rose from his chair and shifted a panel of the false wall forward enough, in the darkness, to walk through. With Terry's assistance, he slid into the room in silence, using only one crutch, which was invisible under the ghost's gauze.

Now the technician's work was up to Terry, but they had gone over every detail carefully. Perspiring with tension, she was nonetheless confident.

Their planned distraction for getting Mike into the room was no longer necessary, because Howard's back was turned to the wall. But Terry decided to use it anyway, if only so that Mike's painstaking efforts would not go to waste. She turned on the hidden film projector and the ghost appeared first on the ceiling and then on the far wall just below the ceiling.

Gil directed Boyce's attention to the reappearance of the spirit, and Boyce stood staring, immobilized by fear.

Mike's first words were on tape with a strong background echo. The voice reverberated through the room calling Howard Boyce's name.

Working the equipment from behind the wall, Terry was becoming nervous about the gun. They had expected Boyce to pull out his gun earlier, when there was nothing live in the room to shoot at. He hadn't. But Mike was out there now— a living target. Once again, Mike's life depended on Gil. Gil would be on full alert. But would he be fast enough, if Howard in his hysteria suddenly decided to go for his gun?

Mike's voice, on tape, echoed through the room. "I'm glad you came, Howard. But if you hadn't, I'd have found you anyway. There's no place you can hide from me now. You can't get away from the dead."

"No!" the man screamed. "No!"

As Terry had feared, he reached wildly for the protection of his gun. Gil, anticipating this desperate move, had stayed within an arm's length of Boyce, primed for trouble. From the peephole it was difficult for Terry to see what was happening in the dusty light, but Gil appeared to grab Howard's gun and then aim it directly at Mike.

Her stomach dropped and she went cold with fright as Gil fired several shots at the ghost. Mike didn't move. Blanks! Terry tried to calm her throbbing heart. Gil must have had his own gun ready and quickly switched guns. The illusion was perfect. The spirit of Colin MacKaine was unaffected by the bullets.

Mike raised an arm. As he did so, the filmy white gauze flapped softly in the breeze of the fan. "Sit down on one of those chairs, Howard," he said in a clear voice, a live voice, without the echo. "Sit down and stop whimpering. I don't like whimpering. Gil, you sit down too, right over there. Forget the gun. What good did you think a gun would do you against a ghost?"

Terry dimmed the lights to almost total blackness for a second or two, then switched to an eerie glow that descended over the chairs where the two men sat, throwing a deeper shadow over Mike. The scent of unseen burning candles filled the room and mingled with the stale odor of the musty old building and dust.

"It's not as different as you might think, being dead," Mike said with a sneer. "What was unfinished on your side is just as important to me over here as it ever was. I've got unfinished business with you. I'm not going to get any rest over here until I get it finished. You two won't be breathing another breath of fresh air until I get what I want."

"What do you want?" Gil asked in a high, weak voice.

"I've got some scores to settle with Howard."

"Gil was the one who killed you," Boyce wailed.

The ghost laughed. "Only to beat you to it. My scores to settle with you go back a lot further than the day I died, and you know it. This scar, Howard. I had to go through life with a scarred face thanks to you. What's more, you could've got me killed that night."

Terry sat forward, listening. Mike had never talked about how he got the scar. He'd changed the subject once when she'd started to ask. Now he was saying it was caused by Howard Boyce.

A silence fell over the room. Then Mike's voice boomed out again so abruptly it startled Terry as well as the two other men. "Remember that day, Howard? The practice football skirmish and the fight afterward on the pier at the lake? I had two guys on me, and I was doing okay. I was getting the better of both of them, until you interfered."

Gil spoke up. "Yeah! Till you grabbed a rope and tripped Colin and he fell off the side of the pier and hit the blades of a boat motor. I saw the whole thing."

Howard's voice rose like a child's wail in desperate self-defense. "How could I know he'd hit a boat motor?"

"You had no business interfering in that fight," the ghost said. "Every time I looked in the mirror I swore I'd get even with you someday. You scarred me for life. That might have been enough for some guys, but not you. Not you, Howard."

"I didn't mean it!"

The ghost laughed a terrible laugh and moved a step nearer the men, to convince Howard that it could come as near to him as it wished. Mike's hobble on the one crutch was hardly noticeable, for a ghost could move erratically, haltingly, any way it wished to move. It asked, "Shall we talk about David's murder?"

Howard slid down onto his knees. "Please! I didn't mean for you to get convicted. I didn't think there'd be enough evidence to convict you."

"You made sure there was enough evidence, by blackmailing Gil into lying for you."

"He did blackmail me," Gil yelled. "But how did you know about it?"

"I can find out anything from over here," the ghost answered. "I can go anywhere, be anywhere. I overheard the two of you talking about it last night in the old company buildings down by the mine."

"We *were* talking about it last night," Gil howled.

The ghost sneered. "No one ever suspected it was the two of you who robbed the grocery store and knocked down old Mr. Stone so hard he broke his hip. I don't think the old man ever walked again. I never suspected you guys, even though I saw how drunk you were that night. I was working at the gas station, remember? You guys came in drunk as skunks, acting all hyped-up and carrying a wad of cash. But I never knew you'd held up a store just for kicks and hurt an old man. Stupid idiots. It was you who shoved him, Gil. That's what Howard had on you. He thought if he ever publicly accused you that the old man might take a second look and identify you. And Howard would have lied out of his part in it like he lied out of the murder. Yeah, Gil, he'd have accused you right out if you hadn't agreed to testify against me. We both know that. His daddy was such a good lawyer, little Howie learned he could get away with anything. Robbery, assault. Even murder."

Mike's voice trembled slightly from emotion or pain; Terry was unable to determine which. She hoped the pain pills were working. She kept a close eye on him, could see no perspiration on his white face. The tremor in his voice might be anger. God knows, his anger had lain dormant long enough. It would be understandable if it tumbled, shaking, out of him. And the tremor was all right; it was ghostly.

"The only thing you hated your cousin for, little Howie," the ghost continued, "was that your daddy liked him as much as if he'd been his son. You couldn't stand that. David had to die for that, didn't he? He'd have inherited some of what you thought should be all yours."

Boyce, still on his knees, hid his face in his hands.

"Look at me!" Mike demanded. "For once in your life stop cowering." He waited until the man was looking at him again, staring up openmouthed, eyes blinking. There were tears of fear misting Howard's eyes. "Yeah..." Mike continued in a slow, deep voice. "I want the world to know about how you deliberately picked a fight with loaded rifles that day we were hunting. I saw that you were acting weird that day, but there was no guessing why or stopping you. Nobody could have stopped you. That's because it was all preplanned. David had to die.''

"I never planned to frame you."

"No? When the police wouldn't buy the accident story, you had to put the blame on one of us, didn't you? And since you had something to blackmail Gil with, I was the lucky choice. I went through seven months of hell waiting for the trial. And eight years of hell in hiding. And for what? To get shot? Oh yeah, we've got scores to settle. Plenty of scores to settle."

Howard Boyce, on his knees, had begun to sob. His body was shaking violently. Gil sat in the chair beside him looking down at him with contempt.

"But I wasn't the one who killed you!" Boyce was onto that again, his only hope for diverting the ghost's wrath away from himself.

"I wouldn't be dead if you hadn't framed me in the first place. I'd be rotting in prison for fifty years, if it was up to you. That's worse than killing me, Howard."

Gil spoke up, "What do you want from us, Colin? You want revenge?"

A frightening silence ensued. It was followed by the ghost's soft, threatening reply. "I'll have my revenge my own way, don't doubt that. But I'm more concerned right now with clearing my name. Thanks to little Howie here, I was estranged from my family and I was branded a killer. For my family's sake, I want my name cleared. I want a confession from the real killer. Go on Howard, let's hear it."

Howard sputtered and sobbed.

Gil said, "What's stopping you, Howard? You think somebody's going to listen to a ghost? Who the hell is going to listen to a ghost?"

"You're a witness to this Gil," Mike said. "This time you're going to be on the side of the truth because if you don't, I won't leave you an hour's peace for the rest of your miserable life."

Gil shoved Boyce's shoulder roughly. "Do what he tells you. He's just a ghost, Howard. How's he going to tell anybody about this, huh? If he wants to hear you confess, then do it!"

Boyce looked back sideways at the other man. "You'll turn on me."

"You got a mad ghost on your back and you're worrying about *me*. Colin is going to get you, Howard. One way or another, he's going to get you and I don't want to be around to see it. If I was in your shoes I'd do what he wants before he gets any madder."

This was Terry's cue to turn on the tape recorder and the movie camera up above.

Howard muttered, "What do you want me to say?"

"The truth, damn you!" Mike answered. "I want you to tell the truth about how David died. I heard a thousand lies pouring out of your mouth during my trial. Now I want to hear the truth."

"I never planned to frame you," Boyce repeated. "The shooting was supposed to look like an accident. But when that didn't work, what choice did I have? There were just the three of us. I figured the word of two against one would work, and I got Gil to say you deliberately killed David."

"Did you use money to convince Gil to lie?" Mike asked, deliberately avoiding the subject of blackmail to protect Gil now that the recorder was on. Luckily there had been a bribe involved as well as blackmail.

"Yes, I gave him money."

"Why did you kill your cousin?"

"You know why."

"I want to hear you say it."

Boyce whimpered again. "David was going to inherit some of my father's estate. I hated him. My father liked him better than he liked me. My father had asked him to live with us and he was always talking to David at breakfast and ignoring me. David was starting to talk about law school, and then he'd have been taken into the firm too, and I'd have had to compete with him for the rest of our lives."

"So you decided to shoot him and hope it looked like an accident."

"Yes."

"I think you planned to frame me before the shooting, if it came to that. Why else would you offer to let me use your new gun and you use my old one? Everybody knew that old gun of mine, and it was the one that killed David. You planned to frame me all along, didn't you?"

"Only..." Howard's voice shook violently. "Only if...I had to...."

Mike was getting tired, feeling pain in his leg, and the discomfort of leaning on the crutch. Moving helped, and he had been moving about while he talked, but it was getting more difficult to hold himself up. Terry could see the perspiration on his face now, and she knew he didn't want to prolong his ordeal too much longer. She was waiting for any signal from him.

"Here in Jerome," Mike continued. "You came after Terry Morse with the intention of killing her. Is that right?"

"She...she is ruining me! Drawing those pictures that look like me. Showing me as a murderer. People were starting to ask about it, and to connect the story with my cousin. I knew if she was that nervy she'd stop at nothing, she'd go as far as she could to make me look guilty of that crime. Nobody does that to me."

"Did you come here tonight to kill her?"

"Yes ... yes ... where the hell is she?"

"She's here," the ghost said. "In this room. She's taping our conversation."

Boyce looked around wildly. Gil stood up, poised stiff and ready for trouble.

Mike limped over to Howard, grabbed the collar of his shirt and pulled him to his feet. "Look at my eyes, Howard. Do these eyes look dead to you?"

The man could not answer. The strength of Mike's arm was the only thing that kept him from crumbling to the floor.

Still staring into Boyce's terrified face, Mike said, "Turn the lights on, Terry."

The room flooded with light. Gil stood with his gun drawn and pointing at Boyce's head. Terry came out from behind the false wall holding the gun Mike had given her in case of an emergency.

Mike shoved Boyce against the wall. He hit with a thud and slid down to the floor.

"I saw ... you die ... saw ... the ghost."

He was staring up at Mike, who dropped, exhausted, onto the chair Terry moved up for him. Mike proceeded to pull off the white gauze and, perspiring, wiped his face with it. The white color came off easily, but the dark eye shadow remained.

Boyce's eyes turned to Gil, who stood legs apart, holding the gun and sneering.

"Gil ... you knew. You tricked me!"

"You know better than to trust anybody, Howard. Nobody can be trusted."

Terry said, "I'm going for the police."

"That won't be necessary," Mike said. "We'll just take the boards off that window we used to climb in and out of, and the bright lights up here will bring the police in a couple of minutes. The town is too used to this upstairs being dark for a sudden light not to be noticed. Especially now, when the police are on alert for trouble."

Handing his gun to Mike, Gil moved at once to remove the boards.

"Well, then," Terry said with a broad smile, "I'll run downstairs and pull the glass away from the stairway so the police won't charge headlong into it and knock themselves out."

While Howard Boyce sat on the floor, his idiotic stare fixed solidly on Mike, Terry returned via the secret back stairs. She expected to feel drained of all energy after the tension of the last hours. Instead, she felt high, exhilarated.

Mike turned to look at her and smiled and it was different from any smile she had ever seen from him. This smile was victory, it was gratitude, and it was love.

Outside they heard a police siren. Mike's shoulders relaxed for the first time all day. "I never thought I'd be saying it," he murmured, "but that siren is one hell of a sweet sound."

OUTSIDE THE EAST WINDOW the sun was rising over the great red bluffs that lined the Verde Valley. Terry woke from a restless sleep to the sight of light streaks in the sky. Beside her Mike slept soundly, more soundly than she had ever seen him sleep. Her stirring didn't wake him. The morning light didn't wake him. His breathing was steady and even. Terry lay watching him, thinking how handsome he was, and luxuriating in her luck that a man as perfect as Mike loved her.

At her tender touch on his shoulder, Mike moved, opened his eyes and smiled at her sleepily.

She asked, "How is your leg?"

"What leg?"

"This one...." She ran her hand across the edges of the bandage on his thigh.

"That feels nice. It must be better." He reached up to touch her face with his fingertips. "You were fantastic last night, honey. I couldn't have pulled off that hoax without you."

"We were a wonderful team, weren't we? All four of us—you and me and Gil and Rosa. We were all wonderful."

"You're a brave lady," he whispered.

The touch of his fingers on her cheek, stroking softly, was a sweeter, more intimate touch than any she had ever known. In response, she reached out to him, letting her fingertips trace the lines of the scar on his temple.

She said gently, "Fighting seems to be second nature to you."

"Huh?"

"So many fights...you even got this scar fighting."

"It wasn't really a fight. Just some of us kids fooling around working off steam after a football game. It was a fight to Howard, I guess; I was captain of the winning side and he could never stand to lose—not even a stupid practice football game. The rest of us were really just playing."

Terry kissed the scar, allowing her lips to linger against the cool of his skin.

He frowned. "Did you mean you think using my fists is a way of life with me? I guess I couldn't blame you for thinking that."

Her voice was soft, preoccupied now with the joy of touching him. "You're very good at it...at fighting."

"And I'll admit it felt damn good. I had years of built-up tension to let out. But the truth is, honey, those two fist-fights you witnessed are the only times in my life I ever resorted to quite that level of barbaric behavior. Not counting the time on the pier. You're thinking men are barbarians, aren't you?''

"I was thinking that you saved both our lives."

His voice lowered. "I killed a man."

"Yes."

"I had to. He would have hurt you."

Terry remembered the look in Mike's eyes when he turned from the sight of the corpse of the man he'd killed. The same expression had been in his eyes when he shoved Howard Boyce against the wall and watched him slide to the floor in total defeat. It was not victory that shone in his pale blue eyes in those strained moments. Strangely, his eyes were filled with sadness, not satisfaction. He had not wanted his life to be like this.

"You did what you had to do," she whispered. "It's over now."

Gently, she kissed him and lay back on his arm, staring up at the ceiling. "You know, you could start a haunted house business," she mused. "Your ghosts would fool anybody. I can't tell you how impressed I am with what you did."

"A fool's folly," he said huskily. "It's time I got on with living a real life, with real goals."

"What will you do?"

"I'm thinking of staying in Jerome."

"You are?"

"I like this town. There are good feelings here. It's starting to come back to life, you know. These last couple of years it's really been starting to live again, and now the valley is starting to grow. It's a damned nice valley. And the town has been good to me. The people have been good friends. There are a lot worse places to live than this old mountain."

"Yes," she agreed. "There are."

"It all looks different to a free man."

She kissed his cheek and felt his arm tightening tenderly around her shoulder.

"You can't imagine what it feels like to be free. I'm free to walk anywhere now. I'm free to love you. Free to let you love me. Free to think about tomorrow—to actually plan tomorrow. Do you know what that means to me?"

"I think I'm only now beginning to understand what it means to you," she said. "I thought I did before, but it was different before. I was so afraid of the future without realizing how afraid I really was, because I wouldn't let myself think about it. This crazy scheme of yours was such a long shot, and I knew it and wouldn't let myself think that either. But we were hanging on to such a thin thread of hope all along, Mike."

"Yeah. We both knew it and didn't dare say it. I owe so much to you."

"And I owe so much to you. I didn't think you'd let me help you; I really didn't, and I was so surprised when you reluctantly agreed to. Thank God you let me stay and help and be part of your life. I know how difficult that was for you at the time—to let me be part of your secret life."

"I was afraid for you."

"I know." She began to run her hand gently over his chest, letting the little curls of hair tickle her fingers. "Are you really going to stay? Finish renovating the house?"

"I kind of like the idea. How do you feel about it? You know, the view from upstairs is so fantastic, we could renovate the entire second floor as one apartment instead of two."

"We?"

"Will you stay with me, Terry?" He threw off the blanket as though throwing off a heavy encumbrance. The cool of the morning air touched their naked bodies with invigorating freshness. She snuggled closer into his warmth.

"Free!" he said, pulling her over onto his chest playfully. "The best part of being free is to be able to ask the woman I love to stay with me. To marry me."

Terry's spirits soared. The beats of her heart sang in rhythm to the bird songs outside the window. Had those bird songs been there all along, or had they started singing only now?

He asked, "Will you?"

"How could I marry anybody else after what we've been through together?" Her kiss on his neck was soft. His skin tasted salty. She felt her insides churning with wanting him again.

"When?" he asked, his hand caressing her breasts.

"Soon...oh, very soon." She kissed his shoulder while her hands were moving through his thick hair, then over his chest, then his stomach....

"I have to go back to straighten all the legal stuff out," he said.

"Um hum."

"You could...we could both go."

"Um hum."

"What are you doing?"

"Loving you."

He responded with a soft moan of pleasure. "Never stop loving me."

"I never will," Terry whispered, capturing him in the magic circles of her touch. "Mike...do I call you Mike? Or Colin? Will I be Mrs. Calhoun or Mrs. MacKaine?"

His voice was raspy and soft, preoccupied with other matters than his name. "Which do you like best?"

She thought for a moment. "I fell in love with Mike Calhoun."

"That's who I am then. That's fine with me."

"That's it? Just like that?"

"Just like that," he repeated as he brought his hand over hers, guiding her gently while she touched him. "Like that, honey. Just like that...."

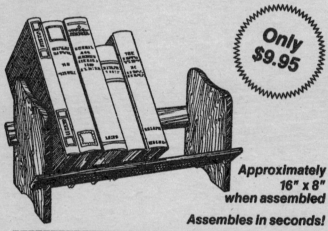

PAMELA BROWNING

... is fireworks on the green at the Fourth of
July and prayers said around the
Thanksgiving table. It is the dream of
freedom realized in thousands of small
towns across this great nation.

But mostly, the Heartland is its people.
People who care about and help one another.
People who cherish traditional values and
give to their children the greatest gift, the
gift of love.

American Romance presents HEARTLAND,
an emotional trilogy about people whose
memories, hopes and dreams are bound up
in the acres they farm.

HEARTLAND ... the story of America.

Don't miss these heartfelt stories: American
Romance #237 SIMPLE GIFTS (March),
#241 FLY AWAY (April), and
#245 HARVEST HOME (May).

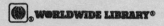